I slowed down shamelessly to eavesdrop

My timing was awful. He turned at precisely the same moment. I could feel myself blushing as our eyes locked and held. Despite his rugged good looks, it was not one of those smoldering occasions you see on commercials. The man was staring at me as though I'd grown two heads.

"Are you all right?" was his peculiar opening remark.

There is no gracious answer to such a question. I said "What are you talking about?"

Now it was his turn to flush. "Aren't you . . . I could have sworn . . . no, never mind. I must've mistaken you for someone else." He turned and left.

I returned to my room and, feeling muddled and exhausted, walked into the bathroom. My tattered nightgown was beside the tub.

I'd almost forgotten about last night's sleepwalking. Now a fresh wave of anxiety flooded through me. I still had no recollection of where I'd gone last night or what I'd done. Maybe that man in the lobby knew something I didn't. Maybe that's why he'd acted so strangely. What if he and I had—

I couldn't finish the thought.

ABOUT THE AUTHOR

Elaine K. Stirling says her Intrigues are always inspired by something that makes her spine tingle. This time, Elaine selected the haunting charm of Bathhouse Row in Hot Springs, Arkansas, to combine with some recent articles she'd read about sleepwalking. From these she created a wonderfully chilling effect. Elaine lives with her two sons in Kelowna, British Columbia.

Books by Elaine K. Stirling

HARLEQUIN INTRIGUE
28–UNSUSPECTED CONDUCT
35–MIDNIGHT OBSESSION
53–FOUL PLAY
85–CHAIN LETTER

HARLEQUIN TEMPTATION
139–ALMOST HEAVEN

HARLEQUIN SUPERROMANCE
261–THIS TIME FOR US
345–MORE THAN A FEELING

Don't miss any of our special offers. Write to us at the following address for information on our newest releases.

Harlequin Reader Service
901 Fuhrmann Blvd., P.O. Box 1397, Buffalo, NY 14240
Canadian address: P.O. Box 603,
Fort Erie, Ont. L2A 5X3

Sleepwalker

Elaine K. Stirling

Harlequin Books

TORONTO • NEW YORK • LONDON
AMSTERDAM • PARIS • SYDNEY • HAMBURG
STOCKHOLM • ATHENS • TOKYO • MILAN

To JoAnn Ross,
my first mentor,
with gratitude and affection

Special thanks
to Cyndee Turnquist,
whose insights and enthusiasm
for Arkansas
made this book possible.

Harlequin Intrigue edition published November 1989

ISBN 0-373-22126-6

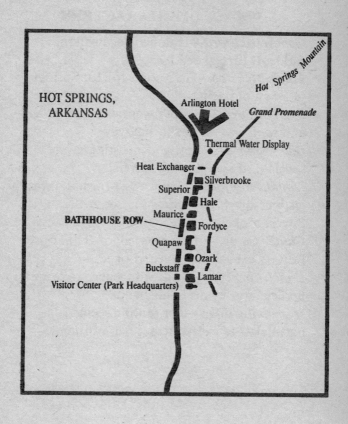

HOT SPRINGS,
ARKANSAS

Hot Springs Mountain

Arlington Hotel

Grand Promenade

Thermal Water Display

Heat Exchanger

Silverbrooke

Superior

Hale

BATHHOUSE ROW

Maurice

Fordyce

Quapaw

Ozark

Buckstaff

Lamar

Visitor Center (Park Headquarters)

CAST OF CHARACTERS

Geneva Ashford—Had her sleepwalking suddenly turned deadly?

Travis McCabe—He'd come to Hot Springs to settle an old debt.

Pearl Tulley—Her story was dead and buried—and *someone* wanted it that way.

Bill Swann—As a private investigator, he specialized in collecting secrets.

Donald Ashford—Geneva's ex-husband was the last person she'd expected to see at the Silverbrooke.

Calder Carson—He owned all of Bathhouse Row . . . except the Silverbrooke.

Enoch Sarrazin—He urged Geneva to leave all her legal problems in his hands.

Hepzibah Tulley—Her ranting seemed harmless—to everyone but her murderer.

Chapter One

I've been sleepwalking for as long as I can remember. No, let me rephrase that. People tell me that I walk in my sleep. I don't actually remember doing it.

My parents, my college roommates and my ex-husband would all vouch for these nocturnal wanderings. They've found me dancing barefoot in snowbanks, warbling "I Am Woman" in the men's dorm at midnight and—so help me—batting my lashes at the concierge during my honeymoon. I'm sure I would have woken up long before anything happened, but try to convince a new husband of that.

Except for this single idiosyncrasy, however, I consider myself fairly well adjusted. I get along with everyone, enjoy my job—but now I'm getting ahead of myself.

Let me tell you the entire story. Then you can decide whether I've been overestimating my sanity for all these years. Eighteen months ago in Minneapolis, my day began like any other. It was a Tuesday, my least favorite day of the week because nothing memorable ever happens on Tuesdays. Except for that one.

We'd had a heavy snowfall the night before which did nothing to improve my mood. Now don't get me wrong. I love Minneapolis, and I adore winter as long as it departs on March 21 when it's technically supposed to. Of course, in

Minnesota, that never happens, and so every year by mid-April, I tend to start muttering vague threats about moving to Tahiti.

The bank where I worked as a mortgage and loans officer had the dignified smell of old money, nothing like those hi-tech banks with glassed-in tellers and ozone-gray decor. My bank had brass rails, oak-paneled walls and real wooden desks with blotters. I once asked my boss for a green visor and arm band, but he said they'd tossed those out along with inkwells and spittoons.

My office was a cubicle formed by those nubbly glass dividers that distort people on the other side and impart the illusion of privacy to one's clients. On my desk was a brass nameplate identifying me as Geneva Ashford.

Ashford is my ex-husband's name. Donald had proved remarkably amenable when I informed him during divorce proceedings that I intended to retain it. It's not that I had anything against my maiden name, Zloczewski. But I'm sure you can appreciate the difficulties inherent in such a handle.

As for the name Geneva, my parents—first-generation Polish Americans—claimed that I had been conceived during a vacation in Switzerland. I've always been grateful they weren't in Zurich at the time.

To get back to that fateful Tuesday, my workday began with a young couple buying their first home. Everything about the interview was routine—they were nervous, I was conciliatory. They didn't have sufficient information with them, so I patiently wrote a list of what else we would require and set up a second appointment for later in the day.

I was getting myself a cup of coffee when the receptionist informed me that I had a walk-in. That was okay with me. According to my appointment book, there was nothing scheduled for hours.

The walk-in's name was Bill Swann, she said. Picturing someone with a long graceful neck, I went out to the waiting area and called him.

A man with no neck stood up. He was short, sixtyish, and dressed in a drab, too-long overcoat. As I ushered him to my office, I noticed that he walked with his head tucked low between his shoulders—more like a turtle than a swan.

I took my usual place behind the desk, smiled pleasantly and said, "What can I do for you, sir?"

The man pulled out his wallet and flashed me a dog-eared piece of identification. "Bill Swann, ma'am, P.I."

My interest perked. "No kidding? You're really a private eye?"

He snorted. "That's what people always say, like bein' an investigator's some kinda glamor job. You can thank them Hollywood phonies for that."

Mr. Swann dragged out his words with a Southern drawl, but I wasn't enough of an expert to identify the state. Meanwhile I restrained my enthusiasm, not wanting to give the impression that I'd been taken in by those Hollywood phonies.

He read from a notepad he'd pulled out from somewhere. "Did your name used to be Geneva Zlo...Zloch..."

"Zloczewski," I said, emphasizing the first *Z* and ignoring the second. "That's my maiden name, yes."

"Could you identify this person?" He showed me a wallet-sized photograph. It was one of those old-fashioned black and white pictures filled in with unconvincing pastels. The photo was of a little girl about two years old with long auburn ringlets, brown eyes and fat cheeks.

"I've never seen this particular portrait, but it's me. Where'd you get this?"

"Are you sure it's you?"

I handed back the photograph. "Mr. Swann, I'd recognize those cheeks anywhere. It's taken me twenty-eight years to outgrow them."

Not entirely a humorless man, he chuckled while flipping through the pages of his notebook. "When's your birthday?"

I was about to reply, but stopped myself. "Mr. Swann, you're not here to inquire about one of my clients, are you?"

"No, I'm definitely here to see you, Miss uh, Ms....Ashford," he said, reading the nameplate with a look of relief.

My stomach knotted with apprehension. "Would you mind telling me why?"

"Not at all. Assuming you are the lady I've been lookin' for, I'm here to inform you that you've come into an inheritance."

My parents had been dead for a number of years, and I knew of no other relatives. But honestly, who hasn't dreamed of a long-lost uncle at least once in their lives?

I leaned forward, fascinated. "What kind of inheritance?"

"A bathhouse."

First I stared, then I laughed. Neither reaction was in keeping with usual professional decorum. "This is a joke, right? Someone set you up. Don't tell me. I'll bet it was Maggie, my old roommate. She's probably in the coffee shop waiting to hear my reac—"

"I assure you, ma'am, this is no joke. I have in my possession a letter authorizing you to assume the lease of the Silverbrooke Bathhouse in Hot Springs, Arkansas."

This was becoming too much to absorb, and I still wasn't convinced the man was for real. "What would anyone do with a bathhouse in this day and age? Health departments are closing them down all over the country.''

Bill Swann gathered his rumpled self into a posture of affront. ''Ms. Ashford, the bathhouses in Hot Springs are nothing like those perverted steam baths in San Francisco. We are talking about hundred-year-old health spas, historic landmarks. Why, the Vanderbilts used to visit them, the Roosevelts, all kinds of upstanding folks.''

I'd obviously, though unintentionally, offended him. ''Are you from Hot Springs, Mr. Swann?''

''Born and raised,'' he admitted proudly.

''Oh. All right, so someone bequeathed someone a bathhouse. What makes you think I'm the beneficiary?''

''I have plenty of evidence that suggests you are. But if you don't mind, I'd like to ask a few questions to be sure.''

''Go ahead,'' I told him, still convinced this was a case of mistaken identity.

''Would you happen to have a copy of your birth certificate?''

''Is the laminated wallet-size okay?'' I asked, reaching under the desk for my handbag.

''Any kind'll do.'' He examined the card, then checked the details against his notes. ''Born in Chicago. Yup, so far, so good. Where'd you grow up?''

''Boston.''

''Battin' a thousand.'' He asked for my parents' names and their dates of birth. When I told him they were deceased, Mr. Swann said he already knew that and offered his condolences, but could I please answer the question anyway.

By now, I felt entitled to ask a few questions of my own. ''Who is this benefactor, anyway? Is he a relative?''

''His name was Festus Tulley.''

''He doesn't sound Polish.''

Bill Swann looked at me strangely. "Don't reckon he was. Festus, who gave me your photo, was an old friend of your parents. They used to visit Hot Springs every year and frequented Mr. Tulley's bathhouse, the Silverbrooke."

"And for that, he wills the place to me?"

"Yeah. It was kinda his way of repaying your parents' patronage."

That struck me as odd, but unfortunately I could no longer ask my parents—or Mr. Tulley—to explain. "Didn't he have any family of his own?"

"Just an old-maid sister, but Hepzibah won't have anything to do with the bathhouse."

Festus and Hepzibah. The names of these people were something else. "Why won't she?"

"Religion," he said. "You know how they get."

Actually, I didn't, but that was irrelevant. "Mr. Swann, I don't recall my parents ever mentioning Hot Springs, let alone Festus Tulley."

The man shrugged. "Yeah, well, we've all got aces up our sleeves somewhere, Ms. Ashford."

Maybe there was a grain of truth to his hayseed philosophy. My parents had always been too busy working to tell me about their younger days. That didn't mean they hadn't had any.

"So you really believe I'm the person you're looking for?"

"No question about it."

Feeling slightly winded, I tried to think of a polite way to handle this. Could one simply refuse an unwanted bequest?

"What do I do now?" I asked.

Bill Swann handed me a letter. "This is from Mr. Tulley's attorney, Enoch Sarrazin, in Hot Springs. It should answer most of your immediate questions, but his number is on the letterhead if you have others. He said to tell you, feel free to call collect.''

The attorney's stationery was of the highest quality vellum. If this was a hoax, someone had gone to impressive lengths to make it look official.

''Now, if you'll excuse me, ma'am, I've got a flight booked for Hot Springs in an hour.''

I looked up, suddenly panic-stricken at the thought of Mr. Swann leaving me with this...this bathhouse. I didn't know why, but I wanted to hand the letter back, tell him I wasn't interested. But Mr. Swann was only the messenger. He'd completed his mission.

''Oh, okay. Well, thank you, Mr. Swann, for uh, informing me. It's not every day one gets a...bathhouse.''

''The pleasure's mine, Ms. Ashford. When you get to Hot Springs, be sure to look me up. We'll have lunch. Here's my card.''

I took his card but didn't bother informing him that my chances of visiting Hot Springs—or any place in Arkansas for that matter—were virtually nonexistent.

AFTER MR. SWANN LEFT, I thought of a dozen questions I should have asked. How had he tracked me to Minneapolis? How did he connect a two-year-old Geneva Zloczewski with the grown-up Geneva Ashford? And why had I never seen that picture of myself before?

That evening my ex-husband asked me those very same questions. But then Donald was, by nature, a circumspect man. He never even paid a utility bill without first establishing the accuracy of the meter readings. Once he had actually found an error, twelve cents in his favor.

I refilled my wineglass and leaned back on the sofa, watching fat snowflakes drift past the balcony doors. ''Why shouldn't I have believed Mr. Swann?'' I asked. ''He seemed legitimate enough.''

Donald glanced at my stockinged feet, propped on the coffee table. If we'd still been married, he'd have instructed me to remove them, but this was my apartment now. He knew better.

''Okay, let's assume the will is legitimate,'' he replied. ''What are you going to do about it?''

''I don't know. That's why I asked you over. To discuss it.''

Donald reached for the bottle and topped his glass. ''Why do you only invite me here when you have a problem?''

''I don't.''

''You do. Last time you called, you'd dropped your Rolex into the toilet.''

I tossed my auburn hair defensively. ''That was hardly the same thing. I wasn't sure if I should use a plunger, and besides, the Rolex was your fifth anniversary gift to me.''

''And the last,'' he added.

''Of course it was the last. No one expects you to buy anniversary gifts for your ex-wife.''

''You're digressing again.''

''Okay, I admit it. Maybe I do tend to rely on you a little more than I should. But, Donald, you have such a sensible head on your shoulders.''

His placid, handsome features fell. ''Gee, thanks, Geneva.''

I hadn't meant to hurt his feelings. Yet so often I managed to do just that. ''Look at it this way. At least we're still friends, unlike most of our divorced acquaintances.''

''Friends.'' He muttered the word as though it were a curse, then stood up and went to the picture window that overlooked Lake Calhoun. ''If you need me so damned much, why aren't we still married?''

Donald, mercifully, didn't see me flinch. "Who's digressing this time?" I said gently.

He turned to look at me, his slim, fair body silhouetted against the twilight. There'd been a time when that body had made me feel special. Now I looked at him in his V-neck cashmere sweater and button-down shirt and, sadly, felt nothing at all.

"You're right," he said. "Let's get back to the bathhouse. You said you spoke with the attorney."

"Yes, I called him this afternoon. He sounded like a very nice man."

Donald rolled his eyes. I should have known such an observation would not impress him. "Did you happen to check his credentials with the Arkansas Bar Association?"

Avoiding his stare, I picked up a container of baklava and tore off some pastry. "I'd have thought of that . . . eventually."

He was kind enough not to call my bluff. "What did the attorney have to say?"

"Well, he explained the conditions of the bequest—"

"Which are?"

"I was getting to that," I said, suddenly recalling how seldom I'd been able to finish sentences when Donald and I were married. "I don't actually own the bathhouse. I own the lease."

"Who owns the bathhouse?"

"Hot Springs National Park."

"Is anyone running the place now?"

"No, it's been closed for twenty-five years."

"Why? What's wrong with it?"

"Nothing, apparently, except neglect. Mr. Sarrazin said that most of the bathhouses have been closed for ages. It's only recently that there's been local interest in reopening them."

"Okay, what are the conditions?"

"They're not unreasonable. If I choose to retain the lease, it's on the condition that I reopen the Silverbrooke as a bathhouse and not as a hotel or museum or whatever. If I want to transfer the lease, my benefactor requests that Enoch Sarrazin be retained to handle the legalities."

Donald sniffed. "Sounds cozy."

"They were old friends. What's wrong with that?"

"Nothing, probably. Go on."

"That's about it. I either become the proprietor of a bathhouse or I give it away. Mr. Sarrazin says I don't even have to go to Hot Springs. We can do whatever is necessary over the phone."

"That's the stupidest story I've ever heard."

"What do you mean, stupid?"

"Think about it, Geneva. The whole thing sounds like a plot from one of those dumb gothics you used to read."

"I thought so, too, at first, but who am I to question Festus Tulley's motives? He obviously thought a great deal of my parents, and the bequest was a way of showing his appreciation."

"Baloney." Donald took a seat across from me. "Why'd you bother calling me? It's obvious what you have to do."

That was news to me. "What do I have to do?"

"Call Mr. Sarrazin, transfer the lease and forget you ever heard of the place."

"Why should I do that?"

"Because you don't know how to handle responsibility. If you'd retained title to your parents' food stores instead of selling out, do you realize how far we could have gone?"

"We?"

"Slip of the tongue. But think about it. The joker who bought your parents' business already has most of New England sewn up. The Atlantic seaboard is just a matter of time."

"That joker, Donald, happened to give me an excellent price for the business. I don't have to work another day if I don't want to. But I *am* working. Which shoots a major hole in your theory that I'm irresponsible."

"Okay, maybe I came down a little hard. What I meant was that you're not the entrepreneurial type, and reopening a bathhouse would definitely require business acumen."

Much as I hated to admit it, Donald had a point. "You're right," I said. "I'll call Enoch Sarrazin tomorrow and tell him to transfer the lease."

Donald watched me get up and begin to clear dishes from the coffee table. "Is this a signal for me to leave?"

"No, of course not. I'm just cleaning up."

He brought his empty wineglass to the sink. "Maybe you should think about this a little longer. There's no need to act hastily."

"There's nothing to think about. I'm not the least bit interested in the Silverbrooke."

"Okay, if that's how you feel. I'd better hit the road. The snow's coming down harder than ever."

I walked Donald to the door. "I really do appreciate your coming over."

Slipping on his coat, he smiled benignly. "Don't mention it. After all, what are ex-husbands for?"

To my surprise, I did something I hadn't done in a long time. I hugged him. "You really are terrific, you know that?"

He returned the embrace, then slid his hand through my hair. Slowly he lowered his mouth to mine.

I turned my face away. "Donald, don't . . . please."

"Why not?"

Because I only like you. I don't love you. But I couldn't have said that without garbling the message.

My silence must have clued him in. He released me, sighing. "My dear ex, still clinging and repelling."

I wasn't sure I'd heard correctly. "What did you say?"

"Clinging and repelling. It's the story of your life, Geneva. No damned wonder things never worked out between us."

Closing the door, I mulled over Donald's parting words. They made no sense to me whatsoever.

A CUP OF HOT CHOCOLATE and a paperback novel accompanied me to bed. I was feeling gloomy, and resented the gloominess because there was no need for it.

My life was perfectly satisfying. Thanks to my parents' initiative, I had no financial worries. I had started dating again, but with no burning compulsion to get emotionally involved. My health was intact, my career secure. . . .

The suspense novel failed to suspend me. I tossed the book aside and turned out the light.

Lying in the dark, I found myself trying to conjure an image of the Silverbrooke Bathhouse—for the time being, mine. It was probably a decrepit old thing with antiquated plumbing inhabited by all sorts of crawly creatures.

And who was this Festus Tulley? My parents, as I remembered them, were not the chummy type. Their few close friends had belonged to the Polish-American society in Boston. Others were little more than business associates.

Oh well, I thought, punching the pillow as I rolled over. There was no point in dwelling on questions with no answers. It just goes to show how little we really know about the people who raised us.

"MOMMY, I thirsty!"
Mommy doesn't answer. She must be sleeping.

I look around my bedroom. It's dark, but I'm not scared. Mommy says darkness is daytime turned inside out. Just like when sometimes my pajamas are inside out.

Why is the floor cold? Where are my slippers? I need Mommy to help me put them on.

I'm going to find her. She'll give me some water, and then she'll tuck me in again.

Everything is made for big people. Big walls, big chairs. It's hard for me to reach the doorknob. But if I stand on my tippytoes and use two hands . . . there, that wasn't so bad.

"Mommy!" She's not in her bed. She must be downstairs.

Now I'm all mixed up. How did I get into this room? It's cold in here, and the walls are scratchy. Not like my walls. "Mommy, where's the door? It's dark! I can't see!"

The door slams shut. The noise scares me.

"Let me out!"

I push and pull. I cry and scratch at the door and cry some more. But no one comes. Not Mommy, not anyone. . . .

I'd only been asleep a few minutes, it seemed, when I was awakened—not by the sound of the alarm, but by someone shaking me gruffly.

"Wake up, Ms. Ashford! Please, try to wake up."

I tried to open my eyes, but the lights were blinding. I lifted an arm to my face. "I'm awake. Stop shaking me." I was still too groggy to be alarmed or curious.

"Are you all right?" a man asked.

"I was until you came along." *You?* Who was I talking to?

My eyes sprang open. Hovering not two feet above my face was a stranger in uniform. Good grief, I was staring at a cop!

Now genuinely alarmed, I hoisted myself to a sitting position—on my sofa, not the bed. "How did I get here? Who are you? What are you doing here?"

"City police, ma'am. Your neighbors phoned us. They were worried."

"Worried? Why?" I glanced around my living room and saw Mrs. Beasley, wringing gnarled hands and wearing an expression of concern.

"Hello, dear. I hope you're not upset, but you had us so very frightened."

"Us?"

"The neighbors. We could hear you all the way down the hall."

"Do you remember anything, Ms. Ashford?" A second officer, I hadn't noticed before, asked that question.

"All I remember is going to bed." Then my face turned an embarrassing shade of crimson. "I was sleepwalking, wasn't I?"

"Appears that way. Do this often?" the officer asked.

"Not lately. At least, I don't think so. Where did I go?"

"Nowhere, dear," Mrs. Beasley replied.

"You didn't leave your apartment," the younger policeman explained. "Your front door was locked and chained. You were pounding on it and screaming."

"I was screaming?"

"Oh, yes," Mrs. Beasley said. "You were begging to be let out. Some of us came over and tried to talk to you through the door, but you didn't seem to hear us. Even while the police were breaking in, you kept right on pounding."

I began to tremble, as much from humiliation as fear. I had no recollection of what they were telling me, but no reason to doubt them, either. I turned to the officer nearest me. "Are you going to arrest me for disturbing the peace?"

He chuckled. "No, ma'am. Sleepwalking's no crime, as far as I know. But you might want to go down to Emergency just to make sure you're okay."

"There's no point. The doctors have tried everything, but there's no cure for my sleepwalking."

"Actually I was talking about your hands."

"My hands?" I looked down. My fingernails were torn, my knuckles scraped raw.

Then I lifted my gaze toward the door where I'd apparently been pleading to get out. The door was off its hinges, propped against the wall and smeared with blood. *My blood.*

Chapter Two

Now I could understand why everyone was looking at me as though I was suicidal or crazy. I was harboring similar thoughts myself.

The police reattached the door while Mrs. Beasley plugged in the kettle for tea. I tried to stammer my assurances. I was fine. Really. All I needed was to be alone.

The alone part was true. But I was far from fine.

As far as I knew, I hadn't walked in my sleep for years. When I had before, I'd never injured myself. I considered taking the policeman's advice and going to the hospital. But I couldn't have handled the humiliation of explaining my behavior to strangers.

Besides, now that I was awake and alert, my hands were hurting. I wasn't sure I could drive—especially on slippery roads in the middle of a snowstorm.

It was best to wait until morning. Then I could talk to my own doctor. Not about my hands, necessarily—about the sleepwalking. Even if there was nothing he could do, I'd feel better if someone told me there was nothing to worry about.

THE NEXT MORNING I sat in Dr. Caldwell's examining room, my hands bandaged like some creature from a B movie. I felt curiously detached from my wounds; as though they were someone else's, and I just happened to be saddled with them.

Dr. Caldwell came in carrying my X rays. "Everything looks okay. No fractures. There might be some minor nerve damage, but it's too soon to tell."

My nerves were damaged all right, but not the ones to which my physician was referring.

"Has anything happened recently that might have upset you?" he asked.

"Not that I can think of." Then I recalled the visit from Mr. Swann. "Well, something did happen yesterday, but I wouldn't call it upsetting. Just weird."

Dr. Caldwell leaned back and listened to my story. "A bathhouse, huh? Have you heard the one about the priest and the rabbi in a bathhouse—"

"No! And I don't care to, thank you." We'd known each other long enough to kid around, but I wasn't in the mood for jokes this morning.

"Sorry. It was a lousy joke, anyway. But seriously, Geneva, I think you should consider getting some help."

"Help?" I repeated suspiciously.

"For your sleepwalking, before the problem gets any worse."

"But it's never been a problem. And anyway, lots of people walk in their sleep, don't they?"

"Certainly. But very few bang their hands until they're bloody."

My face reddened. "I suppose you're right."

"Do you have any memory of what happened when you were asleep?"

"None."

Dr. Caldwell thought a moment. "What I'd like to do, Geneva, is refer you to a colleague of mine. His specialty is hypnosis—"

"Before you go on, I should tell you I've tried hypnosis, and it doesn't work."

"When did you try?"

"When I was a teenager. My parents took me to someone in Boston. But no matter what the man did, I just couldn't go under."

"You're older now. Why not give it another shot?"

I felt a familiar resistance, the same resistance I'd experienced when that hypnotherapist in Boston had swung a gold watch in front of my face. "It'd be a waste of everyone's time. Listen, Dr. Caldwell, I'm sure last night was just an aberration. I'd had a few glasses of wine with my ex-husband who always makes me tense. Combined with that visit from the private eye, it's no wonder I had a strange night. But there's no reason to believe my sleepwalking is becoming a habit again."

"And if it is?"

"If it is . . . I'll consider your advice."

Dr. Caldwell didn't try to mask his disappointment, but this was, after all, my head we were talking about. In the clear light of day, I was convinced that positive thinking would be enough to prevent a recurrence.

"Okay, Geneva, if that's the way you feel. But if you don't mind, I am going to prescribe a mild sedative. It's only to be taken at bedtime, and only if you think you'll have trouble sleeping."

Medication of any kind was abhorrent to me, but I knew the doctor would feel better if I went along with him. And I might even go so far as to buy the stuff. It wouldn't hurt to keep it on hand, just in case.

He scribbled something and handed me the slip. "You might want to consider taking a few days off work. Indulge yourself. Do something relaxing. And if you have any more sleepwalking episodes—I don't care how insignificant—call me, Geneva. I've written down my home number.''

''I will. Thank you.''

Leaving the doctor's office, I decided that time off work was a good idea, but the prime motivation was vanity. My hands looked as though they'd been through a food chopper. I could just imagine how my clients would react.

Outside, the sun was dazzling, but the temperature lay well below freezing. I took the enclosed skywalk from the medical building to the bank, grateful to Minneapolis's city planners for sparing me the cold.

Maybe subconsciously I was feeling boxed in these days. That could explain why I hadn't simply unlocked the door last night and strolled out of the apartment like any normal sleepwalker.

The endless rounds of decision making at work and the eternal winter were probably taking their toll. Furthermore, I hadn't had a real vacation since Donald and I were married.

Thinking of Donald reminded me of how he'd described my behavior the night before. Clinging and repelling. A strange choice of words, but maybe he was right. In some ways I still hadn't caught on to taking responsibility for myself. Maybe it was time I started learning.

It was simple convincing my branch manager that I needed a vacation. He took one look at my hands, listened to my sleepwalking tale and said, ''How much time do you need? A week? Two weeks?''

I stopped him at two weeks, getting the distinct impression that if I let him continue, I'd be off work for a year. Then I visited a travel agency, having decided that a vacation someplace hot was precisely the indulgence I needed.

TRAVEL BROCHURES were spread out like a fan across my coffee table. Puerto Vallarta, Fiji, Honolulu, St. Kitts. Every destination promised more or less the same thing—sun, sand and a welcome rum punch.

Try as I might, it was hard to imagine myself enjoying a beach holiday alone. There would probably be no shortage of men, but I'd witnessed the emotional turmoil of girl friends who'd been through vacation romances. It didn't sound like a remedy for whatever was ailing me.

Making a cup of instant coffee, I noticed Enoch Sarrazin's letter on the counter. Distracted by doctors, bosses and travel agents, I'd almost managed to put the Silverbrooke out of my mind. Now I read the letter again with a new outlook.

Arkansas in the springtime might be quite pleasant. I could combine my vacation with some practical investigating into my inheritance. By seeing the bathhouse, at least my curiosity would be satisfied. Before I could talk myself out of it, I phoned the travel agent and inquired about fares to Hot Springs.

MY PRECONCEPTIONS of Arkansas, I'm ashamed to admit, fell far short of reality. I'd pictured Little Rock, the capital, as a sleepy Southern outpost and found it to be a modern, sophisticated city. The farmland along the interstate was efficiently cultivated, the mountain terrain breathtaking.

I'd flown to Little Rock and rented a car to drive the fifty or so miles to Hot Springs. The trees, the lakes, the clean air were not unlike parts of Minnesota, but here springtime was already giving way to the bloom of summer.

I checked into the Whispering Pines, a small motel on the outskirts of Hot Springs. It was still early in the day. I could have continued on to explore the town, but something—a case of nerves, probably—prevented me. My appointment with Enoch Sarrazin was for the following morning. That was soon enough to face my inheritance and whatever else awaited me in Hot Springs.

I spent a peaceful, solitary evening in my hotel room. Several days had passed since the sleepwalking incident, and my hands were healing nicely. The doctor had been right, I told myself, snuggling into bed. A change of scenery was definitely in order.

Uh-oh, my slippers are wet. Mommy is going to be mad. But I can't help it. The grass and leaves are all wet, too.

I look around, to see where I am. I think my house is down there, but I can't see it. I can't see any lights, either, just Mr. Moon in the sky and giant trees all around me. Their leaves make scary noises like whispers.

"Hey, are you all right?"

I turn to see who said that, and push my curls out of my face. A man is standing under a tree. He's wearing a cowboy hat. I can't see his face, but I think he's a stranger.

He comes closer. The wind is making my nightie stick to me and the man is looking at me funny.

"I'm not going to hurt you. My name's Travis. What's yours?"

I like talking to people. Mommy says I was born talking. But this time I don't. I just look at the man's nice face.

"You're going to catch cold dressed like that. Why don't you take my jacket?"

He seems a little scared. Maybe he's lost like me. He takes his coat off slowly. I let him put it over my shoulders. It feels warm. Like a hug. He's standing so close I can feel him breathing.

"Where's Mommy?" I want to move closer to him. He has a nice smile.

*The man called Travis tips his head like he's thinking
about my questions. "I don't know. Where do you live?"*

I point down the mountain.

"Do you know your address?"

I shake my head. I don't even know what an address is.

"Does anyone know you're up here?"

*Until he said that, I'd forgotten I was lost. Now I'm
scared again. My nose starts dripping. I think I'm gonna
cry. I don't want to cry in front of Travis. He'll think I'm a
baby.*

*"My car's just down the road. Why don't you come with
me? We'll find someone who can help you."*

*I would really like to ride in his car, just like when
Mommy goes for rides with her friends. But I'm not supposed to. So I back away, shake my head no and put my
thumb in my mouth to make me feel better.*

"Hey, what's the matter? You don't have to be afraid."

It's too late. I already am.

*My slippers make funny noises when I run. He yells at me
to wait, so I run faster. I don't think he's nice anymore. Why
would Travis yell if he's nice?*

*Mommy's right. I shouldn't be friendly to strangers when
she's not there.*

*I start crying. I hope Mommy finds me before the man
catches up. . . .*

I woke up aching all over. Must have been the mattress, I
thought, swinging my legs out of bed. Then I reached for my
slippers and gasped. They were sopping wet. At first I
thought the radiator must have sprung a leak during the
night. But no, the carpet was dry. And my slippers were not
only wet. They were caked with grass and mud; practically
worn out. I'd been sleepwalking again!

Barefoot, my heart pounding, I moved cautiously through
the room, looking for some clues as to where I'd gone and

why. The hem of my nightgown was damp. My legs were covered with scratches and mud stains.

"Oh, no!"

A jacket was lying near the bed, a man's denim jacket. I backed away, reaching instinctively for the phone. But who was I going to call? Donald? The police? My doctor?

Granted, Dr. Caldwell had told me to phone the next time I walked in my sleep. But he was in Minnesota, and I was in Arkansas. A fat lot of good that was going to do.

Not knowing what else to do, I went into the bathroom and filled the tub with scalding water. I scrubbed the mud from my legs until the scratches started bleeding. The bath did nothing to ease my state of mind.

I didn't know a soul in Hot Springs, but there was a man's jacket in my room. Where had it come from? And what had I done to get it?

It shouldn't have surprised me that no answers came. My subconscious, or whatever it was that triggered my sleep-walking, seemed as uncommunicative on the subject as ever.

Meanwhile the day loomed before me. My only consolation—and it was a small one—was that I could put off sleeping for a number of hours. Sleep, something no human can do without, was quickly becoming my greatest enemy.

Fumbling through my cosmetic bag, I came across the medication Dr. Caldwell had prescribed. The thought of taking sedatives was still offensive, but I placed the pill bottle carefully on the bathroom counter as though it represented my final link to sanity.

With a shudder, I threw the denim jacket out of sight in the closet and left the room. I had to force myself to enter the motel coffee shop. None of the other guests paid me the slightest attention, but none of them looked as though they might own the denim jacket I'd found, either.

Still feeling shaken, I drove into town and found Enoch Sarrazin's office building. The downtown area was a charming mixture of old and new architecture. Enoch's office was on the third floor of an older, false-fronted building. As I entered his reception area, I hoped that my navy linen suit and white blouse afforded some appearance of dignity. I felt like a nine-car pileup.

Mr. Sarrazin's secretary was a kindly woman who brought me coffee and asked me to make myself comfortable. Mr. Sarrazin, she said, would see me shortly.

I tried to make myself calmer by taking deep breaths between sips of coffee. But it wasn't easy. Enoch Sarrazin kept me waiting ten minutes, by which time I was on the brink of hysteria.

Hands outstretched, he smiled broadly. "Hello, Geneva—may I call you Geneva? Welcome to Hot Springs. It's such a pleasure to meet you."

"How do you do, Mr. Sarrazin." My hand was cold and clammy. The attorney tightened his grip, as though trying to warm me and squeeze out the dampness at the same time.

"Call me Enoch. We don't stand on formalities around here. How was your trip to Arkansas?"

"L-lovely, thank you."

"And the hotel, is it satisfactory?"

"Very comfortable." I couldn't help thinking that I wished I'd stayed *in* it last night. Maybe then I wouldn't be so upset.

Even so, I felt myself relax a little. Enoch was the kind of man whose very presence could put people at ease. Dapper and silver-haired, he stood nearly a foot taller than my own five foot six. He had a golfer's tan and the handshake of someone who'd split rails in his day. A self-made man, I ventured. And from the look of his office, a successful one.

He invited me to take a seat in a leather chair that practically swallowed me whole. Enoch settled himself behind his vast mahogany desk. "I trust you've recovered from the shock of your recent good fortune?"

He meant the bathhouse, of course. He had no way of knowing what other recent shocks I was recovering from. "Yes . . . yes, thank you."

He regarded me silently for a while. I tried not to squirm. To my relief, he eventually turned and picked up a file from the credenza behind him. "Why don't we get our business out of the way *before* we tour the property?" he suggested with a smile. "As you can appreciate, there are a few legal formalities regarding execution of the will, but there's no need for you to make a decision right away. We'll just sign a few papers, then head over to the Silverbrooke and let you take a look. How does that sound?"

"Fine." I was running low on polite rejoinders and wished he'd stop asking my opinion. I was feeling too numb to think and wanted only to get things over with as quickly as possible.

The documents Enoch slid across the desk were worded in typical legalese, but he led me patiently through each one before I signed.

"Naturally," he said, "should you decide to transfer your lease of the Silverbrooke, there would be additional paperwork. But for now the place is officially yours. So we'll leave it at that, shall we?"

Again, I replied lamely, "Fine."

When we'd finished with legalities, Enoch led me outside to where his midnight-blue Lincoln was parked. It reminded me of a hearse, but given my maudlin state of mind, the association was understandable. The car's air-conditioning was on full blast, and I started to shiver. Fortunately our destination was only a few blocks away, so I was able to get out before my skin turned blue.

The sight of Bathhouse Row was enough to dispel everything, even the doom and gloom, from my mind. It was, quite simply, breathtaking. A collection of buildings against the imposing backdrop of a mountain, each structure was unique yet shared that faded elegance of an era long gone.

Held spellbound by the flying buttresses, gargoyles and pillars, I was oblivious to the modern bustle around me. It wouldn't have surprised me to see women with parasols and men with spats stepping out of the bathhouses. French Impressionists would have felt at home setting up their easels on this beautiful Arkansas street.

Only one bathhouse, Enoch explained, was currently open for public use. The rest, with the exception of the Silverbrooke, were undergoing various stages of restoration, as evidenced by the presence of scaffolds and work crews.

I don't know how long I'd been gawking before I realized that Enoch must have better things to do than indulge my newfound enchantment. I turned to him apologetically. "Which one is the Silverbrooke?"

"Down there near the end of the row."

The building was set back slightly from the others which explained why I hadn't noticed it. Built of stone in mottled shades of gray, it had wide front steps and ramps on either side leading to double doors of oak.

The bathhouse must have been handsome at one time. Now, with flying buttresses crumbling, and multi-paned windows smashed, the Silverbrooke looked dejected. Even more dejected than me, which was consoling somehow. I felt almost protective toward the place.

"What do you think?" Enoch asked.

"It's beautiful."

He jingled a set of keys. "Care to go inside?"

"Oh, yes, please."

I ignored the stairs in favor of the gently sloping ramp. "It seems the builders were way ahead of their time in considering the disabled."

"That's 'cause a lot of folks came to the bathhouses in wheelchairs and on crutches, hoping to be cured."

"Do the baths really cure?"

Inserting the key into the lock, he chuckled. "Don't rightly know as they do, but if a person believes, they say the mind can be a powerful healing force."

Or a powerfully destructive one, I mused, thinking of the damage I'd done to my hands, and to my slippers. Then I pushed the grim thought aside. There would be time later on to deal with my other problem. For now I welcomed the distraction of wakefulness.

My heart ached when I saw the Silverbrooke's foyer, filthy with animal droppings and years of neglect. The floor had been laid with a pattern of tiny tiles, many of which were now broken or missing. They had apparently formed a mosaic of some kind, but I couldn't make out the depiction.

Along the far side of the room was a marble counter and behind that were dozens of rusty lock boxes. Enoch explained that they were where people had left their valuables while taking the baths. On the wall behind the counter was a large Baroque-style mirror, miraculously intact.

"You're free to sell the contents of the place regardless of what you do with the lease," he said. "I reckon a mirror like that one could fetch a fine price. You don't find solid lead glass like that anymore."

I looked up and saw two brass chandeliers, tarnished and draped with cobwebs. Removing so much as a single nail from this place struck me as sacrilege. For the moment, however, I wanted to do nothing but absorb.

Two doors on either side of the foyer were marked with gilt letters, Men and Ladies. The Ladies' door was falling off its hinges.

It didn't bother me to learn that my inheritance wasn't Buckingham Palace. What bothered me was the Silverbrooke's pitiful state of disrepair. How could Festus whatever-his-name-was have let this happen?

"Could I see the baths?" I asked Enoch.

"By all means. I'll take you through the ladies' section. The men's is pretty much the same, but it's on another floor and I'm not sure of the state of the stairs."

We entered the appropriate door and arrived at a change room. There were cubicles for dressing and lockers for leaving one's clothes. Everything was grimy, but otherwise looked untouched.

Beyond the change area was a long tiled room containing dozens of claw-footed tubs, the old-fashioned kind you could soak in right up to your neck. Tattered curtains divided them from each other, and there were a few moth-eaten bath mitts and sponges hanging on the walls with faded names tacked above them, undoubtedly for the use of their regular clientele.

"Did anyone famous ever visit the Silverbrooke?" I asked, my sense of romance temporarily outweighing other, more oppressive, emotions.

"Absolutely. During the twenties, the Silverbrooke was known as the literary gathering place of Hot Springs. Festus Tulley's grandparents, the original owners, charged lower rates than the other bathhouses, so starving writers as well as celebrities could afford to indulge themselves. Edith Wharton came here, Fitzgerald, Faulkner...."

"No kidding?" The thought that F. Scott Fitzgerald might have been creatively inspired in *my* bathhouse was titillating.

Next, Enoch brought me to a wood-paneled lounge in the rear of the bathhouse. Huge windows looked out on the lush wooded slope of the mountain. "This was where folks got together after the baths to relax and fraternize."

"What a beautiful view," I said, moving toward the window.

"That's Hot Springs Mountain. A lovely place, but dangerous."

For some reason, I shuddered. "Why do you say it's dangerous?"

"Wild animals and such. People figure just 'cause they're in a city, the mountains must be safe. But this here park's as primitive and natural as when the Indians came to take the waters."

I turned away quickly. "Is there anything else to see?"

"Nothing but the basement and an upstairs apartment. We'd likely die of heat prostration going up there on a day like this."

"Who used the apartment?"

"Whoever ran the place. Bathhouse hours started early and ended late, so it made sense for management to live on the premises."

I noticed Enoch glancing discreetly at his watch. "I've been keeping you from your clients."

"Not at all," he replied unconvincingly.

It was strange, but I felt a certain kinship with the Silverbrooke—not quite familiarity, but close to it. Perhaps I had been here with my parents. That might explain the emotion.

"I wonder, Enoch, would you mind if I looked around on my own?"

He seemed hesitant at first, but masked his reaction with a grin. "The Silverbrooke's yours. You can do whatever you

like. But I should warn you, Geneva, the floors and stair-
wells are in pretty sad shape. Be real careful, y'hear?''

"I will."

He handed me the keys. "If you have any problems or
questions, you know where to find me."

"Yes, thank you."

"I'll come by later on and pick you up."

"That won't be necessary. I can walk to my car. It's only
a few blocks away."

He regarded me with an almost paternal expression, obviously concerned about walking, even a few blocks in that
heat. Then he turned. "All right, if you insist."

My heart was thumping with anticipation as I walked the
attorney to the door. I felt like a kid who'd been given a
playhouse, a make-believe place where all kinds of exciting
things could happen. My giddiness was probably a pendulum reaction to my sleepwalking, but that didn't matter. I
was determined to enjoy the feeling while it lasted.

The apartment had aroused my curiosity. After Enoch
left, I set out to find the stairs, bearing the attorney's warning in mind. There was a side door behind the marble counter that opened onto a spiral staircase. It seemed as good a
place as any to start.

Unfortunately the antiquated light switch didn't work,
and the stairwell was pitch dark. That should have been my
first warning to leave well enough alone, but I was feeling
strangely reckless. At least this was honest-to-goodness
daytime reality, over which I had some control.

Step by step I climbed through the darkness, cringing as
I brushed against cobwebs and other disgusting things I
preferred not to identify. Despite what Enoch had said
about the floors, the steps seemed fairly sturdy. They hardly

creaked at all when I gingerly applied my weight. Fresh air, however, was at a premium, and several times I considered turning back. But since I'd come so far, it seemed a shame to give up.

At the top of the steps was a door, a shaft of dusty light shining from underneath. If nothing else, I knew there had to be a window on the other side.

The door, of course, was locked. Jangling blindly through the key ring, I tried to find one that fit. I was perspiring heavily from the heat as well as my heightened state of nerves.

At last I found the right key and turned it in the lock. The door creaked open slowly, revealing a room thick with dust and muted sunlight. I held my skirt to my face to make breathing easier, then stepped inside.

Depressing was my initial opinion. It was hard to tell if the place had ever been cheery. The wallpaper was a faded yellow floral—I'd always hated yellow floral—and the furniture was all covered with sheets. Before exploring further, I headed for the arched windows on the far wall.

They were stuck shut. In my desperation to unstick them, I nearly wrenched my shoulder. But at last one broke loose and grudgingly lifted. I leaned outside, drew in delicious lungfuls of clear air, then took a few moments to check the view.

While climbing the spiral stairs, I had lost my sense of direction. I'd expected this sitting room to overlook the street. Instead it faced the forested slope of Hot Springs Mountain. The mountain that Enoch had called dangerous.

I could see what he meant. The woods had a disturbing, primeval kind of beauty. Maybe it was simply the power of suggestion, but I didn't like the look of the mountain. The feelings it gave me were eerie.

After propping the window open, I set out to explore the rest of the apartment. The kitchen beyond the sitting room had two small windows overlooking the street. Cupboard space was minimal, and the appliances were definitely of an earlier vintage. The stove was an enamel monstrosity; the refrigerator, a small black ice box.

On either side of the sitting room were two bedrooms, the larger with an ensuite bath. The porcelain tub was similar to the claw-footed variety on the ladies' floor and, except for the grunge on the bottom, it was in remarkably good condition.

Most of the furniture in the apartment was heavy, dark and gloomy. But the master bedroom had a beautiful antique brass bed. The ornate headboard stood nearly six feet high, the footboard about half that height.

An antique dealer would certainly be delighted if I chose to sell it. But darn it, I didn't need the money. Why did I feel obliged to reduce everything to dollars and cents? I'd obviously been married to Donald for too long.

I'd rather keep the bed and have it shipped to Minneapolis. Whacking the mattress for emphasis, I nearly suffocated in the rising cloud of dust.

The disturbance of dust was unsettling in more ways than one. It was as though the apartment had suddenly become too quiet. Just by being there, I sensed I was upsetting the slumber of things better left alone.

Heart pounding, I locked the apartment door and descended the stairs. Going down was less harrowing than going up had been, probably because I knew what was at the other end.

I decided that the basement exploration could wait for another day. Rats and rusty plumbing were not that appealing.

I emerged from the stairwell and gasped. Staring from the antique mirror beside me was a face that could only be described as hideous.

Chapter Three

I whirled around to find a gnarled wisp of a woman standing behind me. In person she was not particularly hideous, just old. But to say she was staring had been an understatement. Glaring would be more precise.

"Are you her?" she rasped in a voice like dried bones.

"Her?" I repeated.

"The one who's come back."

The woman wore a dark printed housedress buttoned to the collar and pinned for good measure with an onyx brooch. Her raisin eyes glittered with an intensity that made my nerves prickle.

"I've never been to Hot Springs before—at least not that I know of. You must be mistaking me for someone else."

Setting a pair of shopping bags on the floor, she folded her arms across a bony chest. "You look like her. Your hair's darker, but it's still curly and you got those same big brown eyes."

"Who is this person I supposedly resemble?"

"Lizbet."

"Who's Lizbet?"

"You, I'd reckon."

The lady was obviously off her beam. Abandoning the circular argument, I decided to try another approach. "My name's Geneva Ashford. I'm from Minneapolis,'' I said, reaching across the counter. "Pleased to meet you."

She glanced at my hand as though it was poisonous, then slid back half a step. "Ashford, Ashford," she muttered as if trying to match the name with some long-buried memory.

Lifting the hinged door of the counter, I stepped into the foyer. "I don't believe I caught your name."

"Hepzibah," she snapped as though I should have known.

The name rang a bell, but there was no great mystery to that. Bill Swann, P.I., had mentioned Hepzibah. And how many Hepzibahs could there be in this world? "Are you Festus Tulley's sister?"

"May God have mercy on his soul."

Recalling Mr. Swann's reference to her religious proclivities, I took the answer to mean yes. "Did you, uh...did you used to work here?"

She snorted. "This den of iniquity? I never set foot in the Silverbrooke unless I had to."

Den of iniquity? I didn't know people still used phrases like that. "Then why are you here now, Ms. Tulley?"

"It's *Miss!*"

I bit my cheek to maintain my composure. "Of course. My mistake."

Hepzibah's eyes had a tendency to dim whenever she retreated to consult her, no doubt, faded memory. They were dimming now. "It was a different name," she mused. "Longer, real foreign."

"Who are you talking about?"

"Your folks."

"Oh." That explained a few things. If Hepzibah remembered my parents, it was possible she remembered me. I must have come to the Silverbrooke with them around the time that two-year-old portrait was taken. "My parents' name was Zloczewski," I offered.

She clapped her gnarled hands. "That's it! They're the ones. I knew it was you all along!"

I didn't bother reminding her she'd thought I was Lizbet. At Hepzibah's age, I suppose, any memory was better than none. "How old was I last time you saw me?"

"About two."

I nodded. "Thought so."

"Are you married? Is that why your name is different?"

"I was. I'm divorced."

Her jaw dropped. "Divorced! That's the devil's handiwork!"

Just what I needed. A Holy Roller expounding on the sanctity of marriage, when I was perfectly capable of conjuring guilt on my own. "Why exactly are you here, Miss Tulley?"

"I wanted to see if it was true about you coming back."

"Guess it is," I conceded.

"Have you talked to Calder yet?"

"Who?"

"Calder Carson. He owns all the leases on Bathhouse Row, except for this one and one down the street. Calder's a good man. He'll likely be wanting to make your acquaintance."

Surprisingly Hepzibah's voice grew gentler as she spoke of Calder Carson. I'd begun to suspect she disapproved of everyone. "Mr. Sarrazin might have mentioned his name. I'm sure we'll have an opportunity to meet before I leave."

"You're not stayin' in Hot Springs?"

"I don't think so." Then, more emphatically, I added, "No, I am definitely not staying." I was surprised to find how sad the thought of leaving made me feel.

"Then you won't be reopening the Silverbrooke."

That seemed to please Hepzibah immensely, which only served to fuel my obstinacy. I was still fuming over that remark about the devil's handiwork.

"Actually, now that you mention it, I haven't made a final decision one way or another. Even if I return to Minnesota, that doesn't mean I won't retain the lease. Why? Do you have some objection to the Silverbrooke being reopened?"

The fanatic glitter came back into her eyes. "The Silverbrooke ought to be burned to the ground."

"Burned?" I said, aghast. This woman wasn't senile. She was a raving lunatic! "What do you have against bathhouses, Miss Tulley? Isn't cleanliness supposed to be next to godliness?"

She rose to her full height of about four foot nine. "Don't blaspheme, girl. This place is an abomination."

"This place," I countered, "is a historic landmark."

Unconvinced, Hepzibah shook her head. "Calder Carson'll know what to do with the Silverbrooke. He'll make things right."

I was beginning to realize that Hepzibah Tulley harbored more than civic admiration for this Carson fellow. Not that this dyed-in-the-wool spinster would ever admit it. "Did Mr. Carson send you here to talk to me?"

The woman's papery cheeks flamed with color. "Most certainly not!"

Her indignation was almost amusing, but not amusing enough to make me want to continue this conversation. "Look, Miss Tulley," I said, edging discreetly toward the front door, "I appreciate your coming to see me, and I look forward to meeting Mr. Carson. But if you'll excuse me, I do have to lock up."

She picked up her shopping bags. "Are you staying in the apartment?"

"Upstairs?" I shuddered. "Heavens, no. I have a room at the Whispering Pines."

Hepzibah gave another of her snorts, then marched smartly past me out the door. "Then you oughta go back where you came from, Lizbet. You should've left things well enough alone."

A FEW MINUTES LATER I left the Silverbrooke, trying to assure myself that Hepzibah's rantings were harmless. So she thought I was someone named Lizbet. Big deal.

The curious thing was that she still remembered my parents after all these years—at least, she thought she did. Hepzibah might have confused that detail as well.

Walking along Bathhouse Row, I turned to glance at the Silverbrooke once more. Strange how a building could evoke an emotional reaction, as though possessing a personality of its own. In her dilapidated splendor, the Silverbrooke brought out a sense of compassion in me I'd neither sought nor expected. It was as though she needed someone who cared.

Good grief, now I was sounding as deranged as Miss Tulley. Buildings did not *need* people. And why was I suddenly referring to the Silverbrooke as "she," like some neglected dowager empress?

Driving to the motel, I decided a hot bath and a cool drink, not necessarily in that order, were long overdue. As I walked through the lobby, I heard my name being called.

"Message for you, Ms. Ashford." The desk clerk was waving a slip of paper at me.

A man in a Stetson was leaning across the counter reading the motel brochure. I glanced at him briefly. For a cowboy, he was gorgeous. Long, lean, with dark brown curls peaking out from beneath his hat.

The message was from Enoch. He wanted me to phone his office at my convenience. As I walked away, I heard the cowboy ask the clerk, "Don't you have any monthly rates?"

"No, sir, I'm sorry."

"Okay, thanks anyway, but these prices are out of my league."

I slowed down shamelessly to eavesdrop, but their conversation was already over. Hearing the man stalk toward the door, I risked a glance.

My timing was awful. The cowboy turned at precisely the same moment. I could feel myself blushing, but our eyes locked and held. Despite his rugged good looks, it was not one of those smoldering occasions you see on perfume commercials. The man was staring at me as though I'd grown two heads. He began to approach me.

For some strange reason I felt like running. But my feet might as well have been nailed to the floor.

"Are you all right?" was his peculiar opening remark.

There is no gracious answer, I discovered, to such a question. Envisioning something worse than spinach between my teeth, I said, "What are you talking about?"

Now it was his turn to go a thousand shades of red. "Aren't you..."

"Aren't I what?"

The man scratched his chin. "I could've sworn...no, never mind. I must've mistaken you for someone else. Sorry 'bout that." He tipped his Stetson, then turned around and left.

I felt like I'd landed in the Twilight Zone. In less than an hour, two perfect strangers had mistaken me for someone else. Since when had my looks become so generic?

The first thing I did upon returning to my room was check the mirror. As far as I could tell, nothing was out of the ordinary. The same brown eyes, a few freckles, shoulder-length auburn hair. I was no raving beauty, but from the way Hepzibah and that man had reacted, you'd think I was a gargoyle.

I abandoned the message from Enoch on the bedside table. Whatever he had to say could wait until after I'd collected my thoughts.

Muddled and exhausted, I walked into the bathroom. My tattered nightgown was beside the tub. In the confusion of Hepzibah and the cowboy, I'd almost forgotten about last night's sleepwalking. Now, a fresh wave of anxiety flooded through me.

The muddy slippers beside the bed. The scratches on my legs. The denim jacket. I still had no recollection of where I'd gone last night or what I'd done. But maybe that man in the lobby knew something I didn't. Maybe that's why he'd acted so strangely.

My cheeks flushed with fear and humiliation. What if the jacket was his? What if he and I had—

I couldn't finish the thought. He didn't look the type to take advantage, but what did I know about him? I couldn't even account for my own nocturnal activities.

Dr. Caldwell was right. My sleepwalking was too serious to ignore. Even if I wasn't doing anything unseemly, the constant worry that I might was as bad as the real thing.

I called his office. He was with a patient. I left a message for him to call me collect.

Then I phoned the desk clerk. "This is Geneva Ashford. Do you remember the dark-haired man with the cowboy hat?"

"The one who asked about the monthly rates?"

"That's right. Do you have any idea who he is?"

"I've never seen him before."

"Did he leave a . . . contact number or anything?"

"No, ma'am, I'm sorry."

It was a long shot anyway, I told myself, hanging up the phone. I felt dangerously close to tears. Somewhere out there a stranger was walking around with a piece of my subconscious—and who knew what else—but I had no way of finding him.

Fortunately Dr. Caldwell didn't keep me waiting long. The phone rang within minutes. "Geneva, how are you?"

"Fine, thanks." What a dumb reply. I decided to start over. "I walked in my sleep again last night."

"What happened?"

"Wish I knew." I described the condition of my nightgown and slippers, the scratches on my legs, the jacket. I couldn't bring myself to admit that I might have just met the owner.

"You have no recollection of a dream or anything?"

"Nothing."

Dr. Caldwell sighed. "When are you coming home?"

"I'm booked for next week, but I can always change the date."

"Are you going to take my advice?"

"About therapy? At this point, I'll do anything."

"Good girl. I'll make an appointment right away with the hypnotherapist and get back to you."

I would have preferred an instant solution, but that was asking the impossible. "Thanks, Doctor."

"Did you get the prescription filled?"

"Yes."

"I'd suggest you take a couple of those sedatives after dinner. Get a good night's sleep, and try not to worry."

Trying not to worry was a tall order, but I loved the idea of a good night's sleep. I thanked Dr. Caldwell again and hung up, feeling a little reassured. At least, his was a familiar voice. I wasn't totally alone with this affliction.

For lack of anything better to do, I filled the tub and climbed in. I tried to concentrate on practical things like the ramifications of reopening the bathhouse. Instead my mind cluttered with images of the man from the lobby.

I'd never cared much for cowboys, not since I outgrew my childhood crush on a young Clint Eastwood in *Rawhide*. My current preference in men ran to pinstripes and wing tips, but the cowboy had certainly done his attire justice. Faded denim clung in all the right places. His shoulders were just broad enough to strain the cambric of his Western-style shirt. I couldn't stop wondering...

That's sick, I told myself. I'd never seen the man before in my life! Scratch that. I probably had, and that made it even worse. I had no way of knowing whether my lustful thoughts were just my imagination or subconscious reminiscence.

I dried myself quickly, feeling the desperate need to hear another familiar voice. I called Enoch. He didn't have any earthshaking news. Just wanted to know how I was doing and make sure I hadn't come to any harm at the Silverbrooke.

He asked if I'd reached a decision about the lease. I said no, but that I would sleep on it and get back to him. I winced at the word *sleep* then changed the subject. "I met Festus's sister."

Enoch groaned. "I was afraid that might happen. I hope she didn't upset you."

Practically everyone was upsetting me lately, but that wasn't his problem. "No, not really," I replied. "But she kept insisting I was someone else."

"Who?"

"Someone called Lizbet."

He muttered some colorful Southern oath. "Don't let her worry you. Hepzibah hasn't been in her right mind for years."

"I gathered as much, but who is Lizbet?"

"Who knows? Festus's sister used to run a home for wayward girls. It was probably someone she knew back then."

Wayward girls, dens of iniquity. This was not only the Twilight Zone; it was another century.

"Did she happen to mention Calder Carson?" Enoch asked.

"Several times."

"Figured as much. Calder's about the only person Hepzibah will associate with. He's an elder at the church and keen on refurbishing Bathhouse Row his way."

"Is my presence going to pose a problem?"

"Not at all. Calder's a gentleman. If you decide to retain the lease and reopen the Silverbrooke, I'm sure he won't give you any trouble."

"That's good." I hesitated before asking the next question, almost afraid of the answer. "What does Hepzibah have against the Silverbrooke?"

Enoch's chuckle was reassuring. "You gotta know the lady to understand. Rumors used to go around that the fraternization between gentlemen and ladies extended beyond the Silverbrooke's lounge, if you get my drift."

Expecting worse, I said nothing at first. "Did Festus encourage that sort of thing?"

"Are you kidding? He partook of indoor sports more than anyone. Festus Tulley had quite a reputation as a gambler and ladies' man, unlike Hepzibah and his folks. But that was back in the days when people took those things more seriously. If he were alive and running the place now, I dare say no one would even care."

I tended to agree with Enoch. If coed baths were the worst that went on at the Silverbrooke, then Hepzibah Tulley really was overreacting. Anyway, I had no intention of following in Festus Tulley's allegedly debauched footsteps.

I thanked the attorney for his concern.

"No problem. If you have any more questions, feel free to call. You've got my home number."

"Yes. Oh, one more thing, Enoch. Did you ever meet my parents?"

There was a pause at the other end. "Why, no. What makes you ask?"

"Nothing. I just thought since Hepzibah seemed to remember them and they used to come here . . ."

"Lots of people came to Hot Springs to take the baths, Geneva. And I didn't work at the Silverbrooke."

"You're right. It was a silly question. Thanks again for your help."

There was nothing worthwhile on television, and the radio was full of hurtin' country songs that did little to ease my restless state of mind. Yet it was too early to take the sedatives. Besides, I was hungry. I needed to get out of the motel, if only for a few hours.

Driving through downtown Hot Springs, I didn't deliberately set out to drive past Bathhouse Row, but something led me there through the confusing network of streets. I slowed as I approached the Silverbrooke. The stonework at dusk had taken on a haunting bluish tinge. Without the din of jackhammers and work crews, the whole street looked different, ethereal somehow.

Careful, Geneva, I told myself. You're getting sentimental again, and that's not like you. It was vital that my decision about the lease be based on sound reasoning. Never mind that sound reasoning, outside of my job, had never come naturally.

I spotted a pancake house almost directly across from the bathhouses. The place looked quaint and homey. The way I was feeling tonight, quaint and homey sounded ideal. I pulled into the nearest parking space.

The restaurant was half-empty. I was trying to decide between a table and a stool at the counter when my heart stopped. So, for that matter, did the rest of me. Sitting all by himself at the counter was the cowboy.

I slid into a chair at the table nearest me. The man hadn't seen me yet, but the restaurant wasn't large. I couldn't hope to get through an entire meal without being noticed.

There was a menu wedged between the bottles of condiments. I snatched it and held it up in front of my face, then realized my behavior was bordering on ridiculous.

Running into him again was a stroke of luck. If my suspicions were correct, the cowboy knew something about what had happened last night. I'd be crazy to pass up this opportunity.

I shook my head ironically. All things considered, I probably was crazy.

The waitress ambled over in leisurely Arkansas fashion to take my order. I mumbled some greeting and settled on the first thing my eyes came to—blueberry buckwheat pancakes with sausage.

She went off to relay the order. On her way to the kitchen, she stopped to refill the cowboy's coffee cup. Apparently lost in thought, he scarcely noticed.

I sat there for a few minutes, trying to decide on the best course of action. I couldn't just go up to the man and ask him if he was missing a jacket. Well, maybe I could, but there had to be a gentler way to ease into the situation.

I could always say I was feeling lonely and wanted someone to talk to over dinner. No, that sounded desperate. Actually the cowboy looked kind of lonely himself. Maybe I could just make it seem like a friendly invitation.

Mustering the courage from heaven knew where, I got up from the table and crossed the room. "Excuse me," I said, tapping him on the shoulder.

The man looked up. His eyes widened. "Cripes. It's you again."

I wanted to bolt, but managed to stand my ground. "Yes, we, uh...we met at the motel."

"You could say that," he replied, looking as comfortable as I felt.

"I thought since, well, both of us seemed to be from out of town and alone..."

A cute grin began to surface. "Yeah, go on."

Dammit, he was enjoying my discomfiture. How many other things about me had he enjoyed? There was only one way to find out. "I was wondering if you'd like to join me for dinner."

"Are you gonna suck your thumb again?"

"I beg your pardon?"

"Never mind, I shouldn't have said that."

Suck my thumb? That hardly fit in with my reconstruction of events. "So will you join me or not?"

"Can't promise I'd be great company."

Something in his tone made me relax a little. "I'm not asking for great company. Regular conversation will do."

"All right, you're on."

My knees were knocking when I realized how close I'd come to being rejected. If he'd turned me down, I'd have probably left the restaurant in utter degradation, knowing he would carry my secret to his grave. He accompanied me to my table and settled into the seat across from me.

"I'm Geneva Ashford," I said.

He shook my hand warmly. "The name's Travis. Travis McCabe."

It was an irrelevant thought, but Travis McCabe was the perfect name for a rugged, masculine man like him. His deep blue eyes were set off perfectly by an even deeper tan. His face, though lined, had an ageless quality that could have put him anywhere between thirty and forty. But since there wasn't a hint of gray in his wavy brown hair, I decided he must be closer to thirty.

"Where you from, Geneva?"

Whatever had happened the night before, he seemed intent on making this a normal occasion. For that I was grateful. There would be plenty of time for careful probing later on.

"Minneapolis," I replied. "And you?"

"Dallas."

A Texan. I should have guessed. Despite his rather world-weary demeanor, he had an expansiveness about him that I'd always associated with Texans. He might be down on his luck, I surmised, but never out.

"Are you just passing through?" I asked.

"Don't know yet."

My determination to discover the truth was wavering. If all his replies were going to be this brief, it could be a difficult evening.

The waitress came over and asked Travis if he wanted to order. He glanced at me with his beguiling boyish grin. "I forgot to ask. Are you buying?"

My heart, so help me, melted. This man couldn't have done anything to hurt me last night. I was almost sure of it. "Order whatever you like," I said quietly.

He picked up a menu and selected a meal of epic proportions—pancakes, eggs, home fries and ham. "And bring us a pot of coffee," he added.

"Do you have decaf?" I asked the waitress.

"No, ma'am, sorry."

Oh well, I could survive the caffeine. After all, I had those knock-out pills waiting for me at the motel.

The waitress left, and Travis leaned back. Suddenly conscious of his miles of leg beneath the table, I tucked my own beneath the chair.

"So," he said. "You're staying at the Whispering Pines?"

"That's right."

"Been there long?"

"Since yesterday."

Travis looked at me strangely.

"What about you?" I said quickly, anxious to keep the conversation rolling. "Did you find someplace to stay?"

"Yeah, a ways out of town."

Travis seemed fascinated with me. I found myself wishing it could just be a physical attraction, but I sensed there was more to it than that. The guy was obviously trying to verify my sanity.

"Is this your first visit to Hot Springs?" I asked, hoping he'd be impressed to see that I could maintain a normal conversation.

His expression told me nothing. "No, I used to come here as a kid. I've got family here."

I wondered briefly why he wasn't staying with them, but not all families felt obligated to house their visiting relatives. And in a resort town like Hot Springs, that was probably doubly true.

"This is my first visit," I said. "From what little I've seen, Arkansas is a beautiful state."

"You're lucky you missed the racing season. It gets a little crazy here when the horses are running."

Good, I thought, another innocuous topic of conversation. "Are you a racing fan?"

"Me? No. I used to raise quarter horses, but just for fun."

Travis must have had money at one time if he could afford to raise quarter horses. Now for some reason, he was reduced to staying "a ways out of town."

"What brings you to Hot Springs?" Travis asked.

"I have . . . legal business here." Until I knew for certain what I'd be doing with the Silverbrooke, it seemed wise not to say too much. If I hadn't already.

"A tycoon, huh?"

"Nothing that exciting. I'm just a humble loans officer."

"No kiddin'?"

"No kidding."

"I hate banks," he said. "They're so damned . . ."

"Pompous?"

For the first time since he'd sat down, he laughed. "Yeah, pompous. That's the word I was looking for."

His laughter was deep and lusty. It lit up his face and crinkled the corners of his eyes. Perversely I thought of Donald. In all the years I'd known him, he never laughed like that.

"How long are you staying?" Travis asked.

"I don't know yet. Maybe a week or so."

Our pancakes arrived, so huge they nearly hung off the plates. For the next little while we ate in silence, while I gathered the courage to bring up my sleepwalking. And waited for him to do the same.

Travis laid down his knife and fork. "Have you had a bath yet?"

My mouth was full of buckwheat and blueberries, but my eyes must have registered surprise.

"At one of the bathhouses," he added.

"Oh, right, that must be a normal question in Hot Springs. No, I haven't. But I thought there was only one in operation."

"Only one on the Row, but there are bathhouses all over town. Not with the same notoriety, of course."

There seemed to be a note of cynicism in his voice, but I might have imagined it. "Are the baths as wonderful as they say?"

His deep blue gaze slid over me. "Oh, yeah. Definitely worth trying at least once."

This was a man who'd mastered the art of visual messages. I picked up my coffee hurriedly, noticing too late it was empty.

"Let me fill that for you." Travis reached over to take the cup. Our hands touched. If the contact was accidental, what followed could not have been. He linked his fingers with mine and drew the cup toward himself as if inviting me to come along.

Outside, I froze. Inside, I ignited. Then I pulled my hand away and Travis poured the coffee as if nothing had happened. Which was, I suppose, understandable. Nothing had.

Even if it was a pass, I had it coming. I'd invited a strange man to join me for dinner, hadn't I?

No! Surely in this day and age, men were more enlightened. An invitation to dinner did not imply an invitation elsewhere, no matter who did the asking.

I couldn't put off knowing any longer. "Travis, I've got to ask you something."

His mouth tightened. "Go ahead."

"Did I . . . that is, did you see me somewhere last night?"

"You don't remember?"

I shook my head.

"Yeah, I saw you."

His confirmation did not have the cathartic effect I'd hoped for. Instead I felt as though the truth might be more than I could handle. And if it was, there was no one here to help me through the fear. "Where was I?"

"On the mountain behind Bathhouse Row."

"Wh-what was I doing?"

Travis shrugged. "Nothing much. Just wandering around."

I exhaled slowly. "That's all?"

"Basically." His eyes narrowed with concern. "Were you on drugs or something?"

His misconception made me laugh. "No, I don't even take aspirin. I'm a sleepwalker."

"Holy smokes."

Travis shuddered as though I'd admitted to being a zombie. But some people had that impression of sleepwalkers. And in some ways, the analogy wasn't inaccurate.

"Do you still have my jacket?" he asked.

"It's in my hotel room."

Travis did something totally unexpected. He reached across the table and took my hand. "Don't look so worried. Nothing happened between you and me. You were cold, I gave you my coat. That's all."

I battled the urge to burst into tears. "Really?"

"Really."

The waitress brought the check, and I picked it up. Now that the truth was out in the open, I didn't know what else to say. I pulled some money out of my wallet and thanked Travis for joining me.

"Thank you," he said. "I really enjoyed this evening."

"Me, too," I admitted quickly.

Travis watched me pay the waitress. I could sense that it bothered him. But his reaction didn't strike me as sexist.

Even if I'd been a man, his pride would still have been ran-kled.

For a moment I forgot my own problems. Travis Mc-Cabe was obviously accustomed to paying his own way in life. I wondered, not for the first time, why he no longer could.

"Do you get out much at night?" he asked. Seeing my reaction, his complexion reddened again. "Sorry, lousy choice of words."

I managed a slight laugh. "That's all right. I just arrived last night."

"Oh yeah, I forgot. Well, listen, if I manage to line up a job before you head back to Minneapolis, would you care to go out some evening?"

I felt flattered. With a man like him, who wouldn't be? But something about Travis McCabe's invitation made me uncomfortable. I couldn't be sure whether he liked me or felt sorry for me.

There were, however, a number of empty evenings loom-ing between now and when I returned home. Anything was better than feeling sorry for myself all alone. "Yes, I'd like to go out with you."

His grin was all boy, but there was nothing juvenile about the spark in Travis's eyes. That part was all man. He walked me to my car, thanked me for dinner and said good-night. All things considered, a perfect gentleman.

I knew I shouldn't have had the coffee, but it was worth it. Travis's honesty had helped put my mind at ease. There was no lurid tale behind the denim jacket. It had just been a casual encounter between a man and a woman who'd been walking in her sleep.

I decided not to take the sedative. So what if I stayed awake all night? At least then I wouldn't sleepwalk. Be-sides, I'd forgotten how good it felt to lie in the dark and fantasize, and Travis McCabe was definitely prime fantasy material.

I found myself imagining how it would feel to hold his face in my hands—the roughness of his whiskers, the satin of his lips. I wondered how he would sound, murmuring words of love in that slow, sexy drawl? Not that I'd necessarily find out, but still there was no harm in pretending.

Before long I started to get drowsy. At first I fought the sensation, concerned about what might happen if I succumbed to sleep. But eventually my exhaustion won out. I whispered Travis's name one last time, as if it were a talisman, then closed my eyes and fell asleep.

The crash and thump that followed occurred almost simultaneously. I leaped up. *Lord, don't tell me, not again!*

But no, I was still in bed, the covers undisturbed.

Switching on the lamp, the first thing I noticed was that the curtains were billowing.

The windows had definitely been closed when I went to bed. But they were obviously open now. I didn't like to think about who could have opened them.

Hardly daring to look around, I got up to investigate. Shards of glass were scattered across the carpet. As I got nearer I saw why. There was a jagged hole in the window.

I turned to look at the bed. A rock, the size of a man's fist, lay on my pillow, mere inches from where my head had been.

Chapter Four

For a few minutes I wasn't even sure if I was awake or whether that rock on my pillow was real. Maybe I'd somehow woken up in the middle of my own nightmare.

But no, if this was a nightmare, it was the waking variety. There was nothing illusionary about the shattered glass, nothing dreamlike in my narrowly escaping injury.

As reality took hold, I began to tremble. Asleep or awake made no difference. I seemed to be losing control in both areas.

Carefully I edged my way to the phone and picked up the receiver. "S-something's happened," I stammered to the clerk. "A rock—"

"Beg your pardon, Ms. Ashford? Couldn't hear you."

Mentally I clung to the cheerful voice at the other end of the line. "A rock through my window...glass all over."

"I'll be right there. Don't move."

True to his word, he showed up right away. Or maybe it took ten minutes, I don't really know. I was too shaken to be aware of mundane things like time.

"Damn kids anyway," he muttered while inspecting the damage.

I was wrapped in a terry robe, virtually cowering in a corner of the room. "What kids?"

"Hooligans, bums. You know how they are."

I hadn't even considered that this might be random vandalism. In my jangled state, I had automatically linked the rock with everything else that had happened lately. My sleepwalking, the Silverbrooke, Hepzibah, Travis. It wasn't a rational assumption, but very few things seemed rational these days.

"Do you really think it's just kids?" I asked in a small voice.

"Sure. Things like this happen. I'm just awfully glad you weren't hurt."

I stared at the fist-sized rock on the pillow, and panic threatened once again. I might have woken up in the hospital—if I'd woken up at all.

"Mind if I call the police?" the clerk asked.

"No...no, of course not."

The night clerk placed the call, then made arrangements to move me to another room.

I was nursing a complimentary brandy when two policemen arrived. I'd calmed down somewhat by then.

At first, their questions were straightforward enough. What time did I go to bed? Did I hear anything outside my window before I fell asleep?

There wasn't much to say, yet I had the craziest feeling that I was deliberately withholding evidence. As though the police would actually care that in Minneapolis I'd beaten my hands bloody. Or that last night I'd walked for miles with no recollection of where I'd gone. Or that the Silverbrooke Bathhouse evoked strange emotions for me, and I didn't know why.

The police had no need to know these things. They were only investigating a rock through a window. "Do you know anyone in Hot Springs who might want to harm you?"

The question startled me. I still hadn't come to terms with the fact I'd harmed myself. "I . . . I've only been here two days."

"You're on vacation, aren't you?"

"Not exactly." So I was going to have to tell them after all. It occurred to me, while apprising them of my inheritance, that I now had a police file in Hot Springs as well as Minneapolis. An alarming realization for someone who had never even let a parking meter expire.

When they requested a list of people I'd been in contact with since my arrival, I felt like screaming. Couldn't they understand? I had no enemies! I was a nice, normal person!

One of the officers must have sensed my agitation. He assured me their questions were routine. He even acknowledged the desk clerk might be right, that the rock throwing was a random act. I just happened to be in the wrong place at the wrong time.

His remark nearly made me laugh. That was precisely the feeling I was getting about Hot Springs.

My list of contacts was short. Enoch Sarrazin, Hepzibah Tulley. At the mention of Hepzibah, the officers glanced at each other.

"Do you know her?" I asked.

"Pretty much everyone in Hot Springs does," was the policeman's tactful reply. "Anyone else you can think of?"

When Travis came to mind, I hesitated. I didn't want to get him involved. None of this was his fault. Then again, none of this was mine, either. "Travis McCabe," I said at last.

The policeman took the name down then clapped his notebook shut. "That's about all we can do for now, Ms. Ashford. Hopefully the remainder of your stay will be more pleasant."

I saw them to the door, naively wondering how things could get worse.

After they left I knew the answer. I was alone again. Alone. With hours of darkness still ahead of me.

Bed seemed the only logical place to wait out the night, but I was afraid to take the sleeping pills. What if someone came after me while I was unconscious? I crawled under the covers, thoroughly convinced that sleep would never come.

But somehow it must have. I awoke the next morning to the sound of a ringing phone.

It was Dr. Caldwell. He had booked an appointment with his hypnotherapist friend in St. Paul. The date was two weeks away. I told him that would be fine. I was sure I'd be home by then.

Hearing his familiar voice felt so wonderful, I wanted to hear another one. I had promised to phone Donald as soon as I arrived in Hot Springs. This was my third day, so I hadn't exactly kept my promise, but I decided late was better than never.

He would probably be frantic by now. For all Donald's complaints about my clinginess, he still seemed to relish the role of mother hen.

There was no answer at his apartment. Surely he'd be up by now, getting ready for work. I took a shower then tried again.

By eight-thirty I gave up, feeling undeniably abandoned. Donald was always there for me, even when I didn't need him. Where the heck was he, now that I did?

My next thought was of Travis. I knew nothing about the man, but I liked him. And somehow I felt he could be trusted.

I wondered whether Travis would actually call. Maybe he was just trying to make me feel better. If he didn't phone, I had no way of contacting him. He'd only said he was staying somewhere in the outskirts of town. Dammit anyway, I should have had the sense to ask where.

Last night's rock throwing still bothered me, but not as much as I'd thought it would. Maybe a good night's sleep had been all I'd needed. There was no evidence that I'd wandered anywhere during the night. That alone was reason to celebrate. But how much nicer it would be to celebrate with Travis.

Outside, a gorgeous day was beckoning. I would have loved to laze around the swimming pool at the Whispering Pines with a good book. But there were decisions that needed to be made first. I'd seen the Silverbrooke, conferred with Enoch, but I hadn't made up my mind about the bequest. Once I had, maybe I could relax—even get some more sleep if I was lucky.

I drove to the Silverbrooke after breakfast. I had no specific plans other than to explore the place more thoroughly and give myself time to think. The familiarity that settled over me when I entered this time felt perfectly natural. I'd been here the day before. The Silverbrooke and I were no longer strangers.

My footsteps echoed through the silent, almost melancholy, bath chamber. The rows of claw-footed tubs stood like mute sentinels of a golden era.

I tried to imagine how it must have been. Steam rising and swirling through the air, muted laughter of patrons and their hardworking attendants. The thermal water would gurgle, the plumbing clang as tubs were emptied and scrubbed for the next bather.

The images were incredibly vivid, but then I'd always had an active imagination. And anyway, the ambience spoke for itself. It fairly echoed with the ghosts of its former glory.

Running my finger along grimy porcelain, I was surprised to experience the same proprietary twinge as I had the day before. It wasn't like me to develop such attachments. After inheriting my parents' food stores, I had felt overwhelmed, totally uninterested and unqualified for the task of managing them. I'd sold the chain at the first opportunity.

Strangely I didn't feel that same urgency about the Silverbrooke. If anything I hated the thought of letting it go. Maybe it was just a sign of maturity, a willingness to accept responsibility. I couldn't imagine any other reason.

I located the stairs leading to the basement. They were nearly rotted away from dampness. It would have been crazy to go down there alone. The rising odor of mildew was enough to make me gag.

Finding some old janitorial supplies in a storage closet, I took a broom and swept the worst of the filth from the tiled lobby. The mosaic, though badly damaged, depicted a lion and a lamb lying together. The peaceable kingdom. Appropriate, I thought, for a place that had once specialized in the repose and rejuvenation of stressed minds and bodies.

I put the broom away, my mind buzzing with possibilities. There was so much that could be done with a place like this, and from a marketing standpoint, the timing couldn't be better. All over the country, people were trying to get more in touch with their bodies and themselves, exploring the ancient truths of holistic medicine and spiritual enlightenment. These thermal baths had apparently been used for centuries by Native Americans who knew and understood their curative effects.

Personally I knew next to nothing about natural spas. But maybe there was something to their claim. And maybe it was time the Silverbrooke had another chance to prove herself.

After locking up, I walked the few blocks to Enoch Sarrazin's office. Fortunately I caught him between appointments and he was able to see me right away.

"Geneva, how are you?" Ebullient and gracious as ever, he led me into his office. "Have you had a chance to make up your mind?"

Accepting his offer of coffee, I took a seat across from him. "I've decided to retain the lease and reopen the Silverbrooke."

He lifted an eyebrow. "You don't say?"

"You seem surprised."

"Now don't get me wrong, Geneva. I'm more than delighted with your decision. But somehow I didn't picture you as the type to take on such an awesome task."

"I admit I'm not the most qualified person in the world, but the Silverbrooke fascinates me. I would love to see her restored and reopened."

"She is a beauty, I'll grant you that."

"Would you be willing to handle the legal work—getting building permits and all of that?"

"That was part of the will's proviso, as you may recall. Not that I'd have had it any other way. Festus Tulley was a dear friend. I'm proud to play a part in carrying out his wishes."

"That's good."

"But now that you'll be heading back to Minneapolis, there's no need to concern yourself with day-to-day details. I know everyone there is to know in the restoration business and, I assure you, the Silverbrooke will be in the best of hands."

My return to Minneapolis was a reasonable assumption on Enoch's part. I had no intention of staying indefinitely in Hot Springs. But I did intend to make the most of what time I had left.

"Actually, Enoch, I was hoping to do some of the groundwork myself. Estimates, hiring, that sort of thing."

"Oh? How long are you planning to stay?"

"Another week and a half."

His smile was indulgent. "Don't know as you'll have much luck getting things rolling that fast, but you could try. Listen, Geneva, have you given any serious thought to the cost of this undertaking?"

"Yes, but money's not a problem. I plan to call my accountant today."

"I understand you got a sizable inheritance from your parents. But even so, a bathhouse is a notoriously expensive proposition. Why, the damage from humidity alone'll cost you thousands each year."

"Every business has its losses. But I still think the Silverbrooke is worth the risk."

"It's your money, and I'm not authorized to tell you how to spend it. I do have one suggestion though."

"I'm certainly open to those."

"If you're serious about doing the hiring and firing yourself, you might want to get in touch with Calder Carson first."

"The man who's restoring the other bathhouses."

"That's right. There isn't anyone in this town more experienced in the restoration business. What's more, folks 'round here respect him. You'd do well to have him on your side."

I appreciated Enoch's suggestion and agreed to take Calder's number. But I was determined to handle this project my own way. After all, my parents had started off with nothing and built themselves a fortune. Maybe I needed to prove that I'd inherited their ingenuity in addition to their wealth.

MY FIRST STOP after leaving Enoch's office was the Hot Springs Chamber of Commerce. The administrative assistant was more than helpful, giving me reams of information about the local business community. I returned to the motel with enough enthusiasm to overcome most of my other doubts.

Granted I knew nothing about construction, let alone restoring a hundred-year-old health spa. The most I'd ever done was wallpaper my bedroom, only to have Donald point out smugly that the vines were growing upside down.

What it came down to was that Donald, Enoch and Calder Carson were all men. I knew myself too well. Whenever there was a man around, I tended to relinquish responsibility for anything I didn't already understand. This time, however, things were going to be different.

The simplest place to start, it seemed to me, was the Yellow Pages. I looked up *Contractors* and was mortified. Who'd have believed there were so many varieties? There were contractors specializing in alterations, brick and masonry, building, concrete, excavating, foundations, heating, insulation, paving, plastering, plumbing and trenching—whatever that was. There was, unfortunately, no one who advertised bathhouse renovation as his specialty.

Undaunted, I called the first alteration contractor. The man was most encouraging, said he'd worked on bathhouses before and would be happy to provide an estimate. Then he asked me which bathhouse. When I told him, the change in his tone was unmistakable.

"The Silverbrooke, you said?"

"That's right."

"The one over on Bathhouse Row?"

"Yes."

He hemmed and hawed for a while, then asked me again how soon I needed the estimate. As soon as possible, I repeated.

"Geez, I'm sorry, lady, but we're booked right through till the end of summer."

"But you just finished saying you could come over this week."

"I know, I musta looked at the appointment book wrong. I'm awful sorry."

Shouldering my disappointment, I thanked him and hung up. I tried the next few numbers, some of which were answering machines. But every contractor I talked to gave me a response remarkably similar to the first one. "The Silverbrooke? Gosh, I'm sorry, ma'am, but . . ."

My frustration grew with every call. By the time I got to the heating specialists, I was convinced there was a massive conspiracy. I tried postponing mention of the Silverbrooke until I'd received a firm commitment, but that didn't help. As soon as I gave the address, all manner of excuses arose.

"What exactly do you have against the Silverbrooke?" I asked a tile setter. "Is it haunted or something?"

He stammered some noncommittal reply, then finally admitted, "It's just that most of us don't feel Hot Springs needs another bathhouse on the Row. We got more than enough in town already."

By that time, I was seething. Who were they to tell me that Hot Springs didn't need another bathhouse? Okay, so maybe the Silverbrooke was a losing proposition, but it was my money. As long as the contractors were paid, why should they care?

I was beginning to develop my own theory about who was behind the boycott of my bathhouse. Hot Spring's favorite citizen, Calder Carson, a man so charismatic he could even quiver the brittle heartstrings of Hepzibah Tulley. He owned all the other leases on Bathhouse Row except one, a powerful position in a town the size of Hot Springs.

I called his office, determined to have a word with the man. His secretary informed me that Mr. Carson was at the bathhouses. Expecting another rebuff, I identified myself as the new leaseholder of the Silverbrooke. To my amazement, she expressed congratulations and offered to page her boss.

She returned to the phone a minute later and told me in which bathhouse I could find him. Mr. Carson was expecting me and would be there for the next half hour.

Her cooperative attitude took some of the wind out of my sails. But maybe that was part of Calder's tactics. No need to play the heavy if he already had the whole town on his side.

The bathhouse where I was to meet him was the largest and grandest on the Row. It stood four stories high with rows of awninged windows, the front exquisitely landscaped with magnolias and holly.

The marble foyer was breathtaking, despite the scaffolds, drop cloths and crews of workmen. I was standing there in open admiration when a small wiry man in a suit and hard hat approached me.

"You must be Miss Ashford," he said, extending his hand and smiling.

"Geneva. You're Mr. Carson?"

"Call me Calder. I'd heard through the grapevine you were in town. A pleasure to meet you."

I'll bet it is. Aloud, I expressed a more courteous sentiment.

He took a spare hard hat from a workbench and handed it to me. "Hope you don't mind wearing this. We're pretty big on safety around here."

The hat was too large and kept sliding down my nose, which did nothing to boost my self-esteem. I gamely held the hat in place and followed Calder to an office in the rear of the building.

"This is a beautiful building," I had to admit.

"Why, thank you. We're hoping to turn it into a casino if we can just get through the red tape."

"But if Hot Springs already has horse racing, why would a casino be a problem?"

"Because Bathhouse Row belongs to the National Park system, and law books are pretty specific about no gambling on their property. 'Course, I get my share of flak from the local do-gooders too."

Grudgingly I had to admit that I liked the man, at least so far. Assuming he wasn't already an adversary, he might even make a good ally.

"Saw Bill Swann just the other day," Calder said, taking a seat across from me. "Said he'd just about given up all hope of finding you."

I made a mental note to get in touch with the investigator. He'd been nice, and it wouldn't hurt to have another contact in Hot Springs. "Yes, I'm sure it was quite a search."

"So you came down to take a look-see, did you?"

"That's right." I searched Calder's small features for signs of resentment, but saw nothing. The man was a closed book.

"What do you think of the Silverbrooke?" he asked.

"I love it. And I've decided to retain the lease."

He didn't miss a beat. "Good for you! I admire a lady with business acumen."

"Thank you. The reason I came to see you, Calder, is that I'm encountering some resistance from the local contractors."

"I'm sorry to hear that. What kind of resistance?"

When I told him, he didn't appear the least bit surprised. If anything, he seemed amused. "You placed the phone calls yourself, right?"

"Yes."

"Then it's not so hard to understand. We pride ourselves on being progressive here in Hot Springs. But in the construction business, well, I'm afraid things don't change too fast."

"What do you mean?"

"At the risk of offending you, Geneva, you are a woman. And a Yankee, to boot."

I couldn't believe what I'd heard. The woman part wasn't too surprising—but Yankee?

"The Civil War ended over a hundred years ago, Calder."

"I know. Like I said, some things don't change fast. Longtimers like to stick with their own kind. I've been here twenty years myself, and they still call me the new kid on the block."

"But you're one of Hot Spring's most important citizens."

"Let me tell you, it wasn't easy earnin' their respect. Not that folks don't welcome outsiders, but you gotta go about things the right way."

"What is the right way?"

He ran a hand through his thinning hair. "Well, for one thing, who you know in this town is just as important as what you know. My wife, God rest her soul, was a longtimer. She did a lot to put me in touch with the right people."

I smiled sweetly. "So I take it you know the right people."

Calder laughed. "Sweetie, I *am* the right people. All I gotta do is put out the word, and you'll have all the help you need."

My fingers tightened around the hard hat on my lap. I could just imagine what "word" he'd put out. *Humor the lady, boys. She thinks she can do this herself.* But if that was what it took to conduct business in the Deep South, who was I to buck tradition?

It rankled, but I didn't see any alternative. "I'd appreciate whatever you can do, Calder. But I'm only going to be in Hot Springs until the end of next week. Does your grapevine work that quickly?"

"You'd be surprised."

No doubt I would.

"It's all settled then. You just let me take care of things, and everything will be fine." Before I could respond, he added, "Seein' as you're here, why don't I give you a tour of my buildings?"

"I'd like that," I replied. It was a great opportunity to scout the competition.

We left Calder's office together. "Tell you the truth," he said, "I'm glad you're reopening the Silverbrooke as a bathhouse. We could use a second one on the Row. Tourists these days seem to love them. Not like a few years ago."

I had to admit Calder's restoration efforts were impressive. He obviously took pride in his work. One of the bathhouses was to be a museum, another a bed and breakfast. The restoration was in keeping with the ambience of Hot Springs in its heyday. If I could keep my stubborn pride out of the way, I might even learn a lot from him.

When the tour was finished, Calder said. "Now that we're neighbors on the Row, you come round and see me anytime, y'hear?"

Resignedly I promised him I would.

"One of these nights, I'll have to take you to the country club, introduce you to the right people."

My first reaction was to turn him down. My parents were once refused membership in a Boston country club because of their Polish ancestry, and I still harbored some of their resentment.

But Calder was right. Elitist or not, country clubs were useful for meeting the right people and that was obviously important in this situation. I swallowed my objection unuttered. "That'd be nice, Calder. Thanks again for your help." So much for my delusions of independence. Yet another man was coming to my rescue.

SINCE I WAS ALREADY in the neighborhood, I decided to visit the Silverbrooke once more. Now it was officially mine. My very own bathhouse.

It gave me a wonderful feeling to unlock the doors and step inside. Whirling through the lobby like a princess at a ball, I pictured the Silverbrooke restored and resplendent. The chandeliers glistening, the lion and the lamb pieced together once again—

"Excuse me," a man said.

The voice caught me midpirouette. Cheeks flaming, I lowered my arms and turned around. There stood Travis McCabe, hat in hand, looking at me as though I was certifiably insane.

Chapter Five

"Is this a private affair," he asked, "or can anyone join in?"

My face turned a hundred shades of crimson, each darker than the last. "Haven't you ever heard of knocking?"

"At a bathhouse?"

"Good point," I admitted. Anyway, there was no reason for me to be upset with Travis. I was the one who'd been twirling. I straightened my skirt and assumed a more friendly expression. "So how are you?"

"Okay." The tone of his reply suggested that he was thinking at least one of us was.

"Is there, uh . . . that is, were you looking for me?"

"Yeah, I heard you were hiring."

"Gosh, he works fast."

"Who?"

"Calder."

Travis's eyes wandered. "You mean Calder Carson?"

"Isn't he the one who sent you?"

"Hardly."

"Then how did you know I was hiring?"

He shrugged. "News travels fast."

Obviously. "So you're looking for work."

"I believe I mentioned that to you last night."

"You did." I didn't quite know what to say next. "What do you do?"

"Just about everything."

Here we go again, with the three-word phrases. For an otherwise nice guy, he sure didn't make conversation easy. The only way to conduct this interview was to abandon the site of my recent embarrassment in favor of neutral territory. I glanced at my watch. It was close enough to lunch time. "Do you like Mexican food?"

"Love it." He grinned. "You buying again?"

If Travis had displayed the slightest condescension or sarcasm, I'd have promptly informed him it was Dutch treat. But that affable cowboy grin of his could soothe even the prickliest of souls.

I tucked my purse under my arm. "Don't I always?"

A short while later, we were munching nachos and drinking draft in a restaurant replete with bullfight posters and sequined sombreros.

The beer was fortifying my slightly bruised ego. "Travis, about what happened in the lobby—"

"There's no need to explain."

"I know, but I'd like to. You see, I had just decided to retain the lease on the Silverbrooke. Guess I was kind of celebrating."

"Didn't bother me any."

Something in his expression suggested otherwise, but I decided not to challenge his remark. I'd be quite happy if the incident was forgotten and never mentioned again.

"How come you didn't mention the Silverbrooke last night?" Travis asked.

"I was still trying to make up my mind."

"Are you a relative of the former owners or something?"

"No. I just inherited the lease."

"How'd you manage that?"

"It's a long story, and I still don't understand the reasons myself. But I'm supposed to be interviewing you. Why don't you tell me about yourself?"

The night before, both of us had managed to skirt the respective details of our private lives. Today, however, I had the right to ask questions. It went without saying, of course, that my interest was strictly professional. Well, mostly professional.

Travis leaned back and stretched out his legs, but I wasn't fooled by the cool wrangler pose. The set of his jaw suggested he was bracing himself for rejection. I found myself hoping that it wouldn't be necessary.

"Where do you want me to start?" he said.

"Anywhere you like."

"All right, I'm thirty-five, divorced, no dependents."

It wasn't easy to appear unaffected. The perfect age and unattached. Both irrelevant to the issue at hand, but interesting nonetheless.

I cleared my throat in the manner of a prospective employer. "You mentioned last night you were from Texas."

"That's right. Dallas."

"What kind of business were you in?"

"Construction."

"Really? For how long?"

"Seventeen years."

"Good grief. You must have been a child when you started."

"Guess I was what you might call a boy wonder. I started right after high school and learned almost everything there is to know. Pipe fitting, tile setting, heavy equipment. When I was twenty-seven, I went into the contracting business for myself."

"That's quite a responsibility."

He shrugged off the remark. "An uncle helped me get started, but pretty soon I was running a million-dollar enterprise on my own. Had the world by the tail. My wife and I owned a house with a hundred acres and a dozen quarter horses."

"What happened?" I asked, anticipating an unhappy ending.

"I don't know if I should be telling my story to a loans officer."

My gaze fell. It wasn't always easy admitting what I did for a living. "If you're talking about foreclosures, Travis, we don't enjoy doing them."

"Yeah, I guess you wouldn't." Travis sighed, and his eyes grew distant. "For a couple years, everything was hunky-dory. Dallas was booming. Real estate prices were soaring."

I knew enough about recent economic downturns to fill in the rest. "You must have gotten caught when the oil market fell."

"Sure did. There I was with a yard full of iron and building supplies without a hope in hell of paying for them. People were moving out of Dallas in droves. You couldn't give real estate away."

"What did you do?"

"Only thing I could do—declared bankruptcy. The bank foreclosed on the house and land. I sold the horses, and my wife moved back home with her family. That was a year ago, but in some ways, it still feels like yesterday."

My heart wrenched. "How long were you married?"

"Eight years."

"I'm sorry."

He swirled the beer in the bottom of his glass. "It's not that I blame her for leaving. I was never at home, never had time for anything but the business."

I reached across the table and lightly touched his hand. "Do you still love her?"

His expression grew pensive. "No. We'd gone our separate ways long before we split up. But there are still days I wake up and wonder where things went wrong."

"I know the feeling."

He looked up. "Are you divorced, too?"

"Yes. I was married for five years."

"What happened? Not that it's any of my business."

"No, that's okay. I'm not really sure what happened. Donald was a perfectly nice man, but every day of our marriage, I felt like I was dying a little. I used to think it was my fault, that I wasn't trying hard enough to love him."

Travis nodded. "I know what you mean. Working at a marriage is one thing. But loving someone—that ought to come naturally, don't you think?"

I couldn't have agreed more. What surprised me was that our philosophies should dovetail so easily.

The waitress brought our Mexican platters, and for the next little while, we were distracted by the sybaritic pleasures of food.

"What else do you want to know about me?" Travis asked.

There was a great deal I wanted to know, but most of it had nothing to do with the interview. Still, it was important to get back to at least a semblance of business.

"Do you have references?"

"Plenty."

"I'd like to phone my accountant as soon as possible with figures. How soon could you draw up an estimate?"

"Today, if you want."

This was almost too easy. "What about getting a crew together? How long would that take?"

"A few days probably. The guys who used to work for me are scattered all over the South."

I was tempted to hire Travis on the spot for the sheer voyeuristic pleasure of seeing him every day. But I salvaged the remaining shreds of my professionalism. "I'll have to gather other estimates first."

"No problem." The slight stiffening of Travis's shoulders belied his nonchalant tone of voice.

"But if your figures are in line," I added hastily, "I'd be happy to take you on."

"Sounds fair enough."

"What would you consider reasonable wages for yourself?"

He quoted a rate that seemed incredibly low, but according to the Chamber of Commerce, it was in keeping with the norm in this part of the country. Suddenly realizing I might lose Travis to someone else, I suggested two dollars an hour more.

"I wouldn't turn it down," he said.

For the second time that day, my heart ached for the man. Despite his lean whipcord exterior, there was something touchingly vulnerable about Travis McCabe.

"Now it's your turn," I said. "You can ask me questions."

"About anything?"

"Sure."

"When do you suppose I could pick up my jacket?"

I stared at him awhile, then burst out laughing. "That's it? That's your question?"

He grinned. "Couldn't think of anything else offhand."

"You can pick it up anytime."

"Okay, how about tonight? We can grab a bite to eat, have a few drinks."

Life was definitely getting more complicated by the minute. "You wouldn't be trying to softsoap a prospective employer."

Eyes twinkling, Travis shook his head. "More like a prospective friend."

"That's nice," I replied in all sincerity. Both of us were silent for a minute or two. "Travis, did I...say anything last night when you found me sleepwalking?"

"You said you were looking for your mama."

A shiver coursed through me. "My mother? But she's dead."

I uttered the statement not to counter Travis but to confirm the fact to myself. I had come to terms with Mother's death ages ago. Why was I looking for her in my sleep?

"Was there anything else?"

"Not really. You seemed lost and scared and..."

"What?"

"Well, you acted like a little girl. I thought at first you were kinda—"

"Dim."

He grinned sheepishly. "Something like that."

His nervousness about my sleepwalking was a natural reaction from people who'd never encountered it. He probably hadn't even noticed he'd started stroking my hand.

But I had. His palms were warm and well callused, but his fingers were gentle. I felt safe in Travis's hands. In some ways I hadn't felt safe since I came to Hot Springs.

"What did I do after you loaned me the jacket?"

"I offered you a ride home, but you didn't want to come. Then you, uh..." Travis looked down, caught sight of my hand in his and released it. "You started sucking your thumb."

A light glimmered in my brain. "So that explains your remark in the restaurant last night. I thought you were just being a jerk."

Travis laughed. "I probably was. It wasn't the nicest thing I've ever said."

"That's okay. How did I get home?"

"I don't know. You just turned around and started running. I thought about following you, then figured it wasn't worth the risk. For all I knew, you could start hollering rape or something."

"A two-year-old wouldn't know anything about rape."

"Two? Is that how old you were supposed to be?"

His question startled me. Travis had only said I behaved like a little kid. He hadn't said anything about my age.

"I don't know," I said. Yet for some reason, deep inside, I knew that was a lie.

I LEFT TRAVIS at the Silverbrooke that afternoon to put together his estimates. As there was no need for me to be in the way, I went downtown to inquire about utilities. No matter who I ended up hiring for the bathhouse, they would need water and electricity. A telephone, too, would be a help.

Running errands helped keep my mind off the strange experience I'd heard about over lunch. Knowing I'd behaved like a two-year-old that night on the mountain was like being given a single puzzle piece and nothing more. Not only useless, but frustrating.

If that one memory could be triggered, why not more? What was I hiding from myself? What was the big deal about being two? I couldn't even remember back that far.

No further answers came, so I abandoned my thoughts to more practical matters like plumbing. Hooking up regular water at the Silverbrooke was no problem. Hooking up the thermal variety was more complex than I'd anticipated.

The water from the underground springs beneath the mountain was too hot to be used directly. It was cooled through heat exchangers and kept in a common holding tank outside, then it was piped at bath temperature to the individual bathhouses.

The Silverbrooke's thermal plumbing, of course, would require updating before the National Park Association could approve reconnection. But the inspector assured me the job was not terribly complicated for an experienced contractor. And they could schedule an inspection as soon as I wanted one.

That was reassuring. I liked the idea of having a thermal bath in my very own spa.

The immediate errands run, I returned to the motel and phoned my accountant to advise him of my plans. His reaction was typical of his profession. He thought I was crazy to get involved in such a major undertaking, particularly one about which I knew nothing.

Naive or not, I was determined. After all, it was my money. My bathhouse. And my life.

Calder had left a message for me at the motel. He'd found several local contractors who were willing to prepare estimates and do the labor. I phoned them and scheduled appointments for the next few days. I was still hoping to hire Travis McCabe, but until I'd seen his figures, I could hardly commit myself.

It was early evening by the time I changed into jeans and returned to the bathhouse. Travis had told me he would lock up and leave the estimates on the counter, but he was still there when I arrived, poring over pages of calculations.

"I thought you'd be gone by now," I said, delighted that he wasn't.

Travis glanced at his watch. "Darn, late, isn't it? Guess I got carried away."

Our eyes met, and I felt my face growing warmer. It was still a little awkward, knowing that only one of us remembered our first meeting. But although elements of my sleepwalking still frightened me, I no longer felt so alone. Travis knew about it, and he was still here.

"This is, uh . . . quite a place you've got here, Geneva."

Good idea, I thought, following his lead. Impending date or not, we could still take care of business. "I think so, too, but my accountant says I should forget it."

"Are you going to?"

"No way. But just how badly off is the bathhouse?"

"I'll be honest with you. It needs a lot of work. Plumbing, wiring, plaster—everything's gotta be replaced. You're looking at a year, at least, before the Silverbrooke'll be operational."

An entire year. The news was disappointing, but I should have realized as much. "Could you explain the figures to me?"

"Sure thing." Travis patiently explained every item and how he'd arrived at the cost projections. The figures were high, but as he pointed out, his calculations were based on a wide margin of safety. There were a number of areas where he could cut corners some if I wanted him to.

In the final analysis, I decided I would not cut corners. But because Travis had provided that option in the estimates, I knew he could be trusted. And having worked with mortgages and loans, I knew that my instincts were reliable.

"Would you be free to follow the project through to the end?" I asked when we'd finished going over the reports.

His gaze met mine. "I'm free as a bird for as long as you want me."

"Goodness," was my inane and slightly breathless reply. "So am I hired?"

Delightedly, I made a mental note to phone the other contractors and cancel the appointments. "The job is yours." It felt terrific to know I wouldn't need Calder's patronizing help.

Travis leaned across the counter and gave me a resounding kiss on the cheek. "I don't know how to thank you, Genny. You're a sweetheart!"

The kiss was sufficient thanks, particularly since he'd already salvaged my pride. And he'd called me Genny. No one had ever done that before.

THE TRANSITION from strangers to friends was so immediate as to go almost unnoticed. Technically we were now employer and employee, but I felt no sense of superiority. Pulling rank wasn't in my nature, anyway, but there was more to our association than that. All I had was money to restore the Silverbrooke. Travis had the skills. Neither of us was mutually exclusive.

Travis seemed as eager as I to get started on the job. It was still a little early for dinner, so first we went to the shopping mall to look for some basic tools, cleaning supplies and sundries. We took Travis's car, a vintage white Cougar convertible, which he'd identified as one of the few assets he'd been allowed to keep after filing for bankruptcy.

I loved the feel of the wind through my hair and the way Travis looked with the wind through his. Being with him felt like playing. Secretly I hoped that working with him would feel the same way.

I had extra sets of keys made up for the bathhouse, one of which I gave to Travis. And we bought mops and buckets and cleaners and paint thinner, hardly what one would call fun purchases.

Yet with Travis, it *was* fun. He had a corny sense of humor, the kind some people find mortifying in public. He danced with a long-haired mop and rode the shopping cart as if it were a go-kart. By the time we were finished, I had a stitch in my side from laughing so hard.

Then it was time for our "date." Travis insisted on paying this time, since I'd given him an advance on his wages. We found a dining lounge downtown and settled into a quiet corner table. Over cocktails, we toasted to the Silverbrooke's future and our happy, productive association. There was still no reason to believe it would be otherwise.

"Now that you're my boss," Travis said, "I've gotta ask you something."

"Go ahead."

"Where does a pretty, brown-eyed loans officer get the money to finance a bathhouse?"

My heart pattered at the compliment while I tried to infuse my smile with mystery. "Why? Do you think I absconded with clients' funds?"

He laughed. "I'm not jumping to any more conclusions about you. But you can tell me to mind my own business if you want."

If anyone else had asked me, I might have said just that—politely, of course. My fortune was something that made people uncomfortable, myself included at times.

But Travis had treated me kindly both when I walked in my sleep and when I had admitted to it. It was as though we'd already shared something intimate. And so I decided to confide in him.

"My parents owned a chain of gourmet food stores in Massachusetts. They died a few years ago, and I inherited everything. It's that simple."

"Are you an only child?"

"Yes."

"Lucky girl—I mean, I'm sorry about your parents and all."

"That's okay. I know what you meant. I suppose you're right, I am lucky. But the money's never really mattered much to me." Now it was my turn to retract my words. "Of course, I never had to go through what you have."

He shrugged. "It was a lesson I had to learn. But you make money sound like a pain in the neck."

"It was for me, in a way. My parents were always so busy working, they never had much time for me."

"Poor little rich girl, huh?"

"That's about it. I had everything a child could want in material things. And I'm sure my parents loved me, but..." I left the thought unfinished, not wanting to sound maudlin.

"Guess I am lucky," Travis admitted. "My folks weren't rich, but they always had time for us kids."

He talked for a while about his family. Travis had brothers and sisters all over Texas. None of them had done as well professionally as he had, but they were close-knit and happy. I envied him that.

Sometime after midnight, we went our separate ways— Travis to his motel, and I to mine. The phone was ringing when I entered the room.

"Geneva, it's Donald. Where've you been? I've been trying to call you all evening."

"You could've left a message."

"I didn't want you to think I was worried."

I smiled. "But you were."

"Naturally. How come you haven't phoned?"

"I did this morning. You weren't home."

"Oh . . . you're right, I wasn't."

I was itching to ask Donald with whom he'd spent the night, but we had made a mutual agreement not to question each other's social lives. Donald generally kept his side of the bargain better than I did.

"When are you coming home?" he asked.

"The end of next week . . . maybe."

"That long? Hot Springs must be pretty exciting."

"Exciting is an apt description," I said, my thoughts actually lingering on Travis, not Hot Springs. I told Donald about my decision to keep the lease and renovate the bathhouse.

"What? I can't believe you'd decide to do that."

"Well, I have."

"Do you have the foggiest notion of what you're doing?"

I gritted my teeth, determined as a matter of pride to keep things friendly. "Not really, but I've hired someone who does. Donald, the Silverbrooke is just beautiful. But you've got to see it to understand."

"No doubt. How've you been otherwise?"

"Fine," I lied.

"Have you done any more sleepwalking?"

Darn, he would have to ask directly about that.

"Only once. But don't worry, nothing happened." I knew Donald. If I'd told him the truth—that I'd wandered on a mountain in my nightie—he would have hopped the next plane to Arkansas. And frankly, I didn't want him intruding on what promised to be a delightful week and a half with Travis.

"Did you advise Dr. Caldwell?" he asked.

"Yes, and if you must know, I've made an appointment with a therapist for when I get home. But there's nothing to worry about in the meantime."

I could sense his hesitation and felt my own impatience rising. Why hadn't I just lied about walking in my sleep? Why was I always so damnably honest?

Fortunately Donald changed the subject. We discussed Hot Springs in general, Enoch Sarrazin in particular and a few other mundane topics related to banking.

When I finally hung up, I felt almost giddy with relief. There was definitely something to be said for divorce. One didn't have to justify meeting people like Travis McCabe.

I got into a clean nightgown. Then I went into the bathroom to brush my teeth.

The sedatives were still sitting on the counter where I'd left them when I unpacked my things after moving to my new room. I picked up the bottle, shook two pills into my hand then, shuddering, put them back. I decided I didn't need tranquilizers. Not tonight when everything seemed to be going my way.

My intuition proved correct. I slept like a baby and never left the bed, waking up more refreshed than I had in months. I slipped into jeans and a cotton sweater, ate a quick breakfast, then sat down to call the other contractors to cancel the estimates.

I wasn't prepared for their surly reactions. But neither was I going to let them get me down. Calder's good-old-boy network would survive quite nicely even without my business.

I placed a call to Mr. Carson, intending to thank him for his efforts. But he wasn't in his office, so I left the message with his secretary. Then I put him out of my mind and drove eagerly to the Silverbrooke where Travis would be waiting.

He was in the lobby with a telephone serviceman. He looked happy to see me. Or maybe he was just happy to have a job again.

"Glad you're here," Travis said.

My heart soared.

"Did you want the serviceman to put jacks in the upstairs apartment?"

Okay, so it wasn't the most romantic greeting in the world. But since when had romance entered our working agreement?

"Jacks in the apartment would be great," I replied, leading the two men upstairs.

I had bought coffee and muffins on the way to the bathhouse. After the technician left, Travis and I shared them at the kitchen table.

He pointed to the ivory touch-tone wall phone. "Mind if I use this to track down some of my old work crew?"

"Of course, and there's no need to ask. Whatever is here, use it. Meanwhile, I'm going to start cleaning this place."

I left Travis in the kitchen and tore an old sheet into dust rags. Although the apartment was noticeably brighter with Travis around, I still found the place abysmal. The wallpaper was a disgrace, and the furniture depressing. Refurbishing the apartment might be a good way for me to spend the next week or so. That way I could still be on the Silverbrooke's premises without being in anyone's way.

After a while, Travis entered the living room.

I stopped dusting. "Any luck?"

"I can get a few guys by the beginning of next week."

"Wonderful."

"You know, I've been thinking," he said. "Seems a shame to let this perfectly nice apartment go to waste. Would you mind if I stayed here while I'm working for you?"

I looked around, trying to stifle my distaste. "You'd actually want to live here?"

"Sure. What's wrong with it?"

"Nothing that a few coats of paint won't cure, I suppose."

"It would sure save me a few bucks—course, I'd pay rent. But I could also put in longer hours, save mileage on the car. And you'd have a built-in security guard."

His suggestion made sense, and I liked the idea of Travis looking after the Silverbrooke. Inanely I wondered if the Silverbrooke felt the same way.

"If you'd like to," I said, "it's fine with me. But I wouldn't dream of charging you rent."

"I'm not looking for handouts, Genny."

"I know you're not. But you'd be doing me a favor by staying here."

He considered this a moment. "Okay, if you say so. I'll take the smaller bedroom."

I thought about the lovely brass bed in the master bedroom, then tried just as quickly not to think about it. "Why don't you take the bigger room? It would be more comfortable."

His gaze lingered on me a moment too long. "Nah, I'll stick to the smaller one for now."

"If you insist."

Travis seemed as relieved as I to have that subject resolved. "How'd you make out with the other utilities?" he asked.

"The water and electricity will be hooked up this morning."

"Terrific," he said. "I'll be able to move in tonight. By the way, I want to show you the basement to give you some idea of what we have to do for the thermal hookup."

We left the apartment, went down the stairs, crossed the lobby and followed the corridor that led to the basement stairs. When Travis opened the door, I was assailed once again by the detestable odor of mildew.

"Enoch says the steps are rotten, Travis. I don't think we should go down there."

"I've used them. They're not bad, as long as you're careful."

Grasping the doorknob, I felt my palm grow clammy.

Travis held out his hand. "Come on, I'll help you."

I took his hand, but my feet remained glued to the floor. "What's the matter?" he asked.

"I don't know..." By now, my pulse was racing and my forehead was beading with sweat. "I just can't..."

"It's only a basement."

I yanked my hand from his, feeling the urge to throw up or faint. "I can't go down there, Travis...please, don't make me!"

Chapter Six

Travis pulled the door shut and wrapped his arms around me. "Shh, Genny, it's okay. I'm here."

I was crying and shaking like a leaf, scarcely aware of his embrace. Never had I experienced such overwhelming panic. Even after a sleepwalking episode, there was an element of surrealism. It was like hearing someone else's story. But this was all too real.

"Has this ever happened before, Genny?" Travis asked.

Through the fog of terror I shook my head, pitifully aware of the contrast between my heaving gasps and Travis's calm. "I . . . I've never tried to go into the basement before."

"We won't go down there if it bothers you. Come on, let's get away from here." With his arm around my shoulders, Travis led me to the lounge at the rear of the bathhouse. He yanked a dust sheet off an old leather sofa, then drew back the drapes to let in the sun.

He sat beside me. "Tell me, Genny, what happened?"

My knees were drawn to my chin, fetal-like, which more or less summed up my feelings. "I can't put my finger on it. It was the atmosphere of something . . . horrible."

His arm had been resting on the back of the sofa. Now he stroked my cheek with his fingertips. "Was there something specific that triggered the feeling?"

As Travis phrased the question, I became aware of two opposing currents within me, each struggling for dominance. One was responding with delirious pleasure to Travis's touch. The other was frigid and afraid, recoiling from a nameless, faceless nightmare.

For the time being I struggled to push aside the reality of Travis touching me. At least he was flesh and blood. He wouldn't vanish into some ethereal vapor while I tried to cope with my darker side.

"The smell," I said at last. "That's what triggered it."

"It smells like a cellar."

"No. It's more than that." I squeezed my eyes shut, daring to resurrect the sensation only because it was daylight and Travis was with me. "There's mildew, things rotting, but there's something else . . . something warm, human."

The image was so close I could almost reach out and touch it. But before I could, the thought had slipped away again.

I shivered once, then opened my eyes. "It's no use. I can't remember."

He played with a lock of my hair. "Don't be so hard on yourself. It'll come."

"Maybe. But, Travis, what really confuses me is that I love this place. It's not just because the Silverbrooke is old and charming. I mean, I have this really strong attachment to my bathhouse. All of it."

"You don't seem too crazy about the apartment."

"Oh, that's just because of the filth. I'm excited about fixing the place up." My mind drifted along the strange spectrum of emotions the Silverbrooke evoked.

"Penny for your thoughts?"

It took me a moment to gather them. "I was just realizing that despite everything that's happened so far, I feel safe here. It's as though the Silverbrooke and I are old friends."

He looked at me strangely. "It's only a building."

"I know. That's what's so odd. But I can walk through this place and feel great. The old tubs make me laugh. I can picture these funny old ladies wearing shower caps, up to their necks in steamy water. I can hear echoes in the hallways. It makes me feel like..."

"Dancing in the foyer?"

His gentle teasing was just what I needed. "Yes, the Silverbrooke makes me feel like dancing."

"So how does the basement fit in with all this?"

"I don't know. I don't understand how any of it fits in. Everything seems so...intense. But if it is, why can't I touch the intensity?"

"I wish there was something I could tell you."

I turned to look at Travis. The concern on his face was almost enough to make me cry again. His being at a loss for words didn't matter. I had no need of words.

Travis drew my body closer. That was what I needed. He tipped my head back; his gaze roamed my face. Then he kissed me. Another need identified and met.

Tender, consoling was the way the kiss began. Then our mouths opened, and the mood intensified. It was as though, by drawing deep into my mouth, Travis could somehow draw out my pain. By crushing my hair in his fingers, he might crush the residue of fear.

His tactics must have worked. In place of pain came passion. Instead of fear, desire. Hearing him moan, I shifted my body closer. With my fingertips, I traced the crags and contours of his face. Every sensation—the rasp of whiskers, the heat of his breath—drew from me an elemental response.

Then Travis cupped my breast. Reason clashed with baser yearnings. I pulled away, not wanting to, but needing to before things could get out of hand.

I stared, wild-eyed, aware of feeling shocked—not at Travis but at myself. He stared back and ran his tongue along his lips as if to savor the lingering traces of our encounter.

"Sweet heaven," he muttered and raked his hands through his hair.

I couldn't tell whether Travis's oath was a prayer for deliverance or a repeat performance. Speaking for myself, I wasn't sure which interpretation I preferred.

Silently we returned to the neutral realm of the apartment—neutral because there were things we could do there to keep busy.

"You've really got to get to the bottom of this sleepwalking thing," Travis said as we scrubbed windows.

"I know. I have an appointment to see a therapist when I get back to Minneapolis."

"Sure you can hang on that long?"

"Why do you ask?"

"I don't know. It's just that this place seems to be bringing things out in you."

Travis was right. Things were coming to the surface here, not as smoothly as I would have liked, but in fits and starts. If there was more to come, I had no way of knowing how well I would cope.

As for Travis, he was proving remarkably sympathetic, but he also needed his job. The prospect of his boss going off the deep end wouldn't do much for his peace of mind, either.

"Don't worry," I said. "Things will work out."

Undoubtedly we both knew I had no basis for that claim whatsoever.

NOBODY CAN FIND ME, nobody can find me! I like it here in my playhouse. It's cozy, and I can put my toys in secret places. But I forgot to bring my toys with me. That was silly.

What I like best of all are my building blocks. Big people keep buying me dollies, but I don't want to be a mommy. I don't want to change diapers and spank my baby when she's bad. I wanta smoke fat cigars like my Unca. And make people jump when I talk in a big loud voice.

It's boring in here. I don't have anything to do. Hide and seek would be fun if only I could find somebody to look for me.

Ooh, look, somebody's coming! I can see his cowboy boots right outside my playhouse. But I'm not sure he wants to play. I think he's worried 'bout something. He's tapping his toes, and big people always tap their toes when they're worried.

I cover my mouth to giggle. Then I back up even farther into my secret room. "Betcha can't find me!"

The man's face looks down at me from the roof of my playhouse. He looks pretty funny with his face upside down.

"Genny, what in blazes name are you doing in there?"

My body felt cramped, as though I'd been shoved into a shoebox. I remembered lying down on the brass bed after we had finished the windows. I must have fallen asleep. But now I appeared to be curled up in some kind of cupboard.

Glancing around, I was almost afraid to ask. "Travis, where am I?"

"In the front lobby, under the counter."

Half an hour later, I was still shaking. Travis had done his best to dismiss the incident, but I knew he was entertaining more doubts about my sanity. Who wouldn't?

Sleepwalking was taking over my life. First the night-time, and now the daylight hours. I couldn't simply stop sleeping, not unless I wanted to hasten my descent into mental oblivion.

What perplexed me, more than anything, was the undeniable connection between sleepwalking and the Silverbrooke. It was as though the bathhouse and my subconscious were in conspiracy. But why? What had I done to either of them to deserve this?

"More brandy?" Travis asked, reaching for the bottle on the coffee table.

"No, thanks." I set down the empty snifter.

"It never occurred to me," he said, "that maybe I shouldn't have woken you up when you were sleepwalking."

"That's an old wives' tale," I replied distractedly. "As long as the person isn't standing on a ledge, there's no problem. Travis, why am I behaving like a two-year-old?"

"I don't know. What about the other times when you've walked in your sleep?"

"I can't recall any set pattern. I just acted out whatever was bothering me at the time." Like my honeymoon, I thought to myself. Even then, I was suppressing doubts about Donald and me.

"So obviously something happened at the Silverbrooke when you were two, and you're acting it out."

"But what?" Travis flinched, and I realized I was shrieking. "Sorry. I'm not usually hysterical."

He was too polite to argue the obvious. "I can understand why you're upset, but getting angry at yourself won't help. Nobody remembers when they were two years old."

"But I obviously do at some level."

Travis fell silent. "Maybe there's someone in Hot Springs who can remember you or your parents being here."

"You could be right, but how do I find them?" I counted off on my fingers. "There's Enoch, Hepzibah, Calder—no, he wasn't around then—and Bill…'' My eyes widened. "Of course, why didn't I think of him earlier?''

"Who?''

"Bill Swann, the private eye who found me. He was born and raised in Hot Springs. If anyone could tell me, he could.''

With a sigh of relief, Travis stood up. "Then let's go see the man.''

I was grateful to Travis for accompanying me. Even more so when I saw what part of town Bill Swann worked in. His office was a rundown house in the seedy section of Hot Springs. The front porch sagged like a hammock, and a couple of upstairs windows were smashed. A brass plaque on the door offered an incongruous touch of gentility—a gift, perhaps, from a satisfied client. They'd have done better to buy him a few cans of paint.

The door was unlocked, so we proceeded into the front room. The office furniture was shabby and piled high with magazines and newspapers. A half-empty bottle of cheap Scotch sat on the desk with a pair of eyeglasses nearby.

"Looks like the Arkansas version of a Chandler novel,'' Travis remarked.

I glanced at him. "You read mysteries?''

"When I get a chance.''

Interesting, I thought, tucking that tidbit away for future reference.

Travis wandered down the hall, calling Bill's name, but there was no answer. He returned to the office. "Do you want to leave a note, or should we wait?''

"Let's wait a few minutes. He left the door unlocked, so he might not be gone long.''

"It's okay with me.''

We cleared a space on a dilapidated sofa and sat down. I blew the dust off a 1965 issue of *National Geographic* and began to peruse an article on Jane Goodall's chimps.

After about fifteen minutes, footsteps clumped up the front porch. Bill Swann walked into the office with a sack of take-out food. If he was surprised to find us there, he didn't show it. But maybe that was part of a private eye's persona. Never let 'em see you sweat.

"Ms. Ashford, how ya doin'?"

I stood up and shook his hand. "Hello, Mr. Swann. Sorry we didn't make an appointment."

He snorted. "Hell, no one ever does. Do you think I could find my appointment book in this place?"

The two men introduced themselves, then Bill sat down and brought out a carton of barbecued ribs. "Care for a rib? They're a little messy, but great."

We declined, but encouraged Bill to go ahead and eat. I'm sure he would have anyway.

"Mr. Swann—" I began.

"Bill."

"Bill, I was wondering if you could tell us a few things about the Silverbrooke."

"Maybe. What do you want to know?" he said, biting into a rib that left a slash of red sauce across his face.

"I'm quite sure that I visited the bathhouse with my parents when I was around two. That would have been twenty-six years ago. Do you have any recollection of my parents or me?"

Bill knotted .his brow. "Afraid not. I never got acquainted with the guests."

I wasn't about to give up that easily. "What about the bathhouse itself? Did anything significant happen around that year?"

He sucked a bit of meat from between his teeth. "Why do you want to know?"

"I've been having these . . . flashbacks," I said, reluctant to go into detail. "Sort of like déjà vu."

"Ya don't say?"

"They're frightening me, Bill. I was hoping you could shed some light."

"Well, there was a scandal at the Silverbrooke about that time."

"What kind of scandal?" Travis asked, linking his fingers with mine.

"Festus had a younger sister by the name of Pearl. She was a pretty thing. Had kind of a crush on her myself. But she, uh . . . came to a bad end. Killed herself."

My stomach lurched. I had to force myself to ask the next question. "Where did she do it?"

"Somewhere in the bathhouse is all I recall." He wiped his face with a napkin but succeeded only in smearing the barbecue sauce.

Travis glanced at me to catch my reaction.

I was cold as ice and trembling. "Would she have killed herself in the basement?"

"Now that you mention it . . . yeah, guess she did."

I waited for a revelation, for some inner dam to break open and confirm what Bill had told me. To my acute disappointment, nothing happened.

It was ghastly, of course, to learn that someone had killed herself in my bathhouse. But I could make no conscious association between Bill's pronouncement and what had happened to me at the top of the cellar stairs. Either Pearl's death and my trauma were unrelated, or I was still suppressing the memory.

"Is there anything you can tell us about her?" I asked.

Just then, the phone rang. Bill swore and began tossing papers off the desk until he found the phone. "Excuse me a minute." He grabbed the receiver. "Swann here."

Bill did more listening than talking. After a few minutes, he disappeared behind his desk and emerged with a plastic glass into which he poured a generous helping of Scotch. He held the glass out, presumably offering to share. We both declined.

"Yeah, well, why shouldn't I?" Bill barked. "He was my client, I got my instructions... Maybe you should have thought of that earlier, huh?" Grunting in disgust, he hung up the phone. "Reprobate. Now, where were we?"

"I asked if there was anything else you could tell me about Pearl Tulley."

He shook his head. "Wish I could, Ms. Ashford, but there's not much to say. Pearl was a lovely lady and didn't deserve to die. But that's the way it goes sometimes." He pushed himself away from the desk. "Hate to give you the bum's rush, but I got a client across town who's getting antsy. Thinks his wife is getting somethin' on the side. The guy refuses to take my advice."

"What's your advice?" Travis asked as we got up to leave.

"Let her get it out of her system. She'll be back soon enough."

I scribbled the Silverbrooke's new phone number on a notepad and handed it to the detective. "If you think of anything else about the bathhouse, could you let us know?"

He took the piece of paper and stared at it. "Sure thing. Nice seein' you again."

Maybe it was the heat that had caused sweat to break out on Bill's upper lip. But as we left the office, I got the distinct impression the detective didn't really think it was nice seeing me. Nor did I expect to hear from him again.

"Don't take it so hard," Travis said when we were back in the car.

I wrapped my arms around my midriff. "I can't help it. I just feel so . . . befuddled."

"What do you propose to do now?"

"I'd like to see the basement."

Travis gave me a sidelong glance. "Sure you're up to it?"

"Yes. I know what happened down there, so it's not going to bother me. Besides, if I'm going to own the place, I can't avoid the cellar forever."

"You've got a point. Listen, I know another way to get down there from the back of the bathhouse. It'll probably be easier for you than the stairs."

"Thank you." What would I have done, I wondered, without Travis to get me through this? The prospect was something I didn't even want to consider.

The two of us walked around to the south side of the bathhouse. There was an iron grill gate at the basement level. Travis found the appropriate key and opened it.

A long windowless tunnel extended about twenty-five feet and opened onto a large room. The ceiling was criss-crossed with pipes and loose wires. There were stacks of rotting lumber, crates and assorted debris, obviously the breeding ground for mildew.

"This place is a fire trap," Travis remarked. "We're going to have to clean it out soon."

My hands were pressed to my stomach. I kept waiting for the nausea to recur, but it didn't. Other than being appalled at the garbage, I felt fine. "I wonder what's in these crates?"

Travis pried open a lid. "Looks like old invoices in this one. Geez, this stuff goes back to the thirties. Some of it could be valuable."

My curiosity was once again clouded by disappointment. Valuable or not, the thirties was long before my time. There was little chance of finding any of the answers I was looking for there.

Travis took my hand and pointed out the work that needed to be done. He explained the thermal hookup, gesturing to the rusted pipes that extended from the stairs to the center of the basement.

"This is where the mineral water will be piped in," he said.

"How long do you think it'll take to replace the pipes?"

"Once my crew arrives, it shouldn't take us more than a couple of days. The upstairs pipes are in much better shape."

"Great. I can't wait to have my first official bath."

"Then we'd better not keep the lady waiting." Travis grinned. His hand tightened around mine, but I tried to keep my imagination in check. The man had only kissed me once. It was a little early to be wondering how it would feel to have a thermal bath together.

I was feeling pretty good about myself. We'd wandered through a seemingly endless succession of hallways and small rooms. We explored storage closets, laundry room, workshops, and I was still feeling just fine. At the center of the basement, we came to a room with metal walls extending floor to ceiling and a heavy steel door.

"What's that?" I asked Travis. "A safe?"

"No, a boiler room."

"I'd like to see it."

"Sure." Travis spent the next few minutes cursing and fumbling with the rusty lock. Finally something gave way, and he was able to pull the heavy door open. "Damn thing anyway. If you're ever down here on your own, Genny, remember to prop the door open. Otherwise, it'll swing shut, and you can't get out from the inside. I just about locked myself in yesterday.''

"I'll remember.''

Travis wedged a piece of scrap wood beneath the door. The room was pitch dark, but he knew where to find the light switch. A single dim bulb hung from the ceiling, casting sickly yellow shadows through the room.

Instinctively I moved closer to Travis.

"There's nothing to be afraid of,'' he said. "Just a mess of old wires and plumbing.''

My stomach was heaving. "It's that smell again.''

"I don't smell anything.''

"Sticky, human...oh, Lord.'' Swallowing bile, I covered my face. "Let's get out of here, Travis!''

He wrapped an arm around my shoulders. "Come on, Genny, take it easy. Nothing's gonna hurt you.''

His words, though soothing, were ineffective. I knew what I was smelling. Finally, he persuaded me to open my eyes. I groaned and clung even tighter. "She's still there.''

"Who?''

I pointed to a gloomy corner. "Don't you see her, Travis? She's bleeding all over!''

Travis pulled me by the arm and pointed. "Look, there's nothing on the floor. No body, no blood.''

He was right, of course. The room was cobwebbed, that was all. The image had vanished from my mind as quickly as it came.

"But I saw her, Travis. I saw Pearl Tulley lying right there!''

I waited for him to offer some logical argument. Bill Swann had told us about Pearl Tulley's suicide. We knew it had happened in the basement. It wasn't difficult to understand the association I had made.

But Travis offered no argument. Instead, stooping, he ran his fingers along the floor.

"What is it?"

"Take a look at these stains."

I knelt beside him. There were large dark splotches on the concrete. They could have been oil or solvent, or almost anything.

"Is it blood?" I asked cautiously.

"Can't tell. The light's too dim."

The stains were hardly proof, but at least they were tangible. "Pearl slit her wrists right in this room," I said. "She was barefoot and wearing her nightgown."

Travis's eyes narrowed with concern as he brought me to my feet. "Then you must have seen her, Genny."

I felt both sick and heartened. "Do you really think so?"

"Bill didn't say a thing about how Pearl killed herself. How else could you have known she slit her wrists?"

Chapter Seven

"Someone must have told me," I said later, when I'd had time to think.

"Told you what?" Travis was reading the local paper.

"About Pearl slitting her wrists. I've heard all kinds of local tales from people at City Hall and the Chamber of Commerce."

"Wouldn't you remember something like that? I mean, when someone tells you about a suicide in your own bathhouse, you're not likely to get it mixed up with other local gossip."

"No, I suppose not." I got up from the sofa and stalked toward the window. "Of course, I must have seen Pearl's body. And that would have been traumatic for anyone, let alone a two-year-old. But why am I still denying it to myself? Why am I not deliriously happy that I've had a breakthrough?"

Travis got up and joined me. He slipped his arms around me from behind. "Because, Genny, you're a good decent person, and you're not going to celebrate someone's death, no matter how healthy it might be for you."

I turned around so we were facing each other. "You're amazing," I said.

"Me?"

"Yes, you. Anyone else would have given up on me after that first night on the mountain. But you're still here."

Travis smiled. "I have my reasons."

"I know. Any job is better than nothing."

"It's not that, Genny. I really do care about you."

"Why?" I whispered. Trusting someone else was almost impossible when you didn't trust yourself.

"Because I do. That's all. And I don't think you should be alone anymore."

I ignored his last remark. I just liked the sensation of being in his arms, of knowing that he cared.

Travis tipped my head back to study me. "Did you hear what I said, Genny?"

"Mmm-hmm."

"There's no way of knowing where you could end up in the middle of the night."

"What am I supposed to do—hire a bodyguard?"

"You've already got one."

"Who?"

"Me."

"You can't keep watch every night while I sleep."

"I wasn't exactly talking about watching you. But if you and I shared the apartment, I might be able to wake up in time and prevent you from sleepwalking."

My mouth dropped open. A delicious sense of mischief wriggled inside me. "Travis, are you suggesting we . . . co-habit?"

His complexion reddened. "We'd each have our own room, if that's what you're worried about."

"Of course, I'm not worried about that." Delicious or not, the notion was unthinkable. I hardly knew the man. Yet I actually found myself considering the notion, and not all of my considerations were chaste.

"You don't trust me, do you?" he said, misinterpreting my silence.

His question, however, merited thought. I'd hired Travis. I'd given him keys and use of the apartment. We were already spending most of our daylight hours together. Was there any real difference in sharing the darkness?

"I trust you," I said at last.

"Good. Think about it some more. In the meantime, I'm going to get back to work."

"I'll come with you," I said, not wanting to be alone even while I thought.

Travis's suggestion was sound. My sleepwalking was fast reaching a crisis stage. There was no one in Hot Springs I could turn to for help—especially not at night, when I needed help most.

As we descended the stairs together, I realized how alone and vulnerable I'd become. By sharing the apartment with Travis, I would no longer be alone. But the growing attraction between us meant I would still be vulnerable—for entirely different reasons.

I returned to the motel that evening and found the emptiness unbearable. I knew that at that moment Travis was in the apartment unpacking his clothes and dishes. I wanted to be there with him.

As soon as I made the decision, I could hardly contain my enthusiasm. I decided to call Donald. He was always the perfect testing ground for my impulsiveness. If I could sway my prosaic ex-husband to my point of view, it generally meant I was doing the right thing.

Besides, he ought to know that I had hired someone and that I'd be staying at the bathhouse for the remainder of my visit. Of course, he didn't need to know Travis's name, nor any of his other vital statistics.

Donald wasn't home. I was surprised until I remembered it was a late night at the bank. As a dedicated branch manager, he was probably still there. I decided to call him at work.

He wasn't there. The lady who answered said he'd taken a few days off and she didn't know when he'd be back. Donald taking time off? Would wonders never cease?

I left a message anyway with my new phone number. If Donald were to call the motel and discover I'd checked out, he'd be frantic.

Next, I called Enoch who also needed to remain informed of my activities. All of them, that is, except my sleepwalking. The fewer who knew about that, the better.

"I just wanted to let you know I've hired a contractor," I said.

"Have you now? Anyone I know?"

"Probably not. He's from out of town, a Texan."

"I heard Calder was going to send you some men."

"He did, but I decided to hire my own."

"Oh, mighty brave of you. What's his name?"

There was no reason why Enoch couldn't know. Unlike Donald, Enoch wouldn't consider Travis potential competition. "His name is Travis McCabe. His crew will be arriving early next week."

"Well, best of luck. I'm happy for you."

The note of disapproval was faint but unmistakable. Given his ingrained Southern ways, I should have known better than to expect anything different.

"There's one more thing, Enoch. Starting tonight I'll be staying at the apartment in the Silverbrooke."

"In that old place? Why would you want to do that?"

"Because I can't . . . that is, I thought it would be fun to stay there and fix the place up."

"Fun, huh?" Enoch laughed. "Sometimes there's just no understandin' young folks."

"There's probably no point in trying," I agreed. By the time I hung up, I was feeling pretty good about myself. The thing about men was that you had to establish your parameters early. Otherwise, they'd just walk all over you.

MY PARAMETERS were not that clearly set when I moved in with Travis that night. He carried my luggage into the bedroom. It reminded me of the time Donald had done the same thing. That was on our honeymoon—an irrelevant parallel, if ever there was one.

Travis placed the bags at the foot of my bed. "Was that the last of them?"

"Yes, thank you."

He stood there awkwardly for a minute. "Well, guess I'll leave you alone to unpack."

"I can do that later." It would give me something to do later when I couldn't sleep, knowing Travis was in the other bedroom.

We probably shouldn't have chosen that setting or that moment to kiss. We were much too aware of each other, and a bedroom was a dangerous place for that kind of awareness.

But neither of us seemed inclined to fight it. We fell into each other's arms, and our mouths came together, open, hungry. The bedroom almost crackled while my senses came alive. I felt a roaring in my ears, weakness in my legs. Travis's hands roamed my body as I clung to him.

This was crazy. It had to stop...and soon. We were two responsible adults who'd decided to enter a temporary, and platonic, living arrangement. So why were we behaving like a pair of beasts in heat?

I pulled away, gasping. Travis staggered back half a step, bumping smack into the brass footboard.

"Maybe your coming here wasn't such a great idea," he muttered.

"Do you want me to move out?"

"Cripes, no!"

The intensity of his reply made me jump.

"Sorry, Genny, but you must know how badly I want you."

"Is that the real reason you invited me to move in?"

Travis pushed a hand through his hair. "No... yes... I mean, that's not why I asked you to move in. I'm attracted to you, but I would never do anything that... you didn't want me to do."

The absurdity of human behavior struck me just then. I wanted to make love with Travis. He wanted to do the same with me. Yet both of us had been conditioned to resist this most natural of human activities.

There were certainly valid reasons for resisting until the time was right. But how were you supposed to know the right time? I would have thought that by the age of twenty-eight, the answer would come more easily.

"You must be regretting your decision to come," he said.

"No, I'm not."

"What are we going to do about..." He gestured as though something in the atmosphere was responsible.

"We could try cold showers."

He laughed, and the laughter eased my tension. Yes, I wanted Travis, more than I cared to admit. But I also needed him as my friend and protector. For now, the role of lover was too much to ask.

I SLEPT LIKE A BABY. Judging from the way my hair looked when I awoke, I'd scarcely moved a muscle all night.

Greeting Travis that first morning felt strange. We emerged from our bedrooms at the same time. I was fully dressed—not the way I liked to begin my day. But I didn't feel comfortable enough yet with our living arrangements to hang around the apartment in a bathrobe.

Travis was doing up the buttons on his shirt. There was nothing immodest about it, but it was impossible not to notice the muscles and the fine sprinkling of hair on his chest.

He started buttoning faster. "Good morning. Have a good sleep?"

"It was wonderful. I woke up right where I was supposed to. How about you?"

"Terrific, thanks. My snoring didn't keep you awake?"

I shook my head. "Not at all."

Our paths merged en route to the kitchen. It occurred to me how natural it would feel to kiss Travis good-morning. Not kissing him required effort. I wondered whether Travis felt the same way. Then I filled the coffee maker and pushed the thought aside.

FOR THE NEXT FEW DAYS, we worked from morning till night. Travis was preparing for the arrival of the crew. I was redecorating the apartment.

We were working so hard that I had no trouble sleeping. It felt good not to sleepwalk. I no longer felt an urgency to tamper with my subconscious. Pearl Tulley had killed herself when I was two. I had seen her body and been traumatized. Seemed to me that was all I needed to know.

Travis and I selected the wallpaper for the living room together, a tranquil stripe of taupe and cream. The kitchen and bedrooms would be painted white. I enjoyed the work and especially enjoyed Travis's company.

Our companionship was as natural and nonthreatening as the colors we'd chosen. As for the nights in separate rooms, we were adjusting. Tacitly, we understood the need to maintain our distance, but that didn't stop us from sharing affection. Evenings, we'd sit close on the sofa, watching TV or listening to music.

I'd bought a portable television and a ghetto blaster. Travis had an eclectic variety of tapes—Jimmy Buffet, the Gatlin brothers, Beethoven and the Kinks. I can honestly say I'd never felt happier.

And then we ran into Hepzibah. Travis and I were downtown buying more hardware supplies. We met her on a street corner.

Dressed as if in perpetual mourning, Hepzibah was handing out religious tracts. I was tempted to drag Travis across the street for his protection, but she saw us before I had the chance.

"You!" she cried, pronouncing the word like a curse.

My teeth clenched in the likeness of a smile. "Hello, Hepzibah. What a pleasant surprise."

Eyes blazing zealously, she thrust a tract into my hands. I glanced at the cover. It had something to do with the Second Coming, an event she apparently expected almost any day.

Hepzibah turned to Travis. I had little choice but to introduce them. Her reaction to him was fascinating. She seemed to curl into herself as though his very proximity was threatening.

"You the one who's fixing the Silverbrooke?" she sniped.

Travis smiled amiably. "That's right."

"May God forgive you."

"Why would He want to do that? What have we done?" I could have hugged Travis.

"The place is an abomination," she answered, "a den of fornicators and adulterers."

Travis glanced my way. *Was this lady for real?* his eyes seemed to ask. I shrugged, almost grateful that he and I had thus far refrained from licentious activity. It made it easier to look Hepzibah in the eye.

"The Silverbrooke's a bathhouse," I informed her. "If any of my guests intend to fornicate, they'll have to do it someplace else."

Travis smothered a laugh while the old woman clutched her tracts to her bosom. "I know what grievous sins the two of you are committin'."

"Beg your pardon?" Travis said.

"She moved in with you. The whole town knows."

"So?" I demanded, not the least bit interested in informing her of the truth. Let her think the worst if she wanted to.

Hepzibah backed away as though I'd admitted to having a communicable disease. "Bad blood will always tell. The sins of the father..."

"What?"

She shoved a pamphlet into the unwilling hands of a passerby. "This is a God-fearing town, missy. And we won't tolerate your type around here."

Travis slipped an arm around my waist while I entertained the notion of punching her in the nose. "Let's go, Genny. We've got things to do."

I grumbled all the way to the car. "That woman ought to be locked up. She's a menace."

"She's harmless enough. We had folks like her in my home town."

"I've got nothing against religion," I said, tossing the pamphlet into the litter bag, "but she carries things too far."

Travis's eyes twinkled. "Don't be too hard on her. The woman's frustrated."

I caught his implication and chuckled. Travis was probably right. But if that was the outcome of chronic frustration, I wasn't about to remain celibate.

WITH BOTH OF US in and out of the Silverbrooke constantly, it was easy to miss important calls. So among my other purchases, I'd gotten an answering machine.

The only message waiting when we returned from town was from Bill Swann. His voice sounded strained, the way people sound who hate talking to machines.

"Uh...Ms. Ashford, it's, er...Bill. Bill Swann, P.I. I was wondering if we could maybe get together. How about the day after tomorrow? Two o'clock, Club Café. Lemme know if that's not a good time. Uh . . . see ya."

I jotted down the message, then erased and rewound the tape. "Wonder what that was all about."

"He must've thought of something else to tell you about the Silverbrooke."

I wrapped my arms around Travis's neck. "Yuck, I'm not sure I want to know anymore. Things have been going so nicely."

"Call him and cancel the meeting."

"I can't do that."

"Why not?"

"I'd die of curiosity. Besides, whatever Bill has to say, I can handle it."

"Are you sure?"

"I've never felt more sure in my life."

Travis kissed me, his hands resting dangerously close to my bottom. "Does this new confidence have anything to do with . . . us?"

I moved my body closer, felt the burning of our mutual desire. "It has everything to do with us."

The tip of his tongue glided along my lips. "I don't know how much longer I can stand this, Genny."

Abstinence wasn't doing anything for me, either. Somehow, in the back of my mind, I'd been half hoping that familiarity would lessen my feelings for Travis. Maybe I was still gun-shy from my failed marriage, but I didn't want to get emotionally involved. Not yet.

Despite my best efforts, the feelings were growing stronger. With every passing day, I was more convinced that we were falling in love.

"You and I only have one more week together," Travis reminded me.

Reluctantly I pulled away and walked to the kitchen window. "I know. But we only met a week ago."

"What does that have to do with anything? I want us to make love."

I nodded, suddenly fighting tears that had no reason to be there. "So do I, Travis. But don't you see? When I go back to Minneapolis, it's going to hurt that we're not making love anymore."

"Why do you have to go back?"

"Because I, well . . . there's my job, for one thing."

"You don't need the money."

"No, but—"

"You have a job here."

"The Silverbrooke? No way. I couldn't possibly live in Hot Springs."

"Who said anything about living here? I'm just asking for a little time. A few more weeks . . . a month."

Though I hadn't told Travis, I'd actually already considered extending my vacation. There were certainly enough practical reasons for staying on. I could finish redecorating the apartment by next week, and I'd be able to see the bathhouse taking shape.

My only pressing engagement in Minnesota was with the hypnotherapist, and that was something I decided I could happily postpone, especially since I hadn't walked in my sleep for days.

"If you really want me to," I said, suddenly bashful, "I can stay longer."

Beaming, Travis lifted me off my feet and whirled me around. "Genny, you are the best thing that's happened to me in years."

So are you, I admitted, if only in my mind.

TRAVIS SPENT that evening hammering pipes in the basement while I did battle with the wallpaper. The damned stuff was determined to break my will. Every strip either stretched or bubbled or ripped in two. I'd only finished half the room when I finally gave up, exhausted.

I did, however, reach a decision about Travis and me. This was going to be the night we made love. He was still downstairs working. I figured that would give me a chance for a hot bath and a short rest beneath the covers.

Crawling into bed, I shut my eyes, dreaming of the magic moment when Travis would come upstairs. Next time I opened my eyes, the sun was shining brightly over Hot Springs Mountain.

"Well, blast it," I muttered, punching the pillow. A whole night wasted, and I hadn't even heard Travis come in.

Donning my bathrobe, I went into the living room. Travis's bedroom door was ajar, but he always left it open so he could hear me if I got up during the night.

I knocked softly. There was no answer.

"Travis, it's me." I waited a few seconds, then pushed the door open and peeked inside. His unmade bed was empty. I'd missed him. What a lousy sense of timing!

There was a pot of coffee on the stove and a plate of muffins on the table, along with a note.

You were sleeping so soundly last night, I didn't want to wake you. Enjoy your breakfast. See you downstairs.

Love, Travis

I touched the note as if it were made of gold.

"Love, Travis," he had written.

"I already do," I whispered in reply.

After breakfast I cleaned the kitchen, humming as I worked. It was amazing how the most routine tasks take on fresh appeal when one is in love. I decided I might even find the wherewithal to face the wallpaper again.

The day promised to be a scorcher. I put on a pair of shorts and wondered whether my peers in Minneapolis were still shoveling snow.

Tripping lightly down the stairs, I came around the counter and stopped dead in my tracks.

The day before Travis and I had swept and cleaned the mosaic floor. Even with the missing tiles, the place had positively glistened.

Now the Silverbrooke's lobby stank to high heaven. The floor was littered with spoiled vegetables and rotten eggs.

Chapter Eight

"Travis!"

Racing down the basement stairs, I completely forgot their rickety condition. A step caved in beneath me. I stumbled and landed on my knees at the bottom.

The pain was excruciating, but this was no time to worry about bruises. I got up from the floor, limping. "Where are you, Travis?"

The whine of the power saw gave me a clue. I headed for the workshop and found Travis sawing two-by-fours. I waited until he had laid down the saw before calling out to him again.

He turned to me and smiled. "Good morning, Genny." Then he noticed I was doubled over, rubbing my knees. "What's wrong?"

"I tripped, but never mind that. Something terrible has happened!"

"What? Did you walk in your sleep again?"

"No, nothing like that. It's the lobby. Come upstairs, I'll show you."

Travis saw the broken step on our way up. "Is this where you fell?"

"Yes, but it was my fault. I wasn't being careful."

"You'd better stay off the steps completely until I get them fixed."

The stairs were the least of my concern. I muttered my assurances and dragged Travis into the lobby. He took one look at the desecration.

"Who on earth would have done this? It's insane."

"I know, but how could you have missed it, Travis? You had to go through the lobby to get to the basement this morning."

He kicked an overripe tomato. "Yes, and the lobby was fine when I came downstairs."

"So how did . . . whoever did it get in?"

"They probably just opened the door. I had to go out and buy sandpaper this morning."

"And you didn't lock up behind you?"

Travis flashed me a look of irritation. "You can't keep this place locked during the day, Genny. What'll you do when the work crew gets here—make up twenty sets of keys?"

"I guess you're right." I stepped over mouldy bread crusts and egg shells to lean against the counter. My bruises were throbbing. So was my head. "If you've already gone out this morning, this must have happened sometime afterward."

"Sometime during the last hour or so, probably."

"Who would be crazy enough to trash a place in broad daylight?"

"Beats me. When did you get up?"

"About an hour ago. Travis, why are you looking at me that way?"

"I was just thinking."

He didn't need to elaborate. "Surely you don't think I did this!"

"How should I know? I've been working all morning."

"Well, for your information, I didn't do it!"

In spite of my indignation, I could understand why Travis might jump to such a conclusion. Several times I'd proven myself capable of bizarre behavior while asleep. But there was also practical evidence as to why I couldn't have managed this one.

"This looks like somebody's compost heap," I said. "Where would I have gotten compost?"

"Good thinking. It's not like you can go out and buy the stuff. So who's got a grudge against the Silverbrooke?"

One person came immediately to mind. "Hepzibah."

"That funny old lady? Nah, she wouldn't do anything like this."

"Don't be so sure. You saw how she treated us yesterday."

Travis scratched his head. "Yeah, I know, but . . . there's gotta be someone else out there with an ax to grind."

"Like whom?"

"What about Calder Carson?"

"He's not that kind of man," I protested. Then I realized Calder hadn't returned my message the day I phoned to thank him. Amidst all the activity, I'd forgotten to call him again. It was certainly poor manners on my part, but surely he wouldn't be *that* put out. "No," I added vehemently. "Not Calder."

"Okay, what about the contractors he lined up for you?"

This time I wasn't so quick to argue. A few of them had been quite abrasive when I'd canceled their appointments for estimates. "But why would they resort to this?"

"Probably to let you know that nobody messes with the good-old-boy system."

"But I'm not. I just happened to hire somebody else."

Travis's expression grew pensive. "Sometimes that's all it takes."

I considered his argument, but my gut feeling told me otherwise. "I still think it's Hepzibah."

"Why? What would she gain by doing this?"

"She wants to scare us away."

Travis laughed. "With rotten eggs? They might stink, but they're hardly lethal."

"I never claimed she was rational. But Hepzibah ranks the Silverbrooke right down there with hell itself."

"And us too," Travis acknowledged grudgingly.

"I'm going to pay her a visit. Would you like to come?"

"Genny, you don't know for sure it was her."

"That's why I'm going. To find out."

"Why don't we just call the cops and let them handle it?"

"I'll do that first, but I still want to talk to Hepzibah."

The woman's histrionics had finally gotten to me. I was craving a confrontation even if it turned out she wasn't responsible for this latest disaster. Probably had something to do with being called a fornicator when I hadn't even gotten around to it yet.

"I'll come," Travis said. "The mood you're in, you could use a witness."

The Hot Springs police arrived a short while later to take our statements. One of the officers remembered me from the night at the Whispering Pines Motel.

So much had happened during the past few days I'd almost forgotten about the rock through my window. It seemed so insignificant in retrospect. Now I began to wonder whether it really was a random act of vandalism. I distinctly remembered telling Hepzibah which motel I was staying in. Maybe that had been her first attempt to drive me out of town.

It was nearly noon by the time Travis and I finished cleaning the lobby. Both of us showered—separately, since this was hardly an occasion to invite intimacy—and decided to postpone lunch until after we'd seen Hepzibah. Rotten eggs have a debilitating effect on one's appetite.

Miss Tulley's name and address was in the phone book. According to my street map, she only lived a few blocks from the Silverbrooke.

"Lovely," I muttered. "We're practically neighbors."

Travis chuckled as he descended the front steps. "You really have it in for this lady, don't you?"

"Honestly, I don't. She's more than welcome to her opinions about righteousness. But that doesn't give her the right to cast stones—or tomatoes, in this case."

The walk would have been idyllic under other circumstances. The sun was shining, and I was with Travis. No matter how bad things were, he usually managed to brighten my spirits. It occurred to me as I limped alongside him that Travis, with his unflappable Southern calm, would never develop an ulcer. Donald, on the other hand, was never without one.

Hepzibah lived in a two-storey house on a wooded lot. There were wrap-around verandahs on both floors and pillars entwined with flowering ivy.

"That's one big house for a little lady," Travis remarked.

"Enoch said she used to run a home for unwed mothers. Maybe this was it."

I was right. A faded wooden sign hung above the door. H. Tulley's Home for Girls. Beneath that was a maudlin passage from Lamentations.

"Nice message," Travis said, ringing the bell.

"Hepzibah's version of a welcome mat," I muttered.

There was no answer to his ring. Travis tried again while I peered through the front window. "Looks like a funeral parlor in there."

"Are you surprised?" he said.

"Not really. Let's check the backyard."

That's where we found her, on hands and knees digging in her roses. For all my negativity, I had to admit that Hepzibah had a marvelous green thumb. I'd never seen a more beautiful garden. Flowers of every conceivable variety and hue were planted in intricate, if severely controlled, patterns throughout the yard.

Hepzibah registered no surprise when she saw us. "What are you doing here?"

"We'd like to talk to you," I said.

"About what?"

"I think you already know."

"If it's about your lobby, the police have already come and gone. I've got nothing more to say."

"What did you tell the police?" Travis asked.

"None of your business."

My hands clenched. "Did you deny throwing garbage into my bathhouse?"

"I didn't deny it."

"So you are responsible."

Her pinched face was expressionless. "What I do and I don't do is between me and the Lord."

I must have lunged. Why else would Travis have grabbed the back of my T-shirt? But no one had ever brought out in me such white-hot rage. I didn't hate Hepzibah Tulley, but I absolutely despised the effect she had on me.

Travis gave me a stern look of warning. Then he went over and stood beside Hepzibah.

"Why don't we talk?" he said. "I'm sure once you realize what Genny's doing with the Silverbrooke, you'll understand she has the town's best interest at heart."

Hepzibah snorted. "That ain't Genny. That's Lizbet."

"I beg your pardon?"

"She thinks I'm somebody named Lizbet," I explained, leaning against the fence.

Travis shook his head and tried again. "Let's just discuss the Silverbrooke. What Genny... what my employer wants to do is to open a respectable family bathhouse. There'll be one side for the men and one side for the ladies. Isn't that what you're worried about?"

Hepzibah stabbed the earth with a trowel and turned to Travis. "Despite what you may think, Mr...whatever-your-name-is, I'm not a senile old biddy. Three generations of Tulleys ran that bathhouse, and I know what went on there. Every member of my family has paid a terrible price for their sins. Some of them are burnin' in hell right this very day."

"But that's just my point, Miss Tulley," Travis continued. "This young lady here has no intention of condoning corruption in the Silverbrooke. But you haven't even given her a chance. And after all, you know what Paul said in Romans, chapter fourteen about judging one another."

Bravo, I cheered silently, impressed with Travis's store of biblical knowledge. I probably couldn't have named the first commandment.

A light flickered briefly in Hepzibah's eyes, then just as quickly vanished. It was a noble effort on his part, but what Travis didn't realize was that some people claimed a monopoly on holiness.

They debated ethics a while longer, but Travis got absolutely nowhere. Hepzibah still refused to confirm or deny doing anything to my lobby. And she maintained that Calder Carson was the only man fit to run the Silverbrooke.

"HEPZIBAH TULLEY is one weird lady," Travis acknowledged on our way home.

"Her fixation with Calder Carson really baffles me. You'd think he was a perfect soul or something."

"She might have trashed the place under his orders," Travis suggested.

"Maybe. But I'll bet we could never prove it."

Travis laughed mirthlessly. "Probably not."

Rotten eggs, cops and Hepzibah had not made for an auspicious beginning to the day. I felt an urge to pamper Travis and myself.

"How about we splurge on a really extravagant lunch?" I said when we reached the Silverbrooke. "And yes, I'm buying."

"Sounds great. Who am I to argue with a lady of means?"

It pleased me to see him taking our respective financial situations lightly. I couldn't help being rich any more than Travis could help being broke. In his case, however, I felt certain the setback was temporary.

"Where would you like to go?" he asked.

"The Arlington."

"Whew, that's big-time."

"I know." The Arlington Hotel had intrigued me ever since my arrival in Hot Springs. Built near Bathhouse Row, the building was old and magnificent and looked like a French chateau.

Travis glanced at his paint-stained jeans. "But I can't go there dressed like this."

"Of course not. You'll have to wear a tie."

He looked at me as though I'd asked him to drown a kitten. "You want me to wear a tie in this weather? It's nearly ninety in the shade."

"Just this once, Travis, please."

"But I've got a million things to do before the crew gets here."

"So we'll skip supper and work late."

His handsome features fell. "Is this an order, Genny?"

I batted my lashes teasingly. "Yes, but it's not from your boss. It's from someone who likes the way you kiss."

The compliment must have worked. "Okay, you win. But this'll be the only time you ever get me into a suit. So enjoy it."

An idiotic thought popped into my head. What would Travis wear when he remarried? As if he actually intended to marry. As if I was going to be there when he did!

THE SIGHT OF TRAVIS dressed up was unforgettable. I'd never seen an instant transition from wrangler to trendy mogul. But in his light gray suit and coral silk tie, Travis looked spectacular. A little irritated, perhaps, but spectacular.

I'd chosen a sleeveless rayon dress in purple and jade, and brushed my hair dramatically behind one ear.

Travis whistled. "I've never seen a lady look so good at two in the afternoon."

"The same goes for a certain gentleman I could mention."

He stroked my cheek with the back of his fingers. "You really are the most intriguing creature I've ever laid eyes on."

I touched his face lightly. "Do you think maybe when we get back from lunch . . ."

He captured my fingers and kissed them, one by one. "We'll lock all the doors and unplug the phone."

What a relief that he hadn't made me put it into words.

THE FOUNTAIN ROOM at the Arlington was everything I had hoped it would be—understated, elegant, with skylights, ferns and a muted decor of peach and spring green.

For all his grumbling, Travis surprised me by knowing his way around haute cuisine. He pronounced the French dishes with only a touch of drawl and selected an excellent Chablis to accompany the meal.

After the wine steward had left, Travis frowned. "Why are you looking at me like that?"

"How?" I asked.

"All funny and dreamylike."

"Oh, I don't know. Guess I've never been swept off my feet by a Texan before."

He grinned. "Lady, you ain't seen nothin' yet."

We were proposing our third romantic toast when I noticed two gentlemen approaching us. The older man was Enoch Sarrazin. The younger one was the last person I'd ever expected to see in Hot Springs. Donald, my ex-husband!

"What on earth is he doing here?"

Travis craned his neck. "Who?"

"My ex."

Just then Enoch caught my eye. His reaction was urbane, but not quite convincing. He obviously hadn't expected to run into me here. "Why, Geneva, what a surprise!"

I couldn't resist matching his syrupy greeting. "Enoch, how *are* you? Isn't it a lovely day?"

Donald's expression spoke volumes. If he'd intended to make his presence known to me, it was obviously not planned to be here or now. The man was on the verge of sinking through the floor.

"Fancy meeting you here, Donald." A cliché, I know, but so very fitting.

"Yes. Surprise." There was an unmistakable wilt to his final word. Then Donald turned to Travis and squared his shoulders as if confronting an arch-rival.

My hopes for an ultimate afternoon were fading fast. It would be too much to expect that Donald was flying back to Minneapolis after lunch. And I had yet to find out why he was here.

"Aren't you going to introduce us?" Travis said in a voice approaching a growl.

Reluctantly I made the introductions. Handshakes were exchanged with all the warmth of superpower peace talks. Then came one of my life's most awkward moments.

Enoch and Donald had already eaten. Travis and I hadn't. Was I supposed to invite them to join us for a drink? I didn't want to. And judging from Travis's scowl, neither did he.

But someone eventually had to say something. "So, Donald," I said with effusive cheer. "Where are you staying?"

"Here, at the Arlington."

Extravagant, I thought—but typical, if only for appearance's sake. Aloud, I said, "For how long?"

"That depends."

"On what?"

"You."

"Oh." That should have been a foregone conclusion.

"When could we have some time alone, Geneva?" He glanced at Travis as though he, not Donald, were the interloper.

I was sorely tempted to kick my ex-husband. "I'm not sure," I said. "Give me your room number, and I'll call you."

"I flew halfway across the country to see you."

"Without so much as a word of warning."

He reddened. "It was supposed to be a surprise."

My resistance finally wore down. "All right, Donald, drop by the Silverbrooke this afternoon. Say around five o'clock."

"Five o'clock's perfect."

"I'll be waiting in the lobby. Don't be late." That last re-mark was a dig. Donald was always disgustingly prompt for everything. Before the two men could skulk away, I called out to Enoch.

He turned once more and smiled painfully. "Yes, Ge-neva?"

"We had kind of a crisis this morning at the Silver-brooke."

"Oh, dear. What happened?"

I told him about the garbage.

"How disgusting! Did you contact the police?"

"Yes. We also went to see Hepzibah."

"Hepzibah Tulley? Whatever for?"

"I think she did it, Enoch."

The attorney lifted a dramatic hand to his heart. "Non-sense. Hepzibah might be senile, but she's not malicious."

"Maybe not, but would you do me a favor? Since you obviously know the woman better than I do, could you per-suade her to take up some new humanitarian cause?"

Enoch gave a strained laugh. "I'll do that, Geneva. Don't you worry about a thing."

THE FOOD at the Arlington was wonderful. Our mood, thanks to Donald, was funereal. So much for salvaging the day. It was obviously determined to be awful. Travis went back to work as soon as he changed into his work clothes.

At one minute to five, I sat waiting for Donald in the Sil-verbrooke's lobby. My tank top was splattered with paint, and my legs still bore the traces of my morning tumble, but I didn't care. I was past the point of primping for Donald.

Either my watch was slow or he was over-anxious. Don-ald came through the doors twenty-seven seconds earlier than scheduled.

"Hello, Donald."

"Hello, Geneva."

My arms were folded, my legs crossed. A sandal was swinging off the end of one foot. "So what are you doing in Hot Springs?" I asked, not willing to waste any time.

"I was worried about you."

"You can see for yourself I'm fine."

"I'm not so sure. What happened to your legs?"

"An accident. No big deal."

He seemed put out that I didn't elaborate. "I saw Ernie last night at the Marquette."

"Ernie?" Ernest Sorenson was my bank manager and boss. He and Donald had been squash partners for years. "What does Ernie have to do with anything?"

"He told me you'd asked for another month's leave."

"He shouldn't have told you."

"I dragged it out of him. Why do you want to stay here another month?"

"Because I decided to renovate the Silverbrooke, and I want to be here while it happens. If you must know," I added emphatically.

He glanced around the dreary foyer. I realized my enthusiasm might be hard for Donald to comprehend. Then the phone rang, postponing further explanation.

"Hello?"

"Geneva, it's Enoch." We exchanged the usual social niceties. Then he said, "I had a little chat with Hepzibah."

"Really? How did it go?"

"She's a stubborn one, I gotta admit. Took me nigh on twenty minutes to get her to admit she'd pelted those rotten eggs."

"But she did admit it?"

"Finally. I warned her of the legal ramifications of her actions. She realizes you and the police have grounds to press charges."

"I don't want to press charges, Enoch. I just want her to leave me alone."

"I understand and must say that's most generous of you."

My ex-husband, meanwhile, was pacing the lobby, clearly disturbed by the nature of my conversation as well as the plaster dust accumulating on his brogues.

"Did Hepzibah agree to give up her campaign against the Silverbrooke?" I asked.

"That's kinda hard to say. She has this habit of fading in and out when you talk to her. I'm not really sure I got through."

When it came to Hepzibah Tulley, I doubted anyone ever had. "Oh, well, that's okay. I appreciate your efforts, Enoch."

"My pleasure. You take care now."

I hung up and said to Donald, "Now, where were we?"

"Trying to establish why you'd jeopardize your security and personal safety for this . . . albatross."

"My personal safety? What are you talking about?"

"Old ladies pelting you with eggs—"

"Not me, the lobby."

"Same difference."

"Listen, Donald, why don't I show you around? Maybe then you'll understand why I love this place."

He looked like a man who didn't want to be persuaded, but what choice did he have? During the hour that followed, I was proud of the way I conducted my tour, reciting Hot Springs facts and figures like an old timer.

Even Donald seemed impressed. My monologue began with an explanation of the thermal water's source. From deep within the earth's core, accumulated rainwater traveled to the surface, making contact with highly heated rock before seeping through the faults of Hot Springs sandstone.

Carbon dating indicated that the water takes four thousand years to reach the springs. The combined flow in all of Hot Springs averages 850,000 gallons per day.

I described the history of Bathhouse Row. The United States had acquired the area from France as part of the Louisiana Purchase. In 1832, the Federal Government had set aside four parcels of land, famous for their curative hot springs.

The first bathhouses were little more than canvas and lumber lean-tos placed over the individual springs. Because of poor drainage, they'd been constantly subject to mud, floods or stagnation.

The grand bathhouses had been built around the turn of the century. Americans were prosperous in those days, and it wasn't uncommon for visitors to indulge in a twenty-one-course bath.

The peak year for "taking the waters" was 1946. From then on, interest in spas declined, and many of the bathhouses were closed. The Silverbrooke hung on longer than most, but eventually it too had been shut down for financial and family reasons. I was a little vague on the reasons but still thought I'd injected a nice air of poignancy to the tale.

I described our plans for the Silverbrooke—repairing the mosaic tile, reglazing tubs, installing stained glass. Donald was so quiet I thought surely he was overwhelmed.

But when we finished the tour, he said, "Why did you keep mentioning that Travis fellow every second breath?"

"I didn't."

"You did."

We'd found Travis scraping putty in the men's bath hall, and admittedly, there had been a certain tension in the air. For one thing, my prospective lover had changed into work clothes while my ex still wore his immaculate linen suit, sufficient justification on Donald's part to look down on Travis.

But I didn't recall mentioning Travis's name all that often. And anyway, my social life was none of Donald's business. We'd made an agreement.

"All right," my ex said while I brewed tea in the apartment. "I'll admit the Silverbrooke has potential, but your costs are going to be staggering."

"I'll eventually recoup my investment, but that's not the issue."

Donald gave me that sanctimonious look I'd always hated. "Then, pray tell, what is the issue?"

"I'm finally doing something for myself. Sure, it's nothing like the grocery empire my parents built, but at least it's mine. And I don't have to go to a dead-end job every day just because I feel obligated to have a job."

"There's nothing dead-end about mortgage and loans. If you applied yourself, you could be branch manager in a few years."

"I don't want to be a branch manager. Banking is boring. And because I've had it all my life, money is boring. At least now I'm doing something enjoyable with my inheritance."

Donald put precisely one and a third teaspoons of sugar into his teacup. "The thrill's going to wear off, Geneva. You'll sink hundreds of thousands into this place and end up with a mildewed white elephant."

"If that's what you think, Donald, fine. But I'd still rather try and fail than never try at all." I was all set to spout off some more pithy bromides when Travis walked into the apartment carrying his hard hat.

"Hi, honey, I'm home!"

Chapter Nine

Donald's jaw dropped. "Honey? Home? Would you mind telling me what's going on?"

Before I could prepare my defense, Travis brought a six-pack of beer into the kitchen and plopped it on the table. Then he marched over and kissed me. Rather loudly, it seemed to me.

Donald's complexion was apoplectic. "I thought this guy worked for you!"

"He does."

"I do," Travis agreed, pulling a beer from the plastic ring. "She's a great boss. Easy to work for, not afraid to pitch in and help."

"Geneva," Donald said. I used to hear that tone of voice whenever I forgot to take meat out of the freezer or put gas in the car.

"Yes, Donald?" My teeth ached with the effort of clenching.

Travis opened his mouth, all set to offer his version of our story. But I glared, and he wisely stayed quiet. There was obviously some male territorial battle in progress, but I wasn't about to end up anyone's quarry. Not unless I chose to be.

"This is not what you think," I told my ex-husband, then groaned. Talk about a hackneyed defense. "Travis is a highly qualified contractor who—"

"Who you've decided to shack up with."

It wasn't like my ex-husband to dangle his participles. Travis took a seat and smugly drank his beer. My gaze flitted from one man to the other. It would serve them both right if I just left the room and let them work things out with their fists. But it wouldn't have been fair for Donald.

"Travis thought it would be a good idea," I explained, "if he used the apartment while he works here. He's putting in long hours, and it would save him a lot of traveling time." I wasn't about to inform Donald of Travis's bankruptcy. Donald had a typical banker's attitude toward insolvency.

"That makes sense," my ex-spouse acknowledged. "But why are *you* living here?"

"I told you before, I've been walking in my sleep again."

"So?"

"Travis thought—and I agreed—that I shouldn't be alone."

"Humph," was Donald's terse rejoinder.

"Besides, it saves me a few dollars, and I like being here, where the action is." Too late I realized the double entendre of my remark.

"Action," Donald repeated with another murderous look at Travis.

"We're in separate rooms," I finally admitted.

"Then what was that kiss all about?"

"I kissed her," Travis said, "because I happen to like this lady a lot. And I'll tell you something else. I would never do anything to hurt Genny."

For that remark I'd have gladly allowed him to kiss me in front of Donald again.

"But you've only known each other a few days."

"So?" Travis countered.

My expression echoed Travis's sentiment.

"Is it true, Geneva? You really like this guy?"

I turned to Travis, and the room grew misty. "Yes, I really like this guy."

My ex-husband fell silent for a moment. "I see. In that case, I suppose there's not much point in my interfering."

"Not really," I said.

He got up from the table. I walked him to the door.

"What are you going to do about your sleepwalking?" Donald asked when we were alone at the top of the stairs.

"I've rescheduled an appointment with a therapist in St. Paul. He thinks we can cure it with hypnosis. I'm not so sure, but we'll see."

"You know I still care about you, Geneva."

"If you care so much, why did you come to Hot Springs without letting me know?"

"It was a last-minute decision. I thought you'd be upset if you knew I was coming."

He was right. I would have been upset. "But why did you contact Enoch?"

"I knew how excited you were about keeping the lease, and I wanted an unbiased professional opinion about the Silverbrooke before I saw you."

That much at least was typical of Donald. He never trusted decisions based on emotion. I was no longer angry at him, only irritated that he hadn't given me the benefit of the doubt.

"Will you be returning to Minneapolis now?" I asked.

"My ticket's good for a week. Enoch says there's good golfing. Might as well play a few holes while I'm here. If it doesn't bother you, that is."

I hoped the conciliatory remark meant that he would leave Travis and me alone, but I wouldn't add insult to injury by asking. "Stay as long as you like. It won't bother me."

"That's good. Bye, Geneva."

"Bye, Donald."

He reached out to touch me, then quickly drew back. I recalled what he had said about my clinging and repelling. When, I wondered, had our roles become reversed?

Returning to the kitchen, I found Travis preparing a Caesar salad. His sidelong glance told me he knew what was coming. A lecture.

I decided to fake him out. I threw my arms around his neck and gave him a smoldering kiss on the mouth.

"Whew," Travis said when it was over. "What did I do to deserve that?"

"Absolutely nothing, turkey. Just wanted to show you what an open-minded, forgiving lady I am."

He resumed crushing garlic. "So you're upset with me, huh?"

"And well I should be. What was that 'Hi honey I'm home' routine all about? You knew I was up here with Donald."

"That was my reason. You were up here with Donald."

"So?"

"You only have to look at the guy, for cripes' sake. He's still crazy about you."

"My ex-husband with whom I shared five years of mediocrity? Don't be ridiculous."

Travis lay down the butcher knife. "I know what I saw, Genny. The only time that guy takes his eyes off you is to shoot daggers at me."

"No. Really?" I wasn't being coy, but it had never occurred to me that Donald might still be carrying a torch. Being so damned practical, he was more likely to carry a rechargeable, waterproof flashlight than a torch. "So you were trying to make him jealous?"

"Darned right. I wanted him to know he'd had his chance with you, and now it was my turn."

"I would have told him about us eventually."

Travis drew me into his arms. "Eventually wasn't good enough. I needed to know the minute I walked in that you still preferred me."

My breath caught as I looked into his craggy, handsome face. "Why would you ever doubt that I preferred you, Travis?"

"Maybe because, so far, you've never really showed me."

I traced the outlines of his mouth. "I can show you now if you like." He smiled, and something responded deep inside me.

"My beautiful, brown-eyed Genny," he whispered. "I can't tell you how much I'd like that."

Hand in hand, we went to the master bedroom. Although the window faced the mountain, I drew the blinds shut. No one, not even Mother Nature, was going to intrude on this private interlude.

I turned and walked slowly toward Travis. Not to tease, but to savor each delicious sensation: the peaceful silence surrounding us; the bold, lean length of him; the magnetic essence of his deep blue eyes.

He ran his hands along my bare shoulders, as if committing my outline to memory. I opened the buttons of his shirt and reveled in the smoothness of his chest.

"You are so sexy," I murmured.

"So are you, sweetheart." He lifted the tank top over my head. I felt sensitized, aware of every curl that fell to my shoulders. When he picked up a lock in his fingers and kissed it, somehow I felt that as well.

"Ever since we met, I've dreamed about loving you," he said, cupping my small, upturned breasts.

"Were they good dreams?"

"They were magic . . . just like you."

Divesting what remained of our clothes, we lay down on the bed. Every motion, every gesture was delight. His tongue on my nipples, his fingers on my thighs.

My hands had never stroked such male perfection. My mouth had never tasted flesh so sweet.

When we came together, length to length, I knew the meaning of a perfect fit. Our legs intertwined, our mouths linked. Wherever we touched, our bodies blended, diminishing the sensation that we were separate beings.

I never will forget how it felt when Travis entered me the first time. The momentary resistance, then the flowering of acceptance. He filled me slowly, surely, with himself, just as I enfolded him.

We were meant to be lovers. I knew that completely as we indulged in the sometimes graceful, sometimes grasping rhythms of our union.

We were partners in a timeless dance of the sexes. Both leading and being led, taking back and giving in. When the magic and passion had reached their peak, we clung together and surrendered. There would undoubtedly be other dances, other rhythms each of us would seek. But I knew from that moment on, I wanted all of mine to be with Travis.

I DON'T HAVE my nightie on! Why did Mommy tuck me in without my nightie? I'm so cold.

I'll wrap this cover around me. The floor is cold under my feet. I have to be careful not to trip. Unca says I trip a lot, but Mommy says that's 'cause I'm just a little girl. I'm not little, I'm two. But I don't know how to make them understand.

My toys aren't in the living room. They must be in the closet by my crib. That's where Mommy puts them when people come.

I don't like it when those strange people visit. They always want to kiss me and hug me and tickle me under the chin. I don't like being tickled. But when I cry or try to tickle them back, Unca gets mad. He says I'm spoiled, but I don't understand that word. Does it mean I'm bad?

The closet door is hard to open. I have to pull and pull. Finally when I use both hands I land smack on my bottom.

The basket of toys is right where Mommy left it, but there's icky stuff all over them that sticks to my fingers. I think it's what spiders make. I look in the basket for spiders but don't see any.

My blocks are here and my cars and the dolly with the blinking eyes whose name is Flossie. I don't want to play with Flossie. She had a cold the other day, and I put a jar of that smelly stuff all over her that Mommy uses when I'm sick. My dolly doesn't have a cold anymore, but now her eyes are stuck shut. I got a big spanking for that.

I like playing with my blocks, especially in the playhouse. But it's dark, so I better not go downstairs. I'll stay right here on the floor. I'll make houses and tables and chairs out of blocks. I can make anything I want to . . .

"Genny, wake up!"

Travis was shaking me by the shoulders. I couldn't understand why he was being so rough. Was this any way to treat a new lover?

I opened my eyes and saw the worry on Travis's face. "Oh, no," I groaned. "Not again!"

"I didn't hear you get up. I thought for sure I would, but . . ."

"Where am I?"

"In the spare room."

It was still dark outside. I sat up, shivering from cold and relief that at least I hadn't left the apartment. Travis wrapped a blanket around me. Then he picked up a piece of wood from a pile scattered on the floor.

"What are these?" I asked.

"Looks like toys. You must have been playing."

"But where'd they come from?"

He switched on a light, momentarily blinding us. We both noticed a small open door on the wall. "I never noticed there was a crawl space in here," Travis said.

The door had been papered to match the room. When closed, it lay flush against the wall. "There was no reason to notice it."

"But you found it in the dark."

I looked up while tears of frustration filled my eyes. Travis was only wearing jeans. He must have thrown them on in a hurry to come look for me. Seeing his beautiful body, remembering how it felt when we made love, I battled with self-directed rage. This was no way to spend our first night together.

"I didn't know about this cupboard, Travis. Or the toys. I don't remember ever seeing them before."

He helped me to my feet. "We've gotta do something, Genny. I didn't even hear you get out of bed."

"That's because I'm good at sneaking out."

"What?"

I shook my head, hardly aware of what I'd said. Or, more importantly, why I'd said it. I wrapped my arms around Travis's neck. "Could we just go back to bed? Please?"

"I think you should call a doctor in the morning."

"Fine, whatever. Just don't make me think about it now."

"I won't, darling. I won't."

He put his arms around me and held me for a long while, probably wondering why he'd gotten involved in the first place. The realization that Travis might give up on me was terrifying. I couldn't abide having this demon inside me much longer. But I didn't want Travis to think it was the only reason I needed him.

Travis shut off the lights and ushered me out of the room. The blocks that I'd scattered in my sleep were still lying on the floor.

I PHONED DR. CALDWELL first thing in the morning. He seemed as upset as the rest of us.

"Haven't you been taking the sedatives I prescribed?"

Frankly, I'd forgotten about them. "No, but I don't want pills, Doctor. I want to stop sleepwalking."

"Until you begin your therapy, I don't know what else to suggest."

"Speaking of therapy," I said guiltily, "I've decided to stay in Hot Springs another month. Is there any chance something could be done down here?"

"Based on the frequency and activity level of your sleepwalking, I think that's a good idea. Something is trying desperately to get out of your subconscious. But you shouldn't be on your own when it does."

I glanced at Travis who sat across the table buttering toast. "I'm not on my own. I have a . . . friend."

Travis gave me a reassuring wink.

"That's good." I could hear Dr. Caldwell leafing through a book. "Here we are. There's a research institute in Little Rock that specializes in sleep disorders. I'm going to refer you to them for consultation. It's crucial, Geneva, that you get to the bottom of this soon."

"Yes, I agree." Dr. Caldwell's analogy of something trying to get out was appropriate. I was beginning to feel this "something's" presence as strongly as my own.

"Are you okay?" Travis asked after I'd hung up.

"I guess so. I'm being referred to a sleep institute in Little Rock."

"That's great, but you don't sound too happy about it."

"Who knows how long I'll have to wait for an appointment? In the meantime, anything could happen."

Travis reached for my hand. "Don't worry. This time, I won't let anything happen."

"Thanks," I replied halfheartedly.

"Did my snoring keep you awake?"

I shook my head, grateful that Travis was trying to make me feel better. But when it came to my nocturnal wanderings, no one could make assurances. Not even me.

THE WORK CREW began to arrive that morning—a motley, friendly bunch of Texans who shared a common loyalty with their former boss. It was like old-home week at the Silverbrooke, the guys swapping jokes as they set up their scaffolds and drop cloths.

Dr. Caldwell phoned me later that morning. It was just as I feared. The sleep institute wouldn't be able to accommodate me for another three weeks. He urged me strongly to start using the sedatives.

I was supposed to meet Bill Swann at the Club Café that afternoon. After all that had happened, it seemed like weeks since he'd left the message to see me.

In the meantime, I'd embarked on a personal search to find out why I'd been playing with blocks the night before. Knowing that Travis was downstairs with the crew helped. No matter what I stumbled on, at least I wouldn't be alone.

There was a basket of toys lying beside the entrance to the crawl space. In the daylight the closed door was barely visible. It seemed incredible that I could have found it in the dark.

Gingerly I examined the toys. They were old, covered with dust and cobwebs. There was a doll whose eyes were stuck shut with some kind of salve. I dropped her into the box and wiped my hands.

Then I forced myself to crawl into the closet. Dust and mothballs made me sneeze and I aimed my flashlight into the corners. All I could see were a few boxes and a collapsed baby crib. I took out the box nearest me and shut the door as if to prevent anything else from emerging, uninvited.

There was nothing of interest in the first box. Ladies' clothes, shoes and belts, mostly of fifties vintage. I returned this to the closet and brought out a second.

This time, I had better luck. There were children's things—little girl's dresses and play clothes. Were these mine, I wondered? Or had I played here with some other little girl my own age? Someone whose name, perhaps, was Lizbet.

Nothing came to me as I pored through the garments. No glimmer of recognition, no sense of déjà vu. Whether they were mine or someone else's made little difference. Seeing them was not enough to spark my subconscious.

The mothballs were irritating my sinuses. I hurriedly removed the remaining contents—little shoes, socks, purses. At the bottom of the box was an envelope from a photography studio in Hot Springs. My pulse quickened. Maybe there would be pictures of people I recognized.

What I found was both disappointing and confusing. They were portrait proofs of a little girl with red ringlets and brown eyes. The same portrait Bill Swann had brought to

Minneapolis, they were all of me. And according to the address on the envelope, they'd been taken in Hot Springs.

I set the envelope aside and finished my exploration of the crawl space. But there were no further revelations in the boxes that remained, only junk.

I threw my dusty clothes into the hamper and showered. Then I changed into a summer skirt and blouse for my appointment with Bill Swann.

Travis would have liked to come with me, but he said he thought he should stay with the crew since this was their first day on the job. He was right of course, but that didn't stop me from missing him as I left the Silverbrooke on my own.

It still astonished me that we were lovers. Every nuance of Travis's lovemaking was fresh in my mind. Every erotic and energetic detail.

What I wouldn't give to indulge myself in daydreams, to do nothing but anticipate our next night together. But for the time being, dreams of any kind were out of the question.

I'd brought the envelope of proofs with me to show Bill. But first I was going to impress the detective with my own sleuthing ability. The address of the photography studio was on the envelope. If their records went back far enough, I might be able to find out who'd brought me for the sitting and when. Not that my quest would be over then, but every bit of information helped.

Hot Springs was not an easy town to navigate. I was lost for a good fifteen minutes before I finally located the right street. I slowed down to read the numbers on the small, commercially zoned houses.

I found the address, but it wasn't a photographer's. The sign read Esther's Esthetics and Hair Salon. I parked the car and got out. Maybe Esther could tell me what had become of the studio.

Inside was a platinum-haired beautician and a lone customer getting a perm. The hairdresser smiled at me. "Hi, sugar."

"Hello. Are you Esther?"

The woman laughed as though I'd said something truly witty. "Esther ain't been here for twelve years. I bought the place from her. My name's Maebelle."

"Oh, I see. How do you do? My name's Geneva. I was wondering if you could tell me about the photo studio that used to be here."

The customer cried out when Maebelle wrapped one of the curlers too tightly. "Oops, sorry, hon. Photo studio, you said?"

"That's right."

"Boy, it *has* been a while since you were here."

My heart leaped. "You mean you've seen me before?"

She gave me a funny look. "I don't know you from Adam. I just meant that first you asked about Esther and then the studio. Both of them have been gone for years."

"But this *was* a photography studio at one time?"

"Sure, ages ago."

"Did they move their premises elsewhere?"

Maebelle thought a moment. "As far as I recall, Mr. Jessup, the owner, retired. I think he went to Oklahoma."

Pulling at straws was so frustrating. "Do you have any idea where in Oklahoma?"

"Not the foggiest. Mr. Jessup was already an old man when I was little. I'm sure he must be dead and buried by now."

Along with what remained of my history in Hot Springs. I thanked Maebelle and left, but it was all I could do not to scream. No matter which way I turned, there was another blind alley.

What worried me most was the feeling that time was running out. That if I didn't find answers soon, my sleepwalking would forever gain the upper hand. I didn't know what happened to people like that, but it wouldn't surprise me if they made their home in padded cells.

I tucked the pictures into my purse and got into the car. The Club Café, where I was to meet Bill, was on Central Avenue, not far from Bathhouse Row. I was still a few minutes early but needed the time to regroup my thoughts.

Most of the lunch crowd had dispersed. I nursed a cold drink and absently perused the menu. The home-cooked smells from the kitchen were fabulous, but I didn't have much of an appetite. I was afraid that Bill's news, whatever it was, would be disappointing. I wasn't sure I could handle another disappointment.

Two o'clock came and went. No Bill. Two-fifteen and he still wasn't there. I ordered another drink and munched on bread sticks, trying to keep my impatience in check. After all, this was the South where time moved more slowly.

By two-thirty, I was livid. There were plenty of other things I could be doing besides sitting here, taking up space. I went to a public phone and called his office. He wasn't in, but I left a tightly worded message on his machine. If he wasn't in, maybe that meant he was on his way.

My patience finally snapped at three o'clock. No one could expect a person to wait for more than an hour. I paid for my drinks, apologized to the waitress and stormed out of the Club Café, promising myself irrelevantly to return with Travis one day. It seemed like a charming restaurant.

I'd never squealed tires before in my life, but on the way to Bill's office, I squealed them three times. I was furious and hoped for his sake that he had an ironclad excuse.

The front door was locked. I knocked, but no one answered. Then I peered through his office window. The desk was empty which struck me as odd. It had been decidedly cluttered the day Travis and I were there.

"You lookin' for Bill?"

I turned to find a lady walking her terrier on a leash. "Yes, do you know where he is?"

She gave me a sympathetic smile and shrugged. "Not precisely, honey. Bill Swann died two days ago."

Chapter Ten

"That's impossible," I said. "He just phoned me two days ago." I had to grab the porch rail to steady myself. *Bill Swann phoned me the day he died.*

The lady knelt to pet her dog. "Were you a friend of Bill's?"

"No, I was his...client. How did he die?"

"Heart attack on the golf course apparently. They say he didn't suffer."

"Did he have family?"

"None that I know of. Folks are always comin' and goin' from Bill's, but I think they were mostly clients. I live just down the street, you see."

Slowly I descended the stairs. The impact of Bill's death was greater than it ought to be, considering the few occasions we'd been together. The timing of his death was a shock, of course. But what shook me just as much was the knowledge that whatever Bill had planned to say to me was now lost forever. Another blind alley, this one permanent.

Then I felt guilty for thinking only of myself. "When is the funeral?" I asked.

"Ain't gonna be one. They cremated Bill's body this morning."

I needed time to make sense of things. For the next few hours, I drove aimlessly along the mountain roads outside Hot Springs, lost in thought—at times, simply lost.

The perverse notion had come to me that I was somehow responsible for Bill's death. That if I hadn't pried, asked so many questions, he would still be alive.

But that was inane. The man had died of a heart attack, for Pete's sake! With his diet of fast food and cheap Scotch, it was little wonder.

Still, even if I had made no impact on him, Bill had certainly changed my life. Since the day he'd appeared in my office, things hadn't been the same. In the space of two weeks, I had injured my hands, wandered Hot Springs Mountain in the middle of the night, had a rock thrown through my window and the lobby of my bathhouse trashed. As if that weren't enough, I had also fallen in love.

Thank heaven for miracles like love. Travis was my one ray of sunshine shining through the nightmare closing in around me. I never could have weathered this series of crises without him.

But it wasn't fair to ask that of Travis. No one could sustain another's emotions indefinitely. He was being supportive and remarkably loving, but how much more could he tolerate before his love turned to pity and finally disgust? I had to regain my balance before that happened.

But how? Where did one begin? With the inner puzzle or the outer one?

Tired of driving, I returned to the Silverbrooke. With the crew there, the place had come to life even more—power saws whining, hammers hammering, men swapping jokes with thick Southern drawls.

I entered the lobby in a disturbed state of mind. I longed to be alone and dreaded solitude. I loved Travis and resented him for not preventing me from walking in my sleep.

I was angry at Bill for dying and angry at myself for being so selfish.

My condition hadn't improved much by the time Travis came up at the end of the day. I was curled up on the living room sofa, staring into space.

"Earth to Genny," Travis said. "Come in, please."

I blinked. "Pardon?"

Travis crossed the room and sat beside me. "Are you all right, Genny?"

"Bill is dead."

"What?"

"Bill Swann. He had a heart attack."

"When?"

"Two days ago."

Travis thought for a moment. "Isn't that the day we got the message from him?"

"Mmm-hmm. He must have died within hours after that."

I suddenly wished we hadn't erased the tape. I thought that if I could hear it again, maybe I could pick up some clue, something to point me in the right direction.

Travis rested my head on his shoulder. "You've had a rough day, haven't you?"

I shrugged.

"I didn't even see you all afternoon. What did you do?"

"Nothing. Drove around." I looked up. "Do you know how I feel, Travis?"

"How?"

"Like I'm functioning with half a brain."

"Don't be so hard on yourself. You're in shock over Bill's death."

"But what if he had something important to tell me?"

"If he did, there's nothing we can do about it now. But don't worry, Genny. We'll get to the bottom of this yet."

Even Travis wasn't sounding too convincing anymore.

I'd hoped he and I could have a quiet evening together, but Travis apologized and said he'd made other plans. He hadn't seen his buddies in three months, and they'd invited him to go out for a beer.

Graciously they invited me too, but I didn't want to put a damper on their evening. And given my state of mind, that's what would have happened.

Travis was concerned about leaving me alone, but I assured him I'd be fine. If I came across like a martyr, he was kind enough not to say so.

I decided to spend the evening searching the Silverbrooke for anything that might explain my continuing repression. Granted, I'd probably suffered psychological damage from finding Pearl Tulley's body in the basement. But I knew about that now. There was no need to suppress the incident. Why did I still feel like there was something more?

My parents must have downplayed Pearl's suicide, just as they had downplayed my sleepwalking. You'll outgrow it, they always said. If you would just stop worrying, you'd stop walking in your sleep.

But I couldn't help worrying. As a child, there's nothing more frightening than waking up in a strange place. My mother found me in a snowbank once when I was five. She carried me inside, holding on so tight I started to cry.

Mother had covered my mouth with her large hand. "Hush, Geneva, you'll disturb your father, and you know how much it upsets him when you cry."

So I'd promptly stifled the tears, just as I'd stifled my memory of the Silverbrooke. Sleepwalking had soon become a regular part of life.

During my teenage years, it was a constant source of embarrassment. The worst incident occurred when I was fourteen.

My parents were having a dinner party with a group of business colleagues. I'd been considered too young to join in and spent the evening reading on my bed. After dozing off, I got up in my sleep and entered the dining room where the table had been set for midnight coffee and desserts.

No one saw me crawl beneath the table. I waited there until the guests had filed in, then grabbed two corners of the linen tablecloth. Mother heard me giggle, but it was too late. I'd given the cloth a yank, and half the china had crashed to the floor.

The next morning Mother told me what I'd done. She and my father were furious, as though I'd done it deliberately to humiliate them. But no one was more humiliated than I. Some of the guests were parents of my classmates. I was certain the news would spread around the whole school.

I pleaded with my parents then to do something about my sleepwalking. Despite their rage, they had refused at first, still convinced I could stop it if I wanted to. But I knew better.

My high school guidance counselor told me that hypnosis was sometimes effective. He agreed to phone my parents and recommend that I get help.

They were livid that I'd actually discussed my problem with an outsider. But why, I wondered, was that worse than behaving like an idiot in front of guests? At times it seemed there was more than just a generation gap between my parents and me. But eventually I convinced them to let me try.

As it turned out, hypnosis didn't work. No matter what the therapist tried, I could not enter a trance state.

He attributed it to tension. I had never considered myself tense, but when a condition is chronic, I suppose one forgets what life was like without it.

My parents interpreted my blockage as a victory for their side. From then on they could safely proclaim there was nothing to be done for my sleepwalking. I suspect there were nights that I sleepwalked and was never told. My affliction became a shameful secret, like the old days when people hid their lunatic relatives in the attic.

I couldn't wait to grow up and leave home. Apart from their attitude toward sleepwalking, my parents were good people and loved me very much. But it wasn't easy to live under their shadow. Superachievers, they saw in their only child an opportunity to aggrandize and display their talents. As for me, I could never do enough to impress them. The memory was depressing.

I WAS GETTING MYSELF a diet cola from the fridge when the phone rang. It was Enoch.

"I've been trying to reach you all day, Geneva."

"The answering machine was on. Why didn't you leave a message?"

"I hate talking into those tomfool things. Listen, I was wonderin' if you would care to join the missus and me at the country club for dinner tomorrow night. I know it's short notice and all."

The invitation didn't appeal to me in the least, but I couldn't think of a polite reason to refuse. "All right, Enoch, I guess I could make it."

"It'll just be Calder Carson, my wife and I. I don't believe you've met Lurlene."

I did some basic calculations. Enoch, his wife, Calder. Add another, you had a cozy foursome. Maybe I was being paranoid, but I'd also been single long enough to smell a potential setup. And Calder Carson was not my idea of a hot date.

"Would you mind if I brought someone, Enoch?"

His silence confirmed my suspicions. "Well, uh...I guess that'd be all right."

"That's great. You see, we sort of made tentative plans for tomorrow evening, and I wouldn't want to cancel altogether."

"Then by all means, bring him along."

After hanging up, I wondered what Travis would say when he learned of the invitation. I didn't usually invite others without asking first. The pressure of the moment must have gotten to me. I knew I would have loathed an evening with Calder as my date.

Putting the invitation out of my mind, I decided to start my search of the Silverbrooke with the basement. While descending the stairs carefully, I reminded myself there was nothing more to fear. What had happened at the Silverbrooke had taken place twenty-six years ago. I was a big girl now. Independent, intelligent. Maybe not as courageous as I'd like to be, but I was working on it.

Travis would be proud when he learned I'd gone downstairs all by myself. It was still no piece of cake. I had to practically force one foot in front of the other.

The boiler room was to my left. I already knew what was in there and felt no desire to see it again. Besides, I'd come down to examine the boxes and crates. There were literally dozens of them all over the basement, a fire hazard that Travis was eager to remove.

I was glad he hadn't had the chance yet. He and the crew had been giving priority to the thermal hookup.

With any luck, somewhere in these crates, I might find something tangible. A picture of Pearl; an article, perhaps. The lids were sealed shut with rusty nails, and the wood was too rough to pull open bare-handed. I found a steel pipe to use as a crowbar and sat down to investigate.

The Tulleys must have been pack rats. I found invoices and registers dating back to the twenties. And to my pleasant surprise, there were a few famous signatures.

F. Scott Fitzgerald and his wife. I wondered with a chuckle whether they'd indulged in a communal bath. The playwrights Eugene O'Neill and Clifford Odets had visited several times. Even Franklin Roosevelt had come to take the Silverbrooke's thermal waters.

For hours I pored through sheafs of old documents and almost managed to forget my problems. The guest registers had been wrapped in heavy paper but were still badly mildewed. I kept the oldest aside intending to bring them to a bookbinder. Despite their condition, many of the signatures would be priceless.

Sometime after midnight, I heard footsteps on the stairs. "Are you down here, Genny?"

His worried tone made me smile. "I'm over here, and don't worry. I'm awake."

Travis found me sitting cross-legged on a carpet remnant. "What a relief," he said. "When I found the apartment empty, I nearly had a fit."

"Sorry."

"You should've left a note."

"I'm only in the basement. No one leaves notes when they go from one room to another."

He laughed. "You're right."

"Did you have a nice time tonight?"

"Yeah, it was great. Wish you'd been there, though."

I crooked my finger. "Come here."

"Why?"

"I want to show you what you missed by going out tonight."

Teasingly he shook his head. "Nah, you come here, and I'll show you what you've been missing."

Fingers jammed in his tight jean pockets, Travis just stood there, looking every bit the cool and cocky cowboy. I felt like melting just from his sheer masculine intensity.

"Okay, you win." I got up and sauntered over. Travis lifted me off my feet and gave me a kiss that could burn a hole through a romance novel.

"Wow!" I exclaimed. "Maybe you should go out with the guys more often."

"I'll bear that in mind, gorgeous. What are you up to, anyway?"

"Just looking for stuff."

"What kind of stuff?"

"Beats me. When I find it, I'll know."

"You didn't get spooked down here all by yourself?"

"Nope."

He tousled my hair. "Good for you, Genny."

"Thanks. Guess what? We have autographs of all kinds of famous people."

"Really? Like who?"

I recited a list of names. None of them made any great impression until I mentioned Raymond Chandler.

"No kidding? My favorite mystery writer actually slept here?"

I laughed. "No, silly, he took a bath. This isn't a hotel."

"Oh, yeah. But somehow it doesn't sound as good. Raymond Chandler washed here. Wonder which tub he used?"

It was endearing to learn that Travis was star struck by the creator of Philip Marlowe. "Who knows?" I teased. "He might have composed *The Big Sleep* while up to his neck in our bathtub."

"Possibly. So are you coming to bed or what?"

"What do you mean, or what?"

Travis gave me his man-child grin. "I mean, would you rather spend the night poking through this stuff or fooling around with me?"

I had really hoped to find something before I went to bed, but it *was* getting late. And there was always tomorrow.

"Well?" he said, standing there, lean and tempting.

Wrapping my arms around his waist, I cupped his bottom. "I'd rather fool around."

IT WAS A RELIEF to wake up the next morning beside Travis. He lay on his stomach, back bare and hair gloriously tousled. No wonder. We'd done a fair bit of tousling the night before.

Snuggling up to him, I kissed his neck. "Good morning, sexy."

He rolled onto his side and nestled his body against mine. "It can't be morning yet," he mumbled. "I just got to sleep."

With a stab of conscience, I remembered Enoch's phone call, the one I'd neglected to mention to Travis. But there was no need to bother him with it now.

I let him sleep a little longer and brought it up over breakfast. "How would you like to go to the country club for dinner tonight?"

"No thanks."

"Enoch's invited us."

"I don't like country clubs."

"Me, neither, but it's a good opportunity for us to meet people."

"Not the kind of people I like to meet."

Travis obviously wasn't going to make this easy. "You might find it interesting. Calder Carson's going to be there. He's the man who—"

"I know who he is." Travis cut into his omelet. "All the more reason to stay home."

"Why? You could learn a lot from someone like him."

His expression darkened. "Are you doubting my abilities all of a sudden?"

His reaction caught me off guard. I'd assumed he was objecting only because he'd have to dress up. "Of course I don't doubt your abilities. It's just that you and Carson are in the same business."

"We're hardly in the same business, Genny. I'm a common laborer these days."

"Don't say that."

"Why not? It's true, isn't it?"

I poured myself more coffee. If this was to be our first argument, I needed some fortification. "Are you saying you absolutely won't come?"

"That's right, honey."

Last time he'd called me honey, Donald had been here. It was not becoming my favorite term of endearment. "Won't you reconsider? I don't like the idea of going there without you."

"Then call Enoch and cancel."

"I can't do that. He'd take it as a personal affront."

Travis dropped two slices of bread into the toaster. "Tell you the truth, that's sort of how I'm taking things right now."

"Oh, for Pete's sake." I folded my arms and glared at the ceiling. My sulk had no effect on Travis whatsoever. So I began to clear the dishes. Noisily.

"Hey, don't take my plate yet. I'm not finished."

I dropped it with a clatter. "Are you always this stubborn?"

"No. If a person handles me right, I can be persuaded to do almost anything."

"You're saying I haven't handled you right."

"You could say that."

"But I've already told Enoch I was bringing a friend."

"Then why not ask Donald to go with you? I'm sure he'd be more than happy to fill in for me."

"Donald? Forget it." I was holding a frying pan full of bacon grease. So help me, I was tempted to pour it over Travis's head. I put it down carefully and stalked out of the room.

FORTUNATELY the Silverbrooke was big enough that we could avoid each other if we wanted to. I spent the morning in the basement looking through boxes. Travis came down a few times for one reason or another, but never to see me.

Whenever he returned upstairs, I felt terrible and promised myself I'd apologize the next time I saw him. But then he'd come down again and I'd see that intractable set of his jaw. The apology remained unspoken.

It was really such a stupid issue. And if anyone was in the wrong, it was me for assuming that Travis would accompany me. I still thought he was being unreasonable, but he was also within his rights.

By noon I couldn't stand it anymore. I brushed myself off, stomped upstairs and found Travis in the men's bath chamber eating pizza with the guys.

Everyone, except Travis, gave me a cheerful greeting. Travis nudged a pizza box with the toe of his boot. "Want some?"

How romantic. I bit my tongue and counted to ten. "No, thank you. Could I see you a moment, Travis?"

"What for?"

"One of the, uh . . . lockboxes is stuck."

"All right." Travis took his time finishing his pizza. Finally he got up and followed me into the lobby. "What's this about the lockboxes?"

"It was an excuse to get you out here."

"Figured as much."

"I, uh . . . I'd like to apologize."

He folded his arms. "For what?"

Damn, he was going to make me spell it out. I'd do well to remember that next time I behaved like a jackass. "For getting angry just because you don't like country clubs." He waited for me to continue. "Okay, I shouldn't have assumed you'd come with me. I should have asked first."

"Now you've got it." If Travis hadn't looked so utterly charming, I'd have punctuated his response to my apology with a poke in the ribs. But knowing he harbored no grudge dispelled what remained of mine.

"So," I said. "Is my apology accepted?"

"Come here." He took me in his arms and tipped my head back. "There's something you gotta know about me, Genny. I don't like fighting. In fact, I'll usually run a country mile to avoid it."

"Me, too."

"But I like to make my own decisions. Would you try to remember that next time?"

"Yes," I said, feeling like a jerk.

"What do you say we forget this ever happened?"

"Yes, please, let's forget!"

"And about tonight—"

"Never mind. I'll go by myself."

"Now hold on just a minute. I told you to let me make my own decisions. I've been doing some thinking, and maybe you're right. Meeting the right folks can't hurt. Besides, I gotta keep an eye on my lady. She's much too pretty to be hanging around country clubs without an escort."

"Are you saying you'll…" Not wanting to press my luck, I fell silent.

"I'll come. But you got to promise me one thing."

"Name it."

"No more fancy outings for the rest of the month."

I kissed him exuberantly. "Consider it a promise."

One advantage of wealth is the freedom to act on impulse. Naturally there are degrees of impulsiveness, some of which I consider excessive. I've never flown to Paris for breakfast or bathed in a tub of champagne—nor do I ever intend to. My parents, having started with nothing themselves, were careful to teach me the value of a dollar.

For me, the ultimate self-indulgence was a complete head-to-toe makeover, something only to be done for special occasions. Not that a dinner at the country club was momentous. But getting Travis to come with me certainly was. I wanted the evening to be unforgettable.

I bought a dress of aquamarine silk with a halter collar, narrow skirt and a slit up the side. I bought new lingerie, stockings, shoes and a handbag.

Then came the part I had especially looked forward to—an authentic thermal bath. It would have been lovely to have one at the Silverbrooke—especially with Travis—but the hookup wasn't quite ready. So I went to the Buckstaff, the only bathhouse operational on the Row. I didn't bother informing them that I'd soon be their competition.

I left my belongings in a lockbox at the front desk. An attendant accompanied me in an old brass elevator to the ladies's chamber. I undressed in the change room and was given a huge sheet to carry with me through the various stages of the bath.

The bath attendant's name was Cindy, a delightful Southern girl who put me at ease right away. She showed me to a tub and invited me to lie back and relax.

Nothing could have been easier. The water was hot, but pleasantly so, and reached my chin in the deep contoured tub. I could feel my skin begin to tingle like millions of tiny fingers massaging me everywhere.

There were cups of spring water to drink while I bathed. The water had no taste and was the same temperature as the bath, but it was surprisingly refreshing.

Twenty minutes later, Cindy returned to wash me. Given my upbringing, I should have been embarrassed to have a stranger scrub my back, arms and legs. I wasn't.

Next came the vapor cabinet. From the neck down, one is ensconced in a steel box and bombarded with hot, soothing steam. A sitz bath was followed by a hot-pack treatment, piping hot towels applied to areas of the body most vulnerable to stress. At the moment, I was feeling anything but stressful, so Cindy placed the packs on my neck, lower back and ankles.

The last of the treatments was two minutes under a needle shower, and then the cooling room where I lay, boneless and indescribably tranquilized.

The only peace comparable to "taking the waters" was lying in Travis's arms after making love. Too bad I couldn't use that metaphor to advertise the Silverbrooke's merits. It would probably do wonders for our business.

My final indulgence was an afternoon at the beauty salon—a cut and style, facial, manicure and, of course, a pedicure. I returned to the apartment feeling like a new woman, or at least a vastly improved version of myself.

Travis was bowled over by the transformation and didn't even complain when the time came to put on his necktie. We drove to the country club in a state approaching bliss.

Enoch and his wife were waiting for us in the club lounge. Calder had yet to arrive.

The attorney greeted me, then looked at my date in surprise.

"You remember Travis," I said.

"Why, yes. What a, er...pleasure."

"You were expecting someone else?" Travis had the nerve to ask.

While Enoch hemmed and hawed, I caught on. He must have thought I was going to bring Donald!

I'd certainly done nothing to promote the notion that Donald and I were reconciling. But if I knew my ex-husband—which I did—that's exactly what he'd want people to believe.

This was not the time or place, however, to set people straight on my relationship with Donald. So I let the matter drop.

Enoch introduced us to his wife, Lurlene. She was the epitome of a Southern belle, beautiful and impeccably presented. Her husband informed us she'd once been Miss Arkansas, a tidbit not easily worked into an introduction, but one he managed with the ease of much experience.

The conversation was stiff as we nursed our cocktails. I wasn't sure why, but it probably had to do with the disparate mix of people. The only thing we really had in common was the table between us.

Enoch began to relate anecdotes from his latest golf game with Donald. That wasn't the wisest choice of topics since Travis didn't care for golf or my ex-husband. Then to my relief, Calder Carson showed up. At least he and Travis could talk construction together.

I had expected Calder to be the convivial gentleman he'd appeared to be when we met. Instead, he scowled darkly at Travis.

Travis grinned wryly in response. "Hello, Uncle Calder."

Chapter Eleven

Calder turned to Enoch. "You never said *he* was coming."

"I thought she was bringing her husband," Enoch replied.

I turned to Travis. "Calder's your uncle?"

"You told me she was divorced," Calder said to Enoch.

"He's my uncle," Travis answered.

"She *is* divorced," the attorney said.

The conversation was too confusing to follow. So were the emotions flying around the table. Enoch looked sheepish while Calder fumed. Travis's expression was unreadable.

Lurlene, oblivious to it all, smiled sweetly. "Isn't this nice? A family reunion."

"Reunion, my foot," Calder sniped. "If I'd known he was comin', I'd have stayed home. If you folks'll excuse me—"

"Now hold on," Enoch said, grabbing his friend's arm. "There's no reason why the five of us can't get along like civilized people."

"There's nothing civilized about my former nephew," Calder said and stalked off to the bar.

Travis watched him go, taking the insult without a flinch.

"Would someone please tell me what is going on?" I demanded, looking around the table.

Lurlene blinked a few times. Enoch stabbed his martini olive. Travis was the one who finally answered.

"I told you about the uncle who helped me start my own construction business."

"Yes, but you never told me it was Calder."

"It never came up in the conversation."

There were obviously strong reasons why it hadn't. "Why is he so upset with you?"

"'Cause I went bust. Uncle Calder doesn't take kindly to people who lose his money. He was the only one in our family who'd made it big. Then I came along with the intention of following in his footsteps. Only I messed up."

"That's no way to look at it," I said, trying to console him. "Lots of people go bankrupt. And I'm sure Calder isn't suffering in the meantime."

"His attorney would know more about that than I would. Enoch, is Uncle Calder suffering on account of my losing his investment?"

Enoch Sarrazin was snipping the end off a cigar, trying to pretend he wasn't hearing our conversation. "I can't reveal information about my clients, but Calder's comfortable. But I don't see why you had to come to Hot Springs and make life miserable for him."

If only we could all be like Lurlene. She was nibbling sugar-coated almonds as if nothing unpleasant was going on. As for Calder, he was at the bar, knocking back Scotch like nobody's business.

"Calder made life miserable for my family," Travis said. "When my business went under, he disowned all of us, even my mother—his own sister. It wasn't their fault, but he vowed never to help another member of our family."

"So you came here to work for the competition," Enoch said.

"What?" Travis asked.

"You're working at the Silverbrooke, the one building on the Row, except for the Buckstaff, that Calder doesn't own. Isn't that why you're here?"

Heart in my throat, I turned to stare at Travis. "Why aren't you answering Enoch's question?"

"Because it's an accusation, not a question. And a false one at that."

"Then tell us your real reason for coming," I said.

Stalling, Travis rotated his glass on the table. "Okay, I'll admit that at the beginning I wanted to make Uncle Calder uncomfortable, remind him by my presence of what he'd done. But I wanted to pay him back, and to do that I needed a job."

"Which you just happened to find at the Silverbrooke," I said. "Your uncle's competition."

Travis reached out to touch my hand. I pulled away.

"It just happened to work out that way—"

"Just happened to? Oh, come on. You wanted to get back at your uncle, and you used me to do it."

"I did not—"

"Ooh," Lurlene squealed as the maître d' approached us. "Looks like our table is ready."

"I'm not staying," Travis said.

"Now, son," Enoch urged. "Why don't we let bygones be bygones and have ourselves a nice meal?"

"Yes, do," Lurlene added. "There isn't nothin' can't be fixed if you put your mind to it."

Speaking of fixing things, Travis and I obviously had some repair work ahead of us. To think I'd actually been surprised when he showed up at the Silverbrooke looking for work.

"It's up to Genny," Travis said. "If she agrees to stay, I will."

He's stalling, I told myself. But as long as we were in a public place, Travis knew I wouldn't cause a scene.

I wanted to stay angry but I couldn't. Okay, so maybe Travis had made a few errors in judgment. We all have. Maybe he should have been straightforward from the beginning. But I still believed he loved me, no matter what his intentions had been the day he'd walked into the Silverbrooke.

We'd still have to talk, of course, but not in front of the Sarrazins. Besides, I'd spent all afternoon getting a makeover and practically twisted Travis's arm to get him here. I decided we might as well make the most of it.

"I'll stay," I said.

"Wonderful!" Lurlene exclaimed.

We settled at the dinner table, then Enoch excused himself to talk to Calder. His cigar fumes lingered after he'd gone. He returned to the table alone. "Guess we'll be a foursome after all. I couldn't persuade him to stay."

"What a shame," Lurlene said. "Calder can be such fun."

I nearly choked on my drink. How could she imagine the evening would be fun was beyond me. As it turned out, *excruciating* might have been a more apt description.

Despite their bumpy start, Enoch and Travis did all right. They launched into a lively series of debates on politics, economics and the local business scene.

Finding the topics fascinating, I did my best to participate, but Lurlene wouldn't let me. She kept interrupting with questions such as, "What's the name of that nail polish you're wearing?"

I said I didn't know.

"Lilac Lagoon is my favorite, but it doesn't go with this shade of pink in my dress."

Eventually I gave up trying to converse with the men and concentrated my efforts on trying to understand Lurlene. It seemed as daunting a task as any I'd encountered that evening.

"Do you work?" I asked.

"Oh, no, Enoch doesn't want me workin'."

"Any children?"

"I have a tipped uterus," she replied as though that were some kind of substitute.

Over duck galantine, I tried again, asking Mrs. Sarrazin how she spent her days.

"I look after the house and the help. 'Course, I also belong to the Horticultural Society. My begonias win ribbons every year. You must come over and see them real soon—the begonias, of course, not the ribbons. They're just little bits of colored satin."

That was an invitation I intended to put off as long as possible, but I responded with appropriate enthusiasm. It was, perhaps, inevitable that the conversation would eventually come around to the Miss Arkansas Pageant.

Lurlene was delicately circumspect about which year her triumph had taken place, but that was the only detail she omitted. I learned the names, ages and measurements of virtually all the participants. Of course, no one could surpass Lurlene's figure. And I listened to a heart-felt rendition of her acceptance speech, full of airy platitudes about Arkansas and world peace. Her reminiscence took us all the way through dessert and cognac. By then I was ready to drown myself in the Courvoisier.

ON THE WAY HOME Travis reintroduced the topic we'd avoided all through dinner. "I'm sorry I didn't tell you about Calder being my uncle."

My head was pounding, and I didn't really feel like discussing anything. "I accept your apology, but you should have told me—preferably the day I hired you."

"If I had, would you still have hired me?"

"I don't know. Maybe not."

"That's what I was afraid of."

"Oh come on, I'm not serious. Why shouldn't I have hired you? You're well qualified."

"You might have thought I was an industrial spy working for my uncle."

"Are you?"

"Hardly. I actually tried to get work with my uncle's subcontractors first, thinking maybe I could pay him back in services. But once they found out who I was, it was a closed shop. No one would give me the time of day."

"Why didn't you confide in me later?"

"I was going to, especially after you and I became... well, close. But then you had all those sleepwalking problems, and—" He hesitated. "Look, Genny, when it comes right down to it, I didn't want to be tossed out of your life just because I was related to my uncle. He'd caused me enough pain already."

"I wouldn't have tossed you out. Well, maybe for a night or two, depending on how you worded things." Travis didn't smile, so I reached across and touched his thigh. "I'm sorry for getting angry."

"You mean you're not anymore?"

"No. But since we're on the subject, how did you find out I was hiring?"

"Just a lucky fluke. I was in this subcontractor's office, trying to persuade him I wasn't there to sabotage my uncle, when you phoned about an estimate. He turned you down, then told me afterward that no one works on Bathhouse Row unless the building belongs to Calder."

I straightened, forgetting all about the pain between my eyes. "Really? The man told you that?"

"His very words."

"How about that?" So Calder *was* behind the boycott of my bathhouse. I shouldn't have been surprised. I'd spent enough years in banking to know the smoothest operators were nearly always the most ruthless. To think Calder had tried to blame it on the Civil War.

"You know what, Travis?" I said as he parked the car.

"What?"

"I love you."

His eyes were glistening when he turned to me. "You've never said that to me before."

"I know," I replied shyly, "and it's always been my policy to make the man say it before I do."

He reached across and took me in his arms. "So in a way, I'm your first, right?"

"In a way."

"That's nice to hear because I love you, too. And my policy, before now, has always been to put off sayin' it for as long as possible."

The walk to the Silverbrooke was short but utterly romantic. The name of the bathhouse seemed especially appropriate that night. A full moon was hanging low over Hot Springs Mountain, infusing the majestic old buildings with an intricate pattern of silver light and shadow.

"It was almost worth going out tonight just to see this," I said.

Travis tugged at his necktie to loosen it. "We could go for a walk any night. There's no need to get dressed up for the occasion."

I laughed, delighted by his unabashedly casual outlook on life. "You're right. Who needs that old country club, anyway?"

At the foot of the stairs, I dug through my handbag for the keys.

"Take a look at that," Travis said.

"What?"

He was pointing at dark streaks on the stone work. "Looks like someone's been doing a paint job."

"Oh, no!"

He was right. A message had been spray painted in huge letters extending from one end of the bathhouse to the other.

"What does it say?" I asked.

"Can't tell. We're standing too close."

Travis took my hand, and we backed up along the sidewalk. As the words came into focus, I could feel my blood pressure rising.

"I'm going to throttle her," I muttered.

"Who?"

"Hepzibah."

"Why are you blaming her again?"

"Read the message," I said.

Sprayed across the Silverbrooke were the words Abandon Ye the Ways of the Wicked.

"Sounds like her philosophy," Travis admitted. "Where are you going?" he said as I stormed off toward the car.

"I'm going to tell that woman off, once and for all!"

Travis caught up to me and grabbed my arm. "You can't go see her at this hour. It's after one o'clock!"

"She obviously stayed up late enough to do this!"

"Calm down, Genny."

"How can you expect me to calm down? That woman is bound and determined to destroy us."

"It takes a lot more than rotten eggs and spray paint to destroy a building."

"Why are you defending her all of a sudden?"

"I'm not defending her, but you can't go making accusations without proof."

"She hates us. That's proof."

"No, it's not. There could be any number of people in this town who don't want to see you open. Uncle Calder's lackeys, for one."

"They wouldn't do this."

"How can you be so sure?"

I had to admit Travis had a point. Maybe I was jumping the gun. Pounding on Hepzibah's door at this hour could do me more harm than good. She'd probably phone the police, and I'd be the one who was charged with mischief.

"Let's go to bed, Genny. We'll talk about this in the morning when you're feeling better."

I seriously doubted that I'd feel better. But the invitation to bed, spoken by someone I loved, improved my outlook considerably.

TRAVIS KNEW BETTER than any man I'd ever met how to make me happy. By the time we fell asleep, my agitation was gone, and I slept soundly the whole night through.

The next morning I reached over and touched my lover's hair. He didn't move.

Still half-asleep, I rolled over. Draping an arm across the mattress, my fingers hit something hard. I opened one eye, then both eyes sprang open. Beside me lay a butcher knife. The handle and blade were covered with blood!

"Oh my God!"

I turned to Travis. He was motionless.

"Wake up!" I screamed, shaking him.

Was it my agitation or was his skin cool?

"Travis, please!"

I couldn't see any stab wounds. I tried to roll him over. His arm flopped.

"What in tarnation are you doing?"

Thank heavens! I hadn't killed him!

Travis peered at me through sleep-filled eyes. "What's the matter, Genny?"

I was examining my own body for signs of injury, but I found nothing. There was no blood on my hands and only a few stains on the sheet.

"Genny," he repeated. "What's wrong?"

I couldn't reply. I could only point, trembling and speechless, to the object that lay beside me.

"What's that doing here?"

"I . . . I don't know. And look, it's all b-bloody."

Travis tried to calm my rising hysteria. But there were limits to what even he could do now. The man was obviously as shaken as I.

"Were you . . . did you—I didn't hear you get up," he stammered.

"You never do," I replied as if this were somehow all his fault.

"Let's get out of bed. There's gotta be a logical explanation."

Backing away from the knife, I got out of bed on Travis's side. My knees were knocking so badly I could scarcely stand.

"I'm positive I didn't go anywhere last night, Travis."

"Don't be too sure." He reached for my dressing gown on the back of the chair. "Take a look at this!"

My new lingerie was no longer pretty. It, too, was smeared with blood.

Chapter Twelve

Travis pulled on a pair of jeans. I simply stood there, naked and shivering.

"Put something on, for cripes' sake."

I was vaguely aware of moving toward the closet and pulling out the first thing I could find—a pair of slacks and a blouse. "Wh-what are we going to do?" I asked, my gaze moving from the knife to the gown.

"Look around the apartment, for starters."

It still hadn't occurred to me that the problem was mine, not ours. Nor was I conscious of Travis's gruffness while we searched the place for traces of blood. Uppermost in my mind was that life, as I had come to know it, was over. The nightmare had finally caught up with reality. There was no place left for me to run.

The bloodstains were limited to my side of the bed, my dressing gown and knife. When we'd finished searching, my shock must have lifted, making way for hysteria. I snatched up my dressing gown. "I've got to wash this before the stains set. Travis, you run the knife under cold water, then put it back in the kitchen. Quickly!"

He grabbed me by the shoulders and shook me. "Stop it, Genny!"

My mouth turned down. "Why do you keep yelling at me?"

"You're not thinking straight."

"What the hell do you expect?"

I wished he were hugging me instead of digging his fingers into my arms. But I didn't dare ask for fear he might walk out of my life altogether. Slowly my breathing returned to normal.

"I'm okay now," I insisted.

"Good. Now listen to me. You can't wash these things. You shouldn't even be touching them."

"Why not?"

"We don't know where the blood came from."

"But if I'm okay and you are, what difference does it—"

"Geneva!"

His use of my formal name made everything snap into place. I pulled away and crumpled to the floor, sobbing. This time I neither sought not expected consolation from Travis. At the moment, I simply despised him for making me face the truth.

Somebody's blood was on my robe. Whose it was, I didn't know. I didn't want to. I only wanted to die on the spot.

But fate never lets a person off that easy. I didn't die. Travis gave me a few minutes to indulge my emotions, then came over and gently lifted me to my feet.

"Let's have some coffee. We'll talk."

Travis steered me into a chair in the kitchen, filled the coffee urn, measured the grounds and plugged in the machine. I couldn't have done a thing. All I could do was stare at the empty space on the knife rack.

A few minutes later he gave me my coffee and sat down across from me. "Okay, Genny, I want you to think. Think hard. Where did you go during the night?"

"I didn't go anywhere."

"You must have."

"If I did, I don't remember!"

"There's no need to shout."

I was tempted to remind him he'd done his fair share of shouting, but under the circumstances, it seemed a moot point.

"Travis, I really am thinking hard, but I don't recall getting out of bed or going anywhere. I slept like a log."

His hands trembled as he sipped his coffee. "I hate to say this, but we are in one big pile of trouble."

The caffeine was clearing my brain. "Not you, Travis. I am."

He laughed bitterly. "I spent the night with you, Genny. Like it or not, we're a team."

It might have been something in his voice or just the workings of a desperate imagination. For one fleeting instant, I envisioned another scenario. What if I *hadn't* walked in my sleep? What if Travis, for some reason, wanted me to believe I had?

I quickly slammed the lid on that ugly thought. Looking back, it's ironic to remember that I was so eager to think well of Travis, yet so willing to believe myself capable of butchery.

"How can we find out... where the blood came from?" I asked, my voice raspy, as if the very words ran against the grain.

"I don't know. Guess we have to call the cops."

The police. I hadn't even thought of them, but he was right. Calling the authorities was the only logical step.

A knock on the door startled both of us, but neither of us got up from the table.

"Do you want to get that?" Travis asked.

I shook my head vehemently.

"Okay, I will."

My fingers were clenched around the coffee cup as I listened to Travis cross the living room and open the door.

"Hoyt!"

"How ya doin', Trav?"

My head dropped to the table in relief. Hoyt was our plasterer, a rotund, jovial fellow. "There's someone downstairs to see Geneva," he said.

"Who?"

"Her ex, I forget his name."

Donald? What could he possibly want?

"Tell him she's busy," Travis said.

"It's okay," I countered, coming into the living room to greet Hoyt. "Did Donald say what he wanted?"

"Nope, he just asked to see you."

Travis placed a hand on my arm. "You don't have to—"

"I don't mind." Not that I wanted to see Donald, or anyone else for that matter. I wanted to get rid of him—figuratively speaking—before we called the police. It was unnerving how often my ex-husband showed up when I was in trouble.

"You stay here," I told Travis.

"Like hell. I'm going downstairs to see how the guys are doing."

I didn't blame him. I wouldn't have wanted to stay alone in the apartment, either. Travis disappeared for a moment to put on a shirt. Then we accompanied Hoyt downstairs.

"Hey, Trav," the plasterer said, "hate to say this, but have you seen the paint job out front?"

"Yeah."

"Want us to clean it up?"

Travis and I glanced at each other. "Just leave it for now, thanks," he said.

Donald was waiting in the lobby, looking his usual impeccable self. He and Travis exchanged brief and hostile looks before Travis headed toward the rear of the bathhouse.

"Hello, Geneva," Donald said. "You look—" he squinted as if doubting his eyesight "—like you haven't had a chance to put on your makeup."

"I haven't. Why are you here, Donald?"

"Uh-oh, someone got up on the wrong side of the bed this morning."

Considering the morning's events, I could have strangled Donald for that remark. But it was, of course, only a cliché.

"Sorry for snapping," I said. "I had a rough night."

"I know. I heard all about it."

"What?"

"I met Enoch for coffee this morning. He told me Calder and Travis caused quite a scene at the country club."

"Oh, that," I said, gasping audibly.

"What did you think I meant?"

"Nothing! Absolutely nothing."

"I couldn't help noticing the graffiti. Is that what's got you down?"

It seemed as reasonable an explanation as any. "Yes, Donald, the graffiti upsets me. Now, would you please tell me why you're here?"

"I wanted to know if you'd like to visit the Mid-America Museum. It's just outside Hot Springs and it's supposed to be quite impressive."

The invitation was so incongruous, I nearly laughed. A day at the museum. What a perfect way to forget my problems.

"I'd like to, Donald, but I can't."

He didn't try to disguise his disappointment. "You've made other plans?"

"Sort of."

"With Travis?"

More like a date with a cop, but it was easier to follow Donald's lead. "Yes."

"Hmm. You know, Geneva, just because you think you're in love doesn't mean you have to give up your friends."

"I haven't. And while I hate to rub it in, I don't *think* I'm in love. I *am*."

"All right, I'll admit it was a cheap shot. But it's such a nice day for a drive. Are you sure you won't change your mind about coming with me?"

"Positive, but you go ahead."

"I'll hold off for now. Maybe we could do it some other day. You could even bring . . ."

"Travis," I offered.

"Yeah, Travis."

"Maybe so. We'll see." As I turned around to leave, a thought came to me. "Donald?"

"Yes?" he said hopefully.

"Have you heard the news this morning?" It wasn't random speculation. Donald never missed the news.

"Certainly, why?"

"Did you happen to—that is, was there any bad news in Hot Springs?"

He thought a moment. "The municipal government turned down another bid to authorize a casino. That's the worst thing I can think of."

I managed a weak smile. "Thanks for dropping by. See you later."

Travis was standing on a scaffold in the lounge, dismantling a chandelier. He still wore the same scowl he'd used to greet Donald. "What did he want?"

"He invited me to go to a museum."

"Just what you need."

"That's what I thought."

"What did you say?"

"I turned him down, of course. What else would I say?"

"You didn't tell him about—"

"Good grief, no. Have you called the police yet?"

"I thought I'd wait for you."

"Then we might as well get it over with."

Travis climbed off the scaffold. "I've been thinking about what happened last night. Maybe you heard a dog outside during the night and . . . wanted him to, well, shut up."

I grimaced. "That's ridiculous. I don't even hear you snoring, and you say that's pretty loud. Besides, I would never hurt an animal." Too late, I realized the absurdity of my denial. I was obviously capable of hurting something, and it wasn't vegetable or mineral.

"It was just a shot in the dark," Travis said.

His remark made me shudder. Strange, I thought, how violence figured so prominently in everyday expressions. I'd never noticed that before.

While climbing the stairs with Travis, I pondered the enormity of what lay ahead. I hadn't even come to terms with my past yet. How on earth was I going to deal with an equally threatening future?

Beneath my surface calm, a battle was raging between me and my subconscious. I needed so desperately to remember. But my subconscious, the rebel force, was still winning. I couldn't remember a thing.

I phoned the Hot Springs Police from the kitchen. "May I speak to . . . someone in charge?"

"What is it regarding, ma'am?"

My voice caught. I hadn't really thought about how to phrase things. "It's, uh . . . regarding a possible crime . . . assault."

There, I'd acknowledged it, actually put it into words. I grabbed a chair to steady myself.

A staff sergeant came on the line.

I spoke like an automaton delivering a message. "My name is Geneva Ashford. I own the lease at the Silverbrooke Bathhouse. There's a knife in my bedroom covered with blood. I don't know how it got there, but someone had better come and take a look."

THEY SAY THAT good things come in threes. Bad things do the same. When the police arrived at the Silverbrooke, I realized it was the third time I'd had reason to deal with them since coming to Hot Springs. First the rock through my motel window. Then the vandalism in the lobby. Number three was by far the worst.

If Travis hadn't been there, I don't know how I would have survived the ordeal. Two officers moved quietly through the bedroom, examining the knife, the bathrobe and everything else. They stripped the sheets to take away as evidence.

Though veteran officers, they were obviously befuddled by the perversity of the crime. Assuming there was one. They were depending on me to shed what little light I could.

I sat down and explained how I'd come to inherit the lease. I told them about visiting the Silverbrooke as a child and my vivid recollection of seeing Pearl Tulley's body in the basement. One of the officers remembered the suicide. He'd been a rookie at the time.

Finally I explained the apparent consequences of my childhood trauma. I was a sleepwalker, incapable of controlling or recalling my nocturnal activities. Returning to Hot Springs had, from all indications, brought my problem to a head.

The police were polite and noncommittal while I told my story. But when I got to the part about sleepwalking, they exchanged glances as if to acknowledge this would not be a run-of-the-mill crime, nor I their typical criminal. It was too soon for me to know whether that would stand in my favor.

They questioned Travis, wanting to know whether he had seen evidence of my sleepwalking. He admitted to having found me under the reception counter and sleeping beside a pile of blocks in the spare room. But no, he couldn't say he had ever actually seen me get out of bed.

Travis was remarkably composed through most of the interview. But it seemed to upset him to tell the police he hadn't been able to intercept my wanderings. "I thought for sure I'd hear Genny in time," he said, "but I've always been a sound sleeper. Turns out I've been no help at all."

The police already knew Travis and I had shared the brass bed. But one of them asked, for the record, "What's the nature of your relationship to each other?"

Travis didn't hesitate. "We're in love."

I nearly started to cry.

At the end of the interview, the older policeman turned to me. "What do you think actually happened last night, Ms. Ashford?"

The question came as no surprise. If anything, I wondered why it had taken them so long to ask it.

"Did you see the message on the front of the bathhouse?" I asked.

"Yes, ma'am. We've got it right here in our notes."

"I've already told you about the incident with the rotten eggs when two other officers came to investigate."

"Yes, I recall readin' the report."

"Well, when we came home from the country club last night and saw the spray paint, I was convinced it was done by the same person who vandalized the lobby."

"How did you react when you saw it?"

There was no point in whitewashing anymore. "I was furious."

"But Genny had calmed down by the time she went to bed," Travis offered.

I placed a hand on his arm. "It's okay, Travis. The police might as well know. He's right. I did calm down eventually, but I must have repressed the anger. That's why it's possible I might have gotten up in my sleep and . . . gone to her house."

"Whose?" the officer asked.

"Hepzibah Tulley's," I replied evenly. "I think you'd better go to see how she is."

During the hours that followed, I agonized over why I'd let so much time lapse before telling the police about Hepzibah. But the truth was until then, I really hadn't associated the butcher knife with a specific victim or deed.

Certainly the evidence was damning enough, as were the motives leading up to the incident. But a person who is otherwise morally upstanding cannot easily accept the possibility of committing a crime she can't remember. Especially one as heinous as this appeared to be.

Until I'd actually uttered Hepzibah's name in the presence of the police, my mind had refused to put two and two together. But I'd gone to bed angry. And I'd woken up with a bloody knife beside me. There were only so many conclusions one could draw.

Travis offered to stay with me in the apartment while we waited to hear from the police, but I didn't want to sit around and wait. I needed to be busy. So busy I couldn't think or feel.

Travis and I joined the work crew downstairs. My contribution couldn't have been terribly helpful, but I set to work methodically, painting baseboards in the hall.

The guys went in and out of the lobby all day for coffee and tools and cigarette breaks, so I became oblivious to the sound of the front doors opening. But although I was some distance away, I knew at once when the police had returned. The door had a different sound when it opened—a kind of ominous thump that brought goosebumps to my skin.

They marched in step as they approached me in the hall, though I'm sure the cadence wasn't deliberate. In fact, the older man seemed genuinely remorseful, removing his hat when he spoke. "We're here to tell you, Ms. Ashford, that Hepzibah Tulley is dead. The cause of death appears to be multiple stab wounds."

Chapter Thirteen

"Are you sure?" My voice was little more than a squeak. "I mean, couldn't there have been some...mistake?"

Neither officer dignified my questions with a reply. Death from stab wounds was not a condition one would likely mistake for something else.

I didn't know how to react. First Bill, now Hepzibah—two people who, until recently, had not been part of my life. Now I was mourning their loss.

Approaching footsteps echoed through the hall. It was Travis; his face went pale when he saw the police. He put an arm around my shoulders. "What is it, Genny?"

"They've...found Hepzibah. She's dead." It was all I could say before collapsing into tears. Travis did his best to console me, but he was upset himself, which only made me feel worse. If he'd never met me, he would have been spared this emotional buffeting. I couldn't help wondering if I was just paranoid or reading his thoughts.

"What happens next?" Travis asked the police.

"An investigation is underway. In the meantime, we'll have to ask the two of you not to leave town."

I felt Travis flinch an instant before he released me.

"We won't," he assured them, as though he would see to it personally that I obeyed their instructions. After the police left, he said, "We've got to get you an attorney."

It was, perhaps, the ultimate test of his feelings that Travis didn't leave me to my own devices then and there. My thoughts were hopelessly muddled. I probably couldn't have found my way out of the room at that moment.

"I'll call Enoch," I said.

"Not him."

"He's the only attorney I know in Hot Springs."

"I don't like him."

"Why not? You seemed to get along well enough at the country club."

"He's arrogant and condescending."

"Well, I think he's nice. And he's obviously successful at what he does."

Travis shrugged. "All right. As long as you're comfortable with him."

"Are you retaining one, too?"

"What for?" Then he blanched. "I'll take my chances. I can't afford any more lawyers in my life."

"I can help—"

"Don't bother," he said emphatically. Then he lowered his voice. "Thanks anyway, Genny, but I'd say you've done more than enough already."

I PHONED ENOCH and told him that something urgent had come up. He agreed to see me right away. Travis, as the closest thing I had to a witness, came with me.

The attorney ushered us into his office and closed the door. He offered us coffee, then took a seat behind the vast mahogany desk. "So tell me, Geneva. What's the problem?"

I started from the very beginning, if only to clarify events in my own mind. I related everything from the day Bill Swann had come to see me in Minneapolis until the moment the police had informed me that Hepzibah was dead. He listened avidly, interrupting only when he needed clarification.

"You say you've never had any recollection of what you've done in your sleep?" he asked.

"None."

"You poor thing. I had no idea what all'd been happening to you here in Hot Springs. Why didn't you tell me about this sooner?"

My cheeks colored. "It's not the kind of thing I like to talk about."

"I expect not. But let me get this straight. The police are of the opinion you murdered Hepzibah in the middle of the night while you were asleep."

"They didn't say anything about who—" I began.

Travis interjected. "If that was their opinion, Enoch, they'd have arrested Genny on the spot."

"Yes, of course. But try to understand, Travis. Playing devil's advocate is part of my job."

He leaned back guardedly. "Fine, as long as you remember that defending your client is also part of your job."

A vein pulsed in the lawyer's temple. "I'll bear that in mind, thank you." Then he turned to me and said, "The state's gonna have one awful time if they decide to press charges. There are only thirty-five documented cases on record of homicide committed during sleepwalking. We can probably avoid conviction—if it comes to that."

Pressing charges, convictions—the words were meaningless, not part of my reality. I had somehow joined this discussion by accident, and sooner or later someone was going to realize it.

Enoch pressed on. "'Course we might be better off plea bargaining."

"Like hell," Travis protested. "That means Genny would have to plead guilty."

"Sometimes it's the best approach."

The two men continued arguing as though it was a tennis match and I was the ball.

"Naturally she wouldn't have to plead guilty," Enoch was saying, "if we could find someone else more likely to have killed Hepzibah."

Travis obviously read something into the silence that followed. "Are you saying I did it?"

"Did you?" Enoch asked just as pointedly.

"Wait a minute," I said, suddenly resenting Enoch's insinuation. "We don't even know for sure that the knife on our bed was the murder weapon."

"That's true," the attorney admitted, "but we have to anticipate that possibility. And if it does turn out that you unknowingly committed the act, the question becomes one of intent."

"Which means what?" I asked.

"Manslaughter."

Another display of semantics. *Manslaughter*, *homicide*, *murder*—they were all fancy words for the same thing. And none of them changed the fact that Hepzibah was dead.

"Travis," Enoch said, "would you mind leaving Geneva and me alone for a few minutes?"

"Yes, I'd mind."

The attorney gave me a look of exasperation. "Could you please explain to your gentleman friend that I'm here to help you?"

"It's okay, Travis," I said, touching his arm.

He finished off his coffee. "All right, I'll be waiting in the reception area." He tossed Enoch a final look of resentment before leaving the office.

"That boy's got a nasty temper, hasn't he?" the attorney said when we were alone.

Good thing Travis wasn't there to hear the word *boy*. "He's just worried about me."

"As are we all, Geneva. But as your attorney, I'm obligated to be honest with you. Depending on what comes back from the lab reports, we've got ourselves one tough row to hoe."

I shut my eyes briefly. "Yes, I know."

"But I don't want you giving up hope, y'hear?"

"I won't."

"I've been an attorney for many years. And a darned good one. So listen to me carefully, Geneva. Have you considered the possibility that you might have been set up?"

"By whom?"

"That's what I'm here to figure out. It's obviously someone who doesn't like your being here."

"Hepzibah fell under that category."

Enoch waved a hand through the air. "She was a harmless old thing. Not that I wished her ill, of course, but she had no real cause to hurt you."

I wasn't convinced of Hepzibah's good will, but that had become an academic argument. "What are you leading up to, Enoch?"

Folding his hands, he leaned across the desk. "This is strictly off the record, you understand, but there are a number of folks in town who could benefit from your absence. What we've got to determine are the lengths to which they'd go to secure it."

"Are you suggesting someone like Calder?"

Enoch shook his head. "I don't know. Calder's a friend, but at times like this, an attorney can't afford to lose his impartiality. I'm honor bound to consider every angle."

"But you're Calder's attorney, too."

"Regarding business matters, yes."

"Even if it were true, how could Calder have gotten into the apartment to leave a knife in my hand and blood on my gown?"

"He wouldn't have to," Enoch replied evenly, "when he's got a nephew there to do it."

My mouth dropped. "No... no, I could never believe Travis had anything to do with this."

"My dear, I understand your infatuation with the man, but you've got to consider this logically."

"I am being logical. Travis wouldn't do anything to hurt me."

"Then look at it this way, Geneva. If he didn't plant that knife, if Travis didn't kill Hepzibah, then we can draw only one other reasonable conclusion."

"Which is?"

"You did it."

"No!" I cried out, pressing both hands to my face.

Enoch came around and bundled me into his arms. "Now, now, honey, it's gonna be all right. I wasn't tryin' to scare you, I'm just preparing you for any eventuality. But you just let your old friend Enoch take care of everything."

I couldn't see what other alternative I had but to trust Enoch. I drew the line, however, at suspecting Travis.

When I'd regained my composure, Enoch continued. "Let's talk about what Travis and his uncle would have to gain by harmin' you."

"Nothing. They don't even like each other."

"That's what we've been led to believe, yes. I've listened to Calder snipe about his nephew for months. But doesn't it seem just a trifle coincidental that Travis showed up at the same time you arrived to claim your lease?"

I was in no frame of mind to weigh such subtleties. All I knew was that Enoch's theory was deplorable. Virtually inarguable, too, which only made matters worse.

"Would you care for some more coffee?" he asked.

"No. Thank you. Just let me think for a minute." I pressed fingers to my temples, trying to review my situation with some objectivity.

Admittedly there were a few coincidences regarding Travis and me. We'd arrived in Hot Springs at practically the same time. He had shown up for a job interview mere minutes after I'd seen Calder. And yes, it bothered me that he hadn't mentioned his relationship to his uncle sooner.

But despite the intimacy of our relationship, Travis was entitled to his privacy. He wasn't obligated to tell me about Calder and given their mutual resentment, I could understand why he wouldn't have said anything right away.

As for the timing of our respective arrivals, maybe it was simply meant to be. Travis was supposed to find me sleepwalking on the mountain that night, just as I was destined to invite him for dinner at the pancake house. Wasn't that how it happened with lovers sometimes?

All right, maybe my defense sounded hokey in light of subsequent events. But I did believe that love brought with it a certain intuition. And mine was telling me in no uncertain terms that Enoch's argument was groundless. For our mutual benefit, I decided to challenge it.

"Okay, Enoch, let's assume that what you say is true. Calder could want me out of Hot Springs so he can take over the Silverbrooke's lease. For some reason, Travis has agreed to conspire with him. Why wouldn't they get rid of me instead of Hepzibah? Nothing could be simpler. I'm a sleepwalker. They could toss me over a cliff at night, and everyone would think it was an accident.''

The attorney leaned back in his leather chair. ''Hmm, interesting premise. I'll have to mull that one over. Maybe they considered that option. But if you were to die soon after coming to Hot Springs, it would have been suspect. And since Calder has the most to gain—on the surface, anyway—the police might have pointed a finger at him right away. No, a man as smart as him wouldn't want to take that kind of risk.''

''But why kill Hepzibah?''

''She's been a thorn in his side for years. And a lot of other people's, for that matter.''

''I thought she adored Calder.''

''She does—or rather, she did—in her funny old-maid way, but she loathed the idea of Calder opening a casino. She'd been pestering him for years to open a church on Bathhouse Row. Kept sayin' that prayer would make him see the error of his ways.''

I'd heard her say things to that effect.

''Of course, there are plenty of subcontractors in this town who would have liked the contract for the Silverbrooke. This doesn't have to be Calder's doing.''

''A few of them weren't too happy when I canceled my appointments with them.''

''So I heard. Could you provide me with a list of names and numbers of the men you talked to?''

''Certainly,'' I said, anxious to turn the tide away from Travis and me—even briefly. I must have fallen silent for a while.

''Are you all right, Geneva?''

I shrugged, not even sure how it felt to be all right. The past two weeks had been the most exciting I'd ever known. Inheriting a bathhouse, falling in love. Now the excitement was replaced by death and a host of unanswerable questions.

"Listen, sugar, why don't you come and stay with Lurlene and me until this thing blows over?"

"No, thank you."

"There's no need to be stuck in that big old bathhouse all by your lonesome."

"I'm not alone."

The attorney laughed awkwardly. "Pardon me for being presumptuous, but surely, you won't be allowing that McCabe fellow to stay on. Not after all we've talked about."

I hadn't thought that far ahead, but I couldn't imagine staying at the Silverbrooke without him. Making Enoch understand, however, was not something I had the strength to attempt. "I haven't made any final decisions."

"Good. Then think about my invitation, won't you? I know Lurlene would be delighted. She thinks you're just the sweetest thing."

I couldn't begin to imagine why. I told him I'd think about it, then got up to leave.

"I'll be getting in touch with the District Attorney's Office to see what's going on. Are you going to be at the Silverbrooke all day?"

"I guess so."

"If the police show up, make sure they read you your rights. Then call me right away, and for heaven's sake, don't say a word until I get there. If I'm not at home or in the office, Lurlene or my secretary'll page me."

"Thanks, Enoch."

"You're welcome. And what we've talked about in here is just between you and me."

I looked at him. "Can't I discuss things with Travis?"

"Lord, no, he's the last person in the world you should be talkin' to. Trust me on this, will you? I know what I'm doing."

Resignedly I left the office, along with what remained of my hopes. The lawyer's secretary flashed me a look of relief. Seeing Travis, I understood why. He looked fit to be tied and had practically worn a path across the carpet.

"What took you so long?" he demanded when we were in the corridor.

I glanced at my watch, but I'd lost all track of time. And now I had the added burden of saying nothing to Travis. "Enoch had lots to talk about."

"Like what?"

"Please don't ask. I'm not supposed to discuss it."

"He wants you to think I killed Hepzibah, right?"

My head shot up. "What makes you say that?"

"Doesn't take any mental giant to figure it out. If you didn't use the knife, there's only one other person likely to have done so. And that's me."

Travis could have been applying reverse psychology. It's what Enoch might have claimed. But as far as I could tell, there was nothing devious about Travis. It was one of the many reasons I loved him.

"I don't think you did it," I said at last.

"Gee, thanks." Travis said nothing more until we were on the street. "So when do I get my eviction notice?"

His tone was cavalier, but there was fear in his eyes. Not fear for his personal safety, but the kind that arises when something precious and fragile is at risk. Was that, I wondered, how he felt about our love?

"There'll be no eviction," I said. "I need you to stay with me."

Later that afternoon we strolled the wooded footpaths of Hot Springs Mountain. There was nothing eerie about the mountain in the daytime. The sun filtered gently through the towering trees, and the air smelled rich and loamy. This was as far from ugly reality as either of us was allowed to go.

"Isn't there some way to make you remember?" Travis asked as we walked hand in hand.

"Remember what?"

"What you did last night. I mean, it's gotta be in your head somewhere, right? It's just a matter of accessing the information."

"Theoretically, yes. I have an appointment with the Sleep Institute in Little Rock, but that's three weeks away."

"Maybe they'd agree to see you sooner. I mean, you really don't have any time to lose."

"Maybe, but even if I could see them, there's no guarantee that therapy would work."

"You have to try something, Genny. I want to be there for you, but there's only so much I can do."

I knew what he was saying. If he thought it would help, Travis would probably have undergone the therapy himself. But he wasn't the one with the problem—unless one counted me as the problem.

Gratefully I wrapped my arms around him. "Have I told you lately how much I love you?"

"No, but let me be the first to say it this time. I love you, Genny, and I'm gonna do everything I can to help you, y'hear?"

"I hear, Travis, and thank you."

I PHONED DR. CALDWELL, hoping he could influence the Sleep Institute to see me sooner. He was shocked to learn what had happened, but sympathetic as well. If I needed a witness or character reference, he'd be happy to help.

His offer reminded me of someone else who might sing my praises if it became necessary—Donald. I had to let him know what was going on. He deserved better than to learn of my implication in Hepzibah's death secondhand.

Meanwhile Dr. Caldwell proved as good as his word. A short while later I received a call from Dr. Glen Peabody, a hypnotherapist in Little Rock. It was hard to guess his age over the phone, but he had a nice voice and no drawl. A Yankee like myself.

"I'm sorry we couldn't accommodate you sooner," he said, "but once Dr. Caldwell explained the situation, I canceled my appointments for the week. I don't get many cases like yours."

Little wonder. "There is one problem, Doctor. The police have asked me not to leave town."

"Not to worry. I have friends I can stay with in Hot Springs. I'll bring the sessions to you."

An appointment was set up at the Silverbrooke for the following afternoon. Travis was delighted. I let him hang on to his optimism. Who was I to rain on his parade?

IT WAS TRAVIS'S IDEA to spend the rest of the afternoon digging through more boxes in the basement. Granted, I had once believed there might be answers lying in those crumbling registers. And I was certainly desperate for answers. But now the possibility that we might find something terrified me more than it reassured. My ability to handle shock was rapidly depleting.

Fortunately Travis's determination took over where mine left off. He knew my feelings about the search and was wonderfully supportive whenever my emotions started to get the upper hand.

"Look at this, Genny. A receipt for a bath and massage signed by Frank Sinatra."

"That's nice," I replied absently. "He was my parents' favorite."

"Mine, too."

"You like Sinatra?"

"I meant my parents."

"Oh."

"Why don't you go upstairs and lie down? I can look through this stuff myself."

"You don't know what you're looking for."

"Sure I do. Anything that has your parents' name on it, right?"

"I guess. But I don't dare lie down, Travis."

"Why not?"

"I might fall asleep and . . . you know."

His expression was a mixture of apprehension and sympathy. "Right, I forgot. Didn't you say you had some kind of pills?"

I recalled the sedatives that Dr. Caldwell had prescribed. They had once seemed so unpalatable. Now, short of a straitjacket, they were my only hope—the one way I could be sure of staying in bed where I belonged.

"I'll take some tonight. How about if I go up and make a pot of tea?"

"Sounds good."

As I climbed the stairs to the apartment, I felt strange waves of energy passing through me—a sensation I hadn't experienced before. They were vague, undefinable, but definitely there.

I'd had flashes of déjà vu in the Silverbrooke—the most notable, of course, being my vision of Pearl's body in the boiler room. But this was more. Almost a complete picture. It felt as near as the other side of the mirror and equally untouchable.

The sensation, however, vanished when I entered the apartment. Though I struggled with all my faculties, the feeling could not be resurrected.

Tears coursed down my cheeks while I filled the kettle. What was wrong with me? Was I losing my mind? Was the descent to insanity really that inescapable?

Asking myself those questions was a total waste of time. That would be Dr. Peabody's job, when he arrived, and I wasn't too sure he would fare any better.

There was a knock on the door. I thought it would be one of the workmen, but it was the police, the same officers I'd seen that morning.

It wasn't easy to remain calm. I invited them inside, knowing from their expressions they hadn't come to apologize.

"The preliminary reports are back from the coroner's office," one said.

"Yes?"

"We're sorry to inform you that you're under arrest, Ms. Ashford, for the murder of Hepzibah Tulley. You have the right to remain silent, you have the right to..."

I listened with a strange detachment. I'd heard those lines recited countless times on television, but they sounded different in real life.

When he'd finished, I didn't know what to do. No one was dangling handcuffs so apparently they didn't consider me dangerous—at least not in the wakeful state.

One of them motioned toward the phone. "Wanta get in touch with your attorney before we go? He can meet you at the station."

"Oh. Yes, of course." Somehow I found my way to the telephone. Somehow I found Enoch's number. He promised to leave for the police station right away.

"Can Travis come?" I asked the police.

"Who's he?"

"My boyfriend. He's downstairs."

"He can follow in his car. You come with us."

The procession of events that followed will be forever engraved in my memory. Fingertips pressed one by one onto an ink pad, a flash for a frontal shot and a profile blinding me. A humorless matron escorting me to a small, windowless room where Enoch and I could confer in private.

A lethargy had settled over me, comparable, I suppose, to the numb demeanor of prisoners on their way to the electric chair. Though still functional, I was beyond feeling, beyond fear.

"I want Travis here," I said to Enoch as he pulled out a chair for me. The last I'd seen of Travis, he'd been pacing in the waiting area.

"Sorry, Geneva. I can't allow that."

"Why not?"

"We've talked about this before. To my mind he's still the number-one suspect. I don't care what the police think. I'd feel much better if you had no further contact with Travis McCabe."

His request punctured my lethargy. "Don't ask me to do that, Enoch, please."

"All right." He leaned across the scarred table. "But just remember, Geneva, anything you tell Travis, he might decide to use against you."

I objected with every fiber of my being, but lacked the strength to verbalize my emotions. So I slumped in my chair and said nothing.

The attorney brought out his briefcase and a pair of half glasses. "Now, then, let's review the police reports. Estimated time of death, 3:00 a.m. Cause of death, bleeding from multiple stab wounds. Fourteen, to be exact."

I flinched, horrified. How could anyone be so brutal?

Enoch continued. "The murder weapon is confirmed to be the butcher knife found in your possession. Blood stains on the dressing gown and knife correspond to Hepzibah's blood type."

"What about fingerprints?" I asked, as though we were discussing someone else's predicament.

"We're still waiting on that one. Meanwhile, the preliminary hearing is coming up. I'm gonna get you released on bail."

I don't know why that particular word finally punctured my lethargy. Bail. It had nothing to do with guilt or innocence, and a lot to do with one's attorney.

But all at once it hit me. They actually thought I'd murdered Hepzibah Tulley! They wanted to lock me away. For all I knew about Arkansas, they might even execute me.

"I didn't do it, Enoch!"

"I know that—"

"No, I mean it." I squeezed his hands so hard he flinched. "You've got to believe me. I did not kill Hepzibah!"

The courts wasted no time. A hearing was scheduled for later that day. We selected trial by jury, and Enoch, true to his word, arranged for my release with a sizable bail.

Emerging from the courthouse, we were instantly assailed by hordes of reporters, shoving microphones in my face and snapping photos. Enoch tried to push them away, but they were like barracudas. Voracious. Without mercy.

My fears escalated. What good was a trial by jury if the public was going to condemn me at once? Even if I were acquitted, how could I ever hold up my head in this town? Scandal always stuck in people's minds.

Enoch told the reporters that all questions regarding the trial were to go through him, not me. He also advised me to inform my work crew. They could help keep the press from entering the Silverbrooke.

That evening Travis prepared steaks and salad for dinner, but I was in no mood to eat. When I refused to answer a question about the preliminary hearing, he reacted with rage.

"I can't handle being shut out like this," he said, swirling the wine in his glass.

"I know, but Enoch's only acting in my best interests."

"Bull roar. Why doesn't he just slap a restraining order on me and be done with it?"

"Now, Travis—"

"Go ahead, Genny. Keep me in the dark. Pretend I'm one of the bad guys. But next time you need a shoulder to cry on, don't come running to me." With that he pushed himself away from the table and stormed downstairs.

I was about to chase after him but stopped myself. After all he'd done, Travis had every right to feel the way he did and to leave if he chose to.

I had no idea whether he'd ever return to the apartment. Neither could I bear the thought of waiting to find out. So I escaped by the only method left open to me. I took two sedatives and went to bed.

The next morning I nearly cried with relief. Travis was sleeping beside me. He had not abandoned me.

Chapter Fourteen

Travis's crew deserved a lot of credit for the way they handled the situation. The latest edition of the *Sentinel-Record* featured a front-page splash on Hepzibah's murder, but most of them still treated me the way they had before. I was amazed that no one quit rather than work for an alleged murderess, and impressed with the way they prevented curiosity seekers from entering the bathhouse. I suspected their loyalty had more to do with Travis than me but, whatever the reason, I was grateful.

The day after my arrest Travis brought some of the crates from the basement into the lounge where I could sort through them at my leisure. I could no longer tolerate the dank and dingy cellar. It was too much like a prison cell. The lounge was relatively comfortable and held no particular memories for me, painful or otherwise.

I sat on the sofa, the only furniture not still covered with drop cloths. As a table for sorting papers, I used the old steam radiator the crew had dismantled the day before.

Shortly before lunch Donald barged in. "Geneva, I just heard the news. Why didn't you call me?"

I set aside the sheaf of papers. "I'm sorry. I was going to."

"But you've always shared your bad news with me."

I'm sure the remark wasn't meant to be amusing, and I wasn't in a funny mood. But I laughed anyway. "I thought you resented that."

"I did. Now I miss it." He took a seat beside me and tried to take my hand. Some reflex made me pull away. "I warned you against coming here," he said. "I told you to leave this place alone."

"I know."

"Don't you wish you'd listened to me?"

I glanced at the paneled walls, the faded opulence around me. "In some ways, of course I do. But I'm still glad I kept the Silverbrooke."

"How can you say that? The sooner you get rid of this place, the better."

"I'm not getting rid of it."

Donald sighed. "There's no point in trying to reason with you. It's not why I came, anyway."

"Why did you come?"

"I was going to fly home tomorrow, but I've canceled the reservation."

"Why?"

"To be with you."

"What?"

"Your old husband Donald is going to get you out of this jam, I promise. Then we can go back to Minneapolis and forget this ever happened. We can make a brand new start."

I couldn't believe I was hearing right. "What on earth are you talking about?"

"You and me. I know we've had our differences, I've been insensitive. But there's nothing that can't be worked out. All we have to do is—"

"Donald, I have no intention of returning to Minneapolis with you, no matter what happens."

"But we've got a lot of history behind us. We used to be so close."

"Listen to me, Donald. What we used to be doesn't matter anymore. I happen to be in love with someone else."

"You're referring to that yokel who's working for you."

I could feel my hackles rising. "Don't you dare say anything against Travis."

"He's really got you under his thumb, hasn't he?"

"What is that supposed to mean?"

"He's set you up for a murder rap. But you're so damned gullible, I'll bet you're still sleeping with him. Whatever became of the level-headed Geneva I used to know?"

That was a question I felt unqualified to answer, but it wasn't the issue, anyway. "Travis did not set me up for Hepzibah's murder."

"Come on, surely you're not that naive. Even in your sleep, you're not strong enough to stab someone fourteen times."

The reference to that gruesome detail made me shudder. "That remains to be seen, but I happen to know Travis. He's warm, loving and would never harm anyone."

My ex-husband snorted. "Anyone's capable of harm with the right motivation."

Something in his tone set my teeth on edge. "All right, Donald. Since we're discussing motivation, what exactly is yours?"

He paled slightly. "What do you mean?"

"When we were married, I had to practically beg you to take a day off work. Suddenly you're languishing in Hot Springs like there's no tomorrow. Why are you really here?"

"I've already told you. I came to talk some sense into you. I still . . . love you, Geneva."

In that regard, nothing had changed. Donald always had trouble saying those words. I didn't want to be cruel, nor did

I like dredging up the past. But what I had to say was long overdue.

"The truth is, Donald, you never loved me. You loved my money."

His jaw dropped. "How can you say that after all we've been to each other?"

"That's just it. We never were anything to each other."

He stood up, backing toward the door as though I were suddenly contagious. "You're wrong, Geneva. Dead wrong. When this is all over, you'll see I was right. Then you'll come begging for my forgiveness."

The man who'd once been my husband stalked out of the room. I didn't hate him. Neither was I particularly angry. But I was more than happy to let him go.

TRAVIS STORMED into the lounge minutes after Donald had left. "Next time that creep comes in here, let me know. I'll throw him out on his ear."

I'd had more than I could take of knights on white chargers. "Calm down, Travis. He's just worried about me."

"Worried, hell. He's mixed up in this, Genny, and I intend to find out how."

"What?"

He pointed to the exposed heating ducts. "I was in the basement. I heard every word the two of you said."

"You were eavesdropping?"

"Yeah, lucky for you. Donald said Hepzibah was stabbed fourteen times."

"So?"

"That little detail hasn't been mentioned in the papers or on the news. Assuming you didn't tell your ex-husband, how did he find out?"

A sick feeling rose in the pit of my stomach. Travis was right. There was no way Donald could have known that detail unless he was involved or had an inside source.

I got up from the sofa. "I'll be right back."

"Where're you going?"

"I don't like this any more than you do. I'm going to phone Enoch."

The attorney was in his office and accepted my call right away. I got to the point at once. "Have you been talking to Donald?"

"We play golf together. We talk all the time."

"I mean, about the murder."

"Of course not, Geneva. Why would you even suggest such a thing?"

"He knew how many times Hepzibah had been stabbed. *I* didn't even know that until you read me the police report."

"Oh, dear, I was afraid somethin' like that might've happened."

"Something like what?"

"Donald was in my office this morning. We were going to play a few holes over lunch. I stepped out to see my secretary for a minute. I'd left your file on my desk. He must have had a little look-see."

"Well, that's just lovely. How many other people had had little look-sees?"

"Now, Geneva, calm down. I would never leave something so confidential out in the open. It's just that I'd been workin' on the file when Donald came in. If it had been anyone else, I'd have been sure to put it away."

"If it had been anyone else, they wouldn't have bothered to read the file."

"You're right, I'm sorry. It was careless of me. But you can be sure nothin' like this'll ever happen again."

It didn't make sense to stay angry. Except for Travis's bruised ego, no real damage had been done. "All right, Enoch, I'll let it go this time. Good-bye."

THERE WERE STILL two hours to go before Dr. Peabody arrived for our first session, so I continued rummaging through musty old crates—anything to keep my hands and mind occupied. Travis had gone back to work, only slightly mollified by my explanation of Donald's involvement.

It was difficult to concentrate on the task. What should have been a fascinating search through Silverbrooke memorabilia had become a chore. A plodding exercise in futility.

But they say that when things seem bleakest, a light will suddenly appear. Actually this was more of a dim glimmer, but I did find the first scraps of evidence linking me to my past.

It was a guest register with my parents' signatures, dated ten years before I was born. I picked up the thread and followed it. They'd come for baths every year, sometimes for a month at a time.

Then they stopped coming. I would have been two years old the last time they visited the Silverbrooke. That would have been when Pearl Tulley committed suicide—when I, for some reason, had come across her body.

But what else did it explain? I sat there and eventually succumbed to disappointment. Yes, it was gratifying to know with certainty that my parents had come to the Silverbrooke. But I hadn't learned anything I didn't already know.

Naturally they wouldn't have returned after Pearl's death. Their only child had been traumatized. Knowing my bombastic father, it was incredible that he hadn't sued the entire Tulley clan for damages.

Which brought me to my next unanswerable question. Given my childhood experience, why would Festus Tulley have willed the Silverbrooke to me? My parents had been regular patrons, but so were a lot of other people. Bill Swann had called it an act of appreciation. To me, it seemed more like one of depravity.

I'D JUST CHANGED CLOTHES and was applying makeup to cover the bags under my eyes when Dr. Peabody arrived, half an hour early.

"Hope you don't mind," he said. "I'm really excited about getting started."

"Not at all. I'm glad you're . . . excited."

I'd expected Dr. Peabody to resemble Freud. He looked more like a high school computer nerd—tall, pimply faced and gangly. But had had a friendly smile and the same mellow voice I recalled from our phone conversation.

Entering the living room, he knocked over an end table and hit his shin on a step ladder. I'm not even sure he noticed.

I caught a table lamp an instant before one of Dr. Peabody's briefcases swung into it. "You'll have to excuse the mess," I said. "We're renovating."

He looked around at the half-papered walls. "Nice place," he said. Then he opened his two briefcases on the coffee table. One was filled with writing supplies, the other held some kind of machine equipped with wires and knobs.

"What does that do?" I asked.

"While you're under hypnosis, this machine will measure and record the intensity of your brain waves."

"What if I don't go under?" Over the phone, we'd discussed my previous attempt at hypnotherapy.

"The machine will register your resistance, and that's just as useful diagnostically. Believe it or not, more energy is expended to resist the hypnotic state than to submit."

It wasn't hard to believe. One look in the mirror was indicative of how much energy I'd been wasting lately.

While we engaged in small talk, Dr. Peabody inserted a cassette into a recorder and instructed me to lie down on the couch. Then he applied electrodes to various spots on my head.

"There's one thing I want you to remember, Geneva, while you're in a trance state. You're the one who's in control, not me. If you feel you can't go on or things are getting too intense, just raise your index finger and you'll come back, just like that."

"Okay."

"On the other hand, when a memory is unpleasant, don't be too eager to avoid it. If you've recalled something painful, it's because your subconscious believes you're ready to expunge the memory. You can only do that by facing it."

I appreciated his straightforward advice and could only hope I'd remember it when the time came.

"Another thing, Geneva. We're not going to explore your recent sleepwalking episodes until I know for sure that you won't block. So don't expect instant results, okay?"

"Okay," I said, determined to keep my spirits up.

The therapist brought out a crystal pendulum—nice New Age touch, I thought—and began to swing it gently in front of my face.

"I want you to relax," he said, "and imagine colors..."

His method worked like magic. I could feel myself going under while I thought of green. The color of leaves and grass and moss on a tree. Green filled my mind and poured over me, filled the pockets of resistance and melted them away. I was fluid, floating, utterly relaxed...

"Very good, Geneva. Tell me where you are."

I heard his voice from a distance, though I knew he was right beside me. But that didn't matter. In trance state, nothing matters.

"I'm in the living room."

"What living room?"

"The upstairs apartment in the Silverbrooke."

"Excellent. Who am I?"

"Dr. Peabody."

"That's right. I'm going to ask you to visit some familiar places, and then I'll ask you to tell me about them."

I waited, hearing the whirrs and clicks of the machine beside me.

"How old are you, Geneva?"

"Twenty-eight."

"I would like you to go back to your twenty-fifty birthday and tell me what you're doing."

"I'm at work . . . the bank. They brought me a cake that says Happy Quarter Century."

"Who's there?"

"The people I work with . . . and Donald."

"Who's Donald?"

"My husband."

"Are you happy?"

I paused. "No."

"Why aren't you happy?"

"Donald won't put on a party hat."

"Why does that make you unhappy?"

"He doesn't know how to have fun, and he doesn't like it when I have fun."

"What else is there about Donald that upsets you?"

"He won't let me do things for myself."

"Do you want to do things for yourself?"

"Yes."

"Very good. Now I want you to go to your tenth birthday. Who do you see?"

"Mother and Father."

"What are you doing?"

"Opening presents. I get lots of clothes and books and some jewelry."

"Are you happy now?"

"A little bit."

"Why just a little bit?"

"Because Mother and Father have no time for me. They don't listen. They're too busy working."

"Do you love them?"

"Sometimes. But sometimes I miss—"

"Who, Geneva? Who do you miss?"

My answer was a long time coming. "I don't know."

"All right, let's go back to when you were two years old. Tell me where you are."

"In my crib."

"What are you doing?"

"Standing up and calling for Mommy."

"Does she come?"

"Yes."

"Where does she take you?"

"Into the living room. Unca is there with two people."

"Who is Unca?"

I paused. "He's just Unca."

"Do you love him?"

No answer.

"Do you love him, Geneva?"

"Yes, sometimes."

"Why only sometimes?"

"He yells at Mommy too much."

"Who are the other people in the room? Do you know them?"

The needle on the machine was scrawling madly.

"It's a man and a woman. I . . . I know them."

"Can you tell me their names?"

"Yes—no, I don't want . . . I don't want to be here anymore."

"If you want to come back, Geneva, you know what to do. When you come back, you'll remember everything you said to me."

I blinked a few times, and the room came into focus. I felt totally refreshed and thought I'd dozed off. But I knew right away that something was different. I had images now of being a baby, waking up in my crib. I'd never had those images before.

"How did I do?"

"Great. How do you feel?"

"Strange, but wonderful. Is that how I should feel?"

"That's entirely up to you. Remember, you're the navigator. I'm just following your lead."

The paper that had emerged from the machine was full of wide, scrawling waves. "What does that mean?"

"It indicates a high level of activity. There's a lot going on in that head of yours."

I laughed nervously. "That's a relief."

We listened to the tape, and I was surprised by the detached monotone in my voice. It sounded as though I was relating someone else's life. Yet I could feel shutters opening in my mind, letting in tiny cracks of light.

Then I heard Dr. Peabody asking if I loved Unca.

I leaned forward, intrigued. But the tape came to an end a short time later. "Who is Unca?"

"Don't you know?"

"No."

"How about the man and woman?"

A thought flickered briefly, then disappeared. "I don't know them, either."

"Do you have any uncles?"

"No. My father was an only child, and my mother had two sisters. But they lived in Canada, and I never met them. I don't even know if they're still alive."

"That's okay. Don't dwell on it. We've made a lot of progress for a first session."

"Why was I able to go under this time and not when I was a teenager?"

"Probably because now your reasons for blocking the memories are outweighed by your need to remember."

I thought of the murder charge hanging over my head. Dr. Peabody was right. My need to remember had never been more desperate.

Chapter Fifteen

We scheduled a second session for the following day.

For the rest of the day, I felt better than I had since the arrest. Not relaxed exactly, but energized, hopeful. I'd felt a similar sensation after my first thermal bath. It was strange that an inner cleansing could have the same effect as an external one.

Travis came upstairs shortly after the therapist left. He looked worried. "How did it go?"

"Pretty good."

"What did you find out?"

"Not much, except that showering a child with expensive presents isn't enough."

"What?"

"It may sound irrelevant, but Travis, I know these sessions are going to work. I can just feel it."

He took my face in his hands. "I'm glad to hear you say that, but how long do you think it will take?"

"Wish I knew."

"There's only two weeks before the trial—"

"I know."

He took my face in his hands. "Hey, don't look so glum. I know you're gonna come through with flying colors. We all will, Genny."

A MEMORIAL SERVICE was held for Hepzibah the following morning. I had mixed feelings about going and phoned Enoch for his advice.

He was appalled. "Why would you even consider showing up?"

"I don't know. Even though I didn't care for her, I knew the woman. And I certainly didn't wish her any harm."

After an awkward silence, I understood Enoch's reaction. I didn't wish her any harm, but Hepzibah was dead. And if you followed the policemen's line of thinking, I had apparently killed her. Why was that unchangeable reality refusing to sink in?

My attorney went on to advise me that the press had been hounding him about the case. I would do well, he said, to lie even lower for the next little while and avoid all reporters. I didn't enjoy feeling cloistered, but at least I wasn't in jail counting the days until my trial began.

Enoch was intrigued by my decision to enter hypnotherapy and asked for copies of the tapes to help prepare his defense. Dr. Peabody said he had no objection as long as he would be allowed to give professional testimony during the trial. The tapes themselves, he said, would be of little value without accompanying reports and a qualified psychiatrist to interpret them.

The doctor had also insisted that Enoch not be given the tapes piecemeal. Once the therapy was concluded and the reports written, then the attorney would be privy to the information. Enoch wasn't pleased about having to wait that long, but neither could he object. When it came to my mental health, Dr. Peabody was officially in charge.

My enthusiasm was greater when we launched into our second session. Travis grudgingly left us alone soon after Dr. Peabody arrived. Travis wasn't pleased at being left in the dark, either, but he'd accepted the situation. I think he must have known that his continued love and support did more for me than all the lawyers and psychiatrists in the world could have done.

This time Dr. Peabody said he was willing to probe my recent sleepwalking episodes. Despite my apprehension, I went into trance effortlessly.

"It's your first night in Hot Springs," he said. "You went to sleep, and now you've gotten out of bed. Where are you going?"

"To the mountain."

"Which mountain?"

"The one behind the Silverbrooke."

"Why are you there?"

"I'm lost. I'm trying to find my way home."

"How old are you?"

"Two."

"Where are your parents?"

"Mommy's at home."

"Where's your father?"

I hesitate. "I don't know."

"Isn't he with your mother?"

"No."

"Are you frightened?"

"Yes. There are animals on the mountain. I'm not supposed to be here."

"Then why are you there?"

"I ran away. I know Mommy's going to be upset, but I can't help it. Sometimes I do things I shouldn't."

"Tell me what you're feeling."

"Cold . . . hungry. I've been out here too long, and now it's dark."

"Does anyone find you?"

"Yes."

"Who?"

"Travis."

"What is he doing?"

"He's coming over to talk to me, but he doesn't know who I am or where I live."

"What is your reaction when he talks to you?"

"I run back to that . . . other place, the motel. But it's not where I live."

"And then what?"

"Then I go to dreamland. When I wake up, I'm not two years old anymore."

"Very good. Now I'd like you to be two again."

I started to whimper.

"What's the matter?"

"Bad things are happening. I don't like them."

"What bad things? Tell me."

"Unca is yelling at Mommy. I'm hiding in my play-house. He doesn't know I'm listening."

"Why is he yelling?"

"Because she had a baby."

"Do you know who the baby is?"

"Yes."

"Who?"

"Me."

"Where is your father while your Unca is yelling?"

"He's not there, and I'm glad."

"Why are you glad?"

"Because he gets angry at Mommy, too. She's so nice. I don't understand why everyone is mean to her."

"Does Unca or Mommy find you in the playhouse?"

"No. They go upstairs. That's when I run away."

"To the mountain?"

"Yes."

"Who finds you this time?"

I shake my head, refusing to answer.

"Think, Geneva. Who finds you and brings you home?"

"I don't want to...I can't..."

"Why are you frightened?"

"They're going to...take me away."

"Who?"

"Those bad people. I don't like them..."

"Do you know who they are?"

My agitation grew, and I started to cry. "They put me in my crib, and I can't see Mommy anywhere."

"Do you know where she is?"

"Yes...no...I don't know. I'm scared! Please don't make me tell you."

"Remember what I told you, Geneva. You can come out of it anytime."

I raised my finger, and the session was over.

THIS TIME when I came out of trance, my body was wringing wet. I felt none of the hopefulness of the last session. The same couldn't be said for Dr. Peabody. He was elated.

"You did really well today," he said.

"I don't feel well."

"That's understandable. You're getting in touch with some pretty heavy emotions."

He was right. I could feel the traces of every emotion described by my two-year-old self—cold, hunger, fear. I sensed the frustration of a child overhearing an argument with her mother and this person called Unca. But there were conflicting images, shadows I still could not understand.

"Do you recognize Unca yet?" Dr. Peabody asked.

"No." The answer felt so close, I could almost reach out and touch it. But the walls were still there, hiding his face and protecting me. All I knew for certain was that I didn't like the man.

"Could we do another session today?" I asked, anxious to progress as quickly as possible.

"I don't think we should. This can be pretty draining."

"I can handle it."

Dr. Peabody thought a moment. "Tell you what. I'll give you a call later this afternoon, see how you're doing. If you're feeling okay, we can try again this evening."

"I appreciate that."

"Are you having problems sleeping these days?"

"I'm taking sedatives, so I don't know if you'd really call it sleep."

"Keep taking them for now. If you have to regress, I'd rather you do it in these sessions instead of in your sleep."

My sentiments exactly.

AFTER THE THERAPIST LEFT, I went in search of Travis but couldn't find him anywhere in the bathhouse. None of the guys knew where he had gone, either.

The day dragged, and I spent much of it wandering aimlessly through the halls of the Silverbrooke. My frame of mind wasn't great, either. I snapped at anyone who tried to cheer me up.

Though I didn't like myself that day, the self-directed rage was almost reassuring. It was as though my latent sense of inadequacy was finally floating to the surface, ready to be acknowledged and exorcised.

I even wandered through the basement, going from room to room trying to unearth long-buried memories. They were there, all right, niggling and poking at the edges of my conscious mind. But something was still suppressing them, and my will power alone was not enough to set them free.

Travis returned to the bathhouse by midafternoon. He was carrying a bulging manila envelope.

I was in the lobby with the tile setter, helping him match new mosaic tiles to the original floor. Maybe I wasn't exactly helping, but he was too polite to ask me to leave.

"Genny, can you come upstairs a minute?" Travis asked, looking like he was fairly bursting with news.

I excused myself, and the two of us went upstairs.

The phone was ringing when we got there. I ran to the kitchen to answer.

It was Calder Carson. "Sorry I've taken so long to get in touch," he said.

"That's all right." Considering the fiasco at the country club, I wondered why he felt obligated one way or another.

He answered my unspoken question. "I wanted to apologize for my behavior the other night. It was . . . reprehensible."

"That's kind of you, Calder, but it's not me who needs the apology."

Travis had been standing there trying to figure out who I was talking to. At the mention of his uncle's name, he rolled his eyes in disgust.

"I'd like to talk to my nephew, too," Calder went on. "That's why I called. I was wonderin' if the two of you could come over for drinks this evening."

"Gee, I don't know."

"I realize it's short notice, but . . . well, the truth is, Hepzibah's tragic demise brought a few things home to me. Number one—that life's too short to bear grudges."

His admission, though noble, made me uncomfortable. Surely he knew that I'd been charged with Hepzibah's murder. How was I supposed to respond? Again, he seemed to read my thoughts.

"'Course, I don't believe for a minute that you had anything to do with Hepzibah's slayin', Geneva."

"Thank you," I said, for all the good it did.

"Do you suppose you could persuade Travis to come over? It would certainly do my heart good."

"Hold on. I'll ask him."

I covered the receiver and informed Travis of the invitation.

"Tell him to shove it."

"I can't do that. He's feeling terrible. He wants to apologize."

"Then tell him his apology's accepted."

I held out the phone. "You tell him."

Travis folded his arms. "I have nothing to say to that man."

"Then, for heaven's sake, don't say anything. Just hold the phone and listen."

Finally, scowling, he took the receiver. "Uncle Calder? It's me."

I couldn't hear what the older man said, but he was obviously carrying the burden of the conversation. Travis's replies were mainly monosyllabic grunts.

"I don't see the point of coming over," Travis said. "We don't have anything to talk about." At last, he sighed. "Okay, you win. What time do you want us over there? Eight o'clock's fine." He hung up the phone and said, "Dammit. Now why did I go and do that?"

"Because it's the only fair thing you can do. He really wants to make amends."

"He should've thought of that a few months ago."

"Now, Travis. That's no way to—"

"I know, I know. Spare me the lectures. Are you sure you're up to visiting tonight?"

"Anything is better than hanging around here."

"Which reminds me. Come into the kitchen, and I'll show you what I found." He carried the envelope with him.

"Where've you been all day?" I asked as I took a seat at the table.

"Putting the pieces of your life together."

I laughed nervously and picked up the envelope. "That's supposed to be my job."

He took the envelope out of my hands. "We're in this together, remember?"

There was a hint of sarcasm in his voice—not that I blamed him. I wasn't happy about not confiding in Travis, either, but my attorney's instructions had been specific. The only people with whom I could discuss details of the case were Enoch and Dr. Peabody.

"I spent the day at the *Sentinel* archives," he said, placing the envelope on his lap where I couldn't reach it. "The lady who works there remembers what happened twenty-six years ago at the Silverbrooke. They say it was quite the scandal."

"Pearl's suicide, you mean?"

"Right. She and Festus ran this place together after their parents retired."

"What about Hepzibah?"

"She had her home for wayward girls."

"Oh yes, I forgot."

"Anyway, Pearl was only eighteen and unmarried when she got pregnant. She wouldn't tell anyone who the father was, only that he was one of their clients. Her family was mortified and wanted her to quit and leave town. But the patrons really liked her, so Festus let her stay on at the Silverbrooke. He was the only broad-minded one of the bunch, apparently."

"Did she have the baby?"

"A little girl. After the child was born, folks sort of forgot about Pearl's indiscretion. The child was a sweetheart, and everybody liked her. The clients used to bring her gifts, and she'd play in the lobby while her mother ran the front desk."

Unaccountably my heart was starting to hammer. I was finding it difficult to be patient while Travis told his story.

"When she was two," he continued, "the little girl went missing."

"Oh, my Lord." I knew what was coming next.

"Volunteers spent two days looking for her. At the end, all they found was a baby sweater on Hot Springs Mountain, shredded and covered with blood. Her body was never discovered. Theory is, a mountain lion got her."

"But that's impossible."

"Why do you say that?" he asked, in the tone of someone who already knew the answer.

"Because... because I... she didn't die!"

Travis had no visible reaction. "Do you want to hear the rest of the story or not?"

"Yes, please!"

"The very night Pearl Tulley was shown the sweater, she slit her wrists." He pulled out an old newspaper from the envelope. "Take a look at this."

The banner headline read "Disconsolate Hot Springs Mother Kills Herself." There was a picture of a smiling young woman. Beneath it, the photo of a child, the same one Bill Swann had shown me in Minneapolis.

"But... that's me!"

"No, Genny, that's Lizbet Tulley. And you're Lizbet."

Chapter Sixteen

My eyes blurred. I shook my head. "No, Travis, that's impossible."

"Has any of this come out in therapy?"

"No," I said emphatically. I could feel my thoughts shifting, opening up. "What I don't understand is, did I die on that mountain or not?"

"You're here, Geneva. Figure it out."

The absurdity of my remark sank in. Only then did I realize that I'd inadvertently acknowledged being Lizbet. "But if I'm her, who are my parents? And how did they end up being my parents?"

"I don't know," Travis replied, "but if you're Lizbet, it would certainly help explain why Festus willed you the Silverbrooke."

I nodded. "Because he's my uncle."

Uncle, Unca. That had to be the link, but I felt no emotional reaction to this knowledge. *Unca*, apparently, frightened me at times, but *Festus Tulley* aroused nothing in the grown-up version of me. The mental blocks were not all broken yet.

"When's your next session?" Travis asked.

"Tonight, hopefully."

"We're supposed to visit Uncle Calder's tonight."

"Shoot, I forgot." There were too many things on my mind these days—not the least of which was how to stay out of prison.

"We'll cancel the visit," Travis offered, too eagerly.

"Don't do that. Calder would be terribly disappointed."

"He can learn to live with it."

"Don't be that way, Travis. He's really anxious to make things right. Anyway, I don't know for sure whether I'll have a session. It depends on whether Dr. Peabody thinks I'm up to it."

"I'm not leaving you alone in this place after dark."

"I won't be alone. Dr. Peabody will be here."

"Let's just play it by ear for now. If we take a look at this other stuff, it might trigger something."

We leafed through articles describing the search for Lizbet Tulley. I read Pearl's obituary and scanned the announcement for the child's memorial service. The final clipping showed a picture of the Silverbrooke with Festus Tulley standing out front. The bathhouse was being closed for personal reasons, he was quoted as saying. The photo was too grainy to make out his features.

To say I had no reaction to it would be inaccurate. But the most I could conjure from this assortment of tragedies was confusion. Who were these people to me? Could it just be coincidence that Lizbet and I were identical—a modern variation on *The Prince and the Pauper*? And whatever lay in our respective pasts, was it so tragic that I was driven to murder in my sleep?

"I wonder if there's anyone who knows exactly what happened," I remarked.

"You do."

"Besides me."

"Bet you any money Enoch does."

Travis's attitude toward my attorney was no great mystery. Enoch had sidelined Travis, and that didn't sit well with him. But this time the remark seemed particularly snide.

"Are you implying he's hiding things from me?" I said.

"Implying is not a strong enough word."

"But why?"

"I don't know. It's just a gut feeling. Something else I'm pretty sure of is that Bill Swann knew the whole story."

I shuddered. "Do you think so?"

"He had Lizbet's photo—or yours, and had been instructed by Festus to find you. He must have known everything, or he could never have conducted the investigation."

"What a shame he's dead."

Travis raised one eyebrow. "Yeah. Coincidence, too."

His sarcasm piqued my curiosity. "What are you talking about?"

"I asked a few questions about Bill today. Did you know he had his heart attack on the golf course? And he just happened to be playing with Enoch and my Uncle Calder that day."

"So? People have been known to die on golf courses."

"But don't you think it's strange that Bill happened to kick the bucket the very day he was supposed to talk with you?"

A chill slithered down my spine. Of course I'd entertained those same misgivings when I'd first learned he was dead, but I'd since dismissed them as one of fate's cruel twists. "You've been reading too many Chandler novels, Travis."

"Maybe so, but I'm keeping an eye on you all the same."

I got up from the chair and wrapped my arms around his neck. "You can keep more than an eye on me anytime."

He turned his face to kiss me. There was love in his eyes, a profound, almost sad kind of love. Thanks to me, the spark of humor wasn't there. I wondered whether I would ever light that spark again.

DR. PEABODY CALLED a short while later. He asked me whether I'd experienced any flashbacks. I told him about the articles Travis had unearthed.

"That's great," the therapist said. "That stuff about Lizbet could be just what you need to break through."

"So can we do a session tonight?"

"Why not? You sound like you've got a handle on things. I've still got some notes to finish writing up, but I can be there by seven."

"Seven's fine," I said and hung up. "You don't mind going to Calder's alone, do you, Travis?"

"Uncle Calder I can handle. It's leaving you alone that bothers me."

"But I've already told you. Dr. Peabody will be here."

"Only for as long as the session takes. I'm talking about afterward."

The truth was, I didn't like the idea of being alone in the house, either, so I came up with an alternate suggestion. "Why don't I come over to your uncle's as soon as Dr. Peabody leaves?"

He thought a moment. "That sounds good. But promise you won't change your mind."

"I promise."

We spent a few precious moments holding each other, forgetting our respective problems. Then one of the guys came up to tell Travis they were ready to turn on the thermal hookup.

"One more thing," he said on his way out the door.

"What?"

"Tonight, after everyone's gone home, let's have our first thermal bath together."

I tangled my fingers through his dark brown curls. "You've got it, cowboy."

ALONE IN THE APARTMENT I phoned Enoch. The articles Travis had found disturbed me more than I had let on. So much was happening lately, my emotions were scattered.

Enoch's secretary informed me that he was with a client. "It's Geneva Ashford," I said. "I've got something urgent to discuss with him."

"Oh, okay, just hold on."

Enoch came on the line a minute later. "What is it, Geneva? Is something wrong?"

I described the contents of the articles in front of me, then paused before saying what was on my mind. "So what I need to know is—who am I?"

There was a slight pause. "I'm not sure I understand. Are you sayin' you think you're Lizbet Tulley?"

"I was hoping you could tell me."

"Listen, Geneva, it's a long story, and unfortunately I don't have the time to go into it right now."

"So you do know something."

"Only what Festus admitted. But rest assured, you are Geneva Ashford. Lizbet died when she was two."

"But how—"

"Tell you what. Why don't I drop by later on this evening and I'll tell you what little I know?"

Something made me hesitate. I'd promised Travis I would go to his uncle's. But surely he would understand that I couldn't pass up this opportunity to learn the truth, once and for all. Besides, Travis's main concern was that I not be alone. With Dr. Peabody here and then Enoch, I wouldn't be.

"I have a therapy session at seven," I said, "but I don't know how long it's going to take."

"No problem. I'll give you a call before I come over. It'd be a good opportunity for me to meet your therapist, see how things are progressing."

TRAVIS WAS NOT PLEASED when I told him over dinner that Enoch was coming over. "So he has known something all along," he grumbled.

"That doesn't mean he's been lying to me. He just didn't want to upset me with old rumors."

Travis seemed unimpressed. "Why can't his visit wait until morning?"

"You're being positively paranoid. Are you jealous or something?"

"Come on, Genny, give me some credit. But if you insist on staying home and entertaining your attorney, go ahead. I can't stop you."

FOR THE REST OF THE DAY I tried my best to soothe Travis's feelings. He was in a terrible mood to visit his uncle, given their stormy history. But Travis would not be appeased, and I finally gave up and let him stay cranky.

The therapist arrived with his glasses halfway down his nose and his collar crooked. Travis excused himself to work in the basement. It was still too early for him to go to Calder's. "Phone me at my uncle's," he insisted, "as soon as Enoch has left."

I promised him I would.

Before we began the session, I showed Dr. Peabody the articles. "How do you feel about them?" he asked.

"I don't feel much of anything about them, but I can sense that the memories are struggling to get out."

"That's what I like to hear. We'll get started now, but don't be too anxious to know everything. There's still a possibility you'll block if we move too quickly."

Dr. Peabody clumsily applied the sticky goop to the electrodes and attached them to my head. Then I lay on the sofa and waited for him to settle into the seat across from me. "Now remember, Geneva, anytime you feel the need to come back—"

"I know. Raise my finger."

"That's right. Okay, I want you to relax and think of colors . . ."

"What's your name?"

"Geneva Ashford."

"Tell me where you are."

"I'm in the living room."

"How old are you?"

"Twenty-eight."

"Very good. Now I want you to go back to when you were a child. Find a happy time, and tell me about it."

"I have a puppy."

"How old are you?"

"Three."

"Who bought you the puppy?"

"Mother and Daddy."

"Is it your birthday?"

"No, they just bought it."

"For no reason at all?"

"They were trying to make me happy."

"Were you sad before you got the puppy?"

"No."

"What were you feeling?"

"Lonely."

"Okay. Now I'd like you to go back to your second birthday. Who do you see?"

"Lots of people."

"Are your parents there?"

"Just Mommy."

"Where is your father?"

"I don't know."

"Where is the party being held?"

"Here."

"In this living room?"

"Yes."

"Is this your home when you're two years old?"

"Yes."

"Is Unca at the party?"

"Yes. He's helping me blow out the candles."

"Okay, now I'd like you to go back to the night when you were in your crib crying for Mommy. She brought you into the living room. Unca was there with two people. Do you remember that night?"

A pause. "Yes."

"Are you happy?"

"No. The lights are bright. I'm crying, and I don't like those people."

"Do you recognize them?"

"Yes."

"Who are they?"

I didn't answer right away. When I did, my voice was small. "They're a lady and my daddy."

"Is Mommy there?"

"No, she's gone downstairs."

"What happens to you?"

"Unca puts me on her...on the lady's lap."

"Do you like being on her lap?"

"No. She hugs me too hard, and she's crying. I start to cry too."

"What is your father doing?"

"He's patting me on the head, but he's angry."

"Why is he angry?"

"I don't know. He's saying mean things to...to the lady."

"What happens after the lady hugs you?"

"Unca picks me up and brings me to bed."

"Do you go back to sleep?"

"No."

"Tell me what happens next."

"I wait until dark. I wait until they're gone."

"Then what?"

"I climb out of my crib."

"Does anyone hear you?"

"No, I'm real quiet."

"Where are you going?"

"Downstairs to look for Mommy."

The machine's graph scribbled frantically.

"Do you find her?"

"No. I want to tell Mommy about Daddy and the lady, tell her I don't like them. But I don't know where she is."

"What do you do?"

"I wait in the playhouse, hoping she'll come. When she doesn't, I go outside to look for her. Unca hasn't locked the gate yet."

"Where is the gate?"

"In the basement at the end of the tunnel."

"You're only two years old. Do you know your way around the whole bathhouse?"

"Yes."

"Where do you go when you get out?"

"Up the mountain. I can't find Mommy, but I want to hide until that lady goes away."

"Why?"

"Because she . . . scares me."

"Why does she scare you?"

"I don't know."

"All right. You're on the mountain. Tell me about it."

I started to shiver. "It's cold and dark. I'm hungry. I don't want to be there anymore, but I can't find my way home."

"How long are you on the mountain?"

"All night, all day, another night."

"Who finds you?"

"Unca."

"What does he do?"

"He takes off my sweater. Mommy sometimes puts a sweater over my pajamas."

"Unca has taken off your sweater. What is he doing?"

I began to whimper. "He's cutting up the sweater...now he's hurting me."

"How is he hurting you?"

"With the ... knife. He's cutting my fingers and squeezing real hard."

"Go on."

"He wipes them on the sweater. Then he carries me home."

"Does he say anything?"

"Yes."

"What does he say?"

"He tells me to be quiet or he'll hurt me some more. He tells me if I'm real good, I can have anything I want."

"What do you say?"

"I want Mommy, but I'm trying so hard not to cry, I can't say anything."

"Is it day or night when Unca takes you home?"

"Night."

"Does he bring you to bed?"

"No, he takes me to the ... laundry."

"Where is the laundry?"

"In the basement."

"Then what?"

"He stuffs something in my mouth so I can't talk or cry. Then he closes the door and leaves me there."

Dr. Peabody scribbled a few notes before continuing. "Does someone come to get you?"

"Yes."

"Who?"

"My other unca."

"You have two?"

"Yes."

"How do you tell them apart?"

"One lives with me. The other one is . . . bigger."

"Which unca takes you this time?"

"The bigger one."

"Where are you going?"

"Upstairs to my crib."

"Do you see anyone else?"

"No."

"Are you crying?"

"I want to, but I still have that thing in my mouth."

"Tell me what happens after Unca puts you to bed."

"He shuts off all the lights. I try to call for Mommy, but I can't. So I go to sleep."

"And then?"

"I wake up. It's still dark, and I'm thirsty. I pull the thing out of my mouth—"

"How did you do that?"

"I don't know. I just did."

"All right, go on."

"I ask Mommy for a drink, but she doesn't hear me. I get out of bed to look for her. She's not in her room, so I go downstairs."

"Does anyone see or hear you?"

"No. I'm real quiet because I don't want Unca to catch me out of bed."

"Where do you go next?"

"I look for Mommy at the desk where she works, but it's dark and she's not there. I go through all the rooms looking for her. I'm trying hard not to cry."

"You're being very brave. Please continue."

"I don't want to."

"You need to find your mommy."

"I'm scared."

"No one is going to hurt you. You know you're perfectly safe talking to me. So please go on."

I sniffled before continuing. "I open the door to the basement. I'm really scared. It's dark and cold down there. And I'm so thirsty..."

"You're doing fine."

"Mommy, where are you?"

"You'll find her. Tell me where you're going."

"I'm going downstairs. It's hard because the steps are for big people. My fingers hurt, and I'm shivering."

"You'll be warm soon. Go on."

"I smell something."

"What is it?"

"I don't know. It smells warm and sticky. I call for Mommy some more, and then I...then I..."

"You're almost there. What do you see?"

"A light in the boiler room."

"Is that where you go?"

"Yes."

"What do you see when you get there?"

"I see my...my mommy." I began to hyperventilate.

"It's okay. You'll be fine," the doctor said. "Take a deep breath...blow it out...that's it. Now, you've found your mommy. Tell me about her."

''She's on the floor, and there's blood all over. That's what smells sticky. I try to wake her up, but she doesn't hear me. And then . . .''

''Then what?''

''The big door slams shut. Mommy and I are stuck in there. We can't get out.''

''What do you do?''

''I bang and scratch and cry for a long time. Mommy doesn't do anything except lie there. Finally Unca comes down to get us.''

''Which unca?''

''The bigger one.''

''What does he do?''

''He picks me up and takes me through the gate at the end of the tunnel. I ask where we're going, but he just says to trust him. We take a path to the mountain. There's a car up there waiting for us.''

''Go on.''

''Unca opens the front door and drops me on her lap.''

''Whose lap?''

''The lady I don't like. The lady who wants me to call her Mother.''

Dr. Peabody fell silent for a while.

''Where did they take you?''

''To my new house.''

''The house where you grew up?''

''Yes.''

''I have two more questions. These are very important. What was your name after you went to live with your new mother and father?''

''Geneva Zloczewski.''

''And what was your name before you went to live with them?''

''Lizbet Tulley.''

"Very good. Now I'd like you to relax for a while. Just think about happy things."

I watched the therapist scribble notes in a shaky hand while I thought happy thoughts. After a while, he continued.

"All right, Geneva, I'd like you to go back to the night that Hepzibah Tulley was killed."

I waited as usual for a direct question.

"What did you do that evening?"

"We're at the country club for dinner."

"Who?"

"Travis and me."

"Who else is there?"

"Enoch and Lurlene Sarrazin—and Calder Carson, but he won't stay."

"How long do you stay at the country club?"

"About four hours."

"Are you enjoying yourself?"

"Not very much."

"Why not?"

"Lurlene is a bore, and she won't let me talk to the men. Travis is tense because he's angry with his uncle."

"Does anything unusual happen over dinner?"

I thought a moment. "No."

"Tell me what happens when you get home."

"We see that someone spray-painted the front of the Silverbrooke. I'm upset."

"Do you express your anger out loud?"

"Yes."

"What do you say?"

"I'm going to throttle that woman."

"Who do you mean by that woman?"

"Hepzibah."

"Are you speaking literally?"

"Of course not."

"Does Travis know you were just using a figure of speech?"

"Yes."

"What do you do next?"

"I head for the car."

"Why?"

"I want to confront Hepzibah."

"Do you?"

"Travis stops me. He says I'd be crazy to disturb anyone that late at night."

"Do you agree with him?"

"After a while, yes."

"What happened next?"

"We go upstairs, have a drink and then go to bed."

"Then what."

"We make love twice. First Travis is on top—"

Dr. Peabody cleared his throat. "You can skip that part."

I did.

"Tell me what happens after you fall asleep."

"Nothing for a while. I just sleep."

"And then what?"

"I hear a noise outside the bedroom door."

"What kind of noise?"

"A floorboard squeaking."

"Do you get up?"

"No."

"This is very important. Are you awake or asleep when you hear the noise?"

"Asleep."

"Go on."

"The door is opening. Someone is coming in. I sit up in bed."

"Are you awake yet?"

"No."

"Then what happens?"

"He whispers my name."

"What does he call you?"

I paused. "Lizbet."

"Go on."

"He is so quiet. I can hardly hear what he's saying. He says not to move or he'll have to hurt me. Says he doesn't want to hurt me."

"And then?"

"He says he has a little surprise for his Lizbet. All I have to do is lie back down and close my eyes. The surprise will be there when I wake up in the morning, but I won't remember where it came from."

"Do you see the surprise before you close your eyes?"

"Yes."

"What is it?"

"A knife. He takes it out of a plastic bag, wipes it on my dressing gown, then leaves it on my bed."

"Do you try to stop him?"

"No, I don't want him to hurt me anymore."

"Then what?"

"He leaves, and I lie down again."

"Do you know who that person is?"

"Yes."

"Who?"

"It's my... unca. Unca Enoch."

"Excellent recall," another voice said. "Might as well shut the tape off, Doctor."

Dr. Peabody spun around.

I raised my finger to come back from trance, but it didn't work. Unca Enoch was still there!

Chapter Seventeen

Actually I *had* come out of trance, but the past was now fresh, vivid in my mind. Enoch looked every bit as threatening now as he had the night I was dropped into the car on Hot Springs Mountain.

Before I could react, the attorney slammed a pistol butt against the back of Dr. Peabody's head. The therapist slumped to the floor.

I was yanking off electrodes, about to escape, when Enoch raised the gun. "Stay right where you are."

Then he reached over, pressed the eject button on the recorder and dropped the cassette into his pocket. "You folks won't be needing this anymore."

"You gave me away," I said, the immediate question of survival eclipsed by the astonishment of remembering. "How could you?"

"You ought to thank me," he replied, sneering.

"Are you really my uncle?"

"Just a close family friend. Festus was your blood uncle." He brandished the gun. "Now get up."

"Why should I?"

"Same mouthy little Lizbet, aren't you?" He cocked the trigger. "Does that make things any clearer?"

My fingers pressed into the nubble of the couch. My senses focused on the small black hole at the end of Enoch's gun. "Travis is due back here any minute."

"Nice try, but I know he's at Calder's. He won't be back for hours. *Now get up!*"

I did as I was told, making no sudden moves and keeping my gaze fixed on Enoch. "Where are we going?"

"Just trust me."

My blood froze. I could recall Enoch saying those very words the night I was taken away. Even a two-year-old comprehends trust—and the betrayal of it.

"That's it. Nice and easy." He directed me toward the door. I had to obey. There was no other way out.

"You'll never get away with this."

"Oh, I expect I will. You're the last one who knows our little secret."

I did some swift mental calculating. Enoch was right. My parents, Festus, Pearl, Hepzibah, Bill—they were the only ones who knew my real identity. And they were all dead. The odds did not look good.

A few feet from the door, Enoch grabbed my arm and wrenched it behind my back. *Travis, Donald, somebody, please come!*

He pressed the gun to my neck. "All you've got to do is relax, Geneva. Everything'll be just fine."

We began to descend the stairs. Our progress was slow. My arm ached, and my neck, courtesy of the firearm, was angled painfully to one side.

"Wh-why did you kill Hepzibah?" I ventured.

"I didn't kill her. You did." His burst of laughter was like a gunshot in the stairwell. "Don't you remember?"

"Was she talking too much? Was that why you had to silence her?"

"The old biddy was crazier than a coot. I did her a fa-vor."

No, she wasn't, I realized too late. If I'd paid attention, asked the right questions when Hepzibah called me Lizbet, maybe both of us would still be alive.

I stumbled, and Enoch got angry. "Watch your step, girl. We can't have the coroner finding any broken bones now, can we?"

"What are you going to do with me?"

"Nothing messy. Not the way your addle-headed mama did it."

Grief mixed briefly with my fear. It was like finding my mother and mourning her in the space of a few minutes.

I thought suddenly of my father, the man I'd witnessed arguing with Mommy. "Did Pearl and my father have a . . . relationship?"

Enoch laughed. "Let's just say he partook of more than the thermal waters while visitin' the Silverbrooke."

Disgust joined the list of my emotions. "But if he was my natural father, why all the secrecy?"

"He didn't want his wife finding out about his peccadil-loes. He paid all of us off handsomely to make sure she didn't."

We reached the bottom of the stairs. "Are you saying my father bought me?"

"That's one way of puttin' it."

Our reflection in the mirror was like the grown-up ver-sion of my childhood nightmare. Unca Enoch again taking Lizbet where she didn't want to go.

We came around the corner. Enoch's attention wavered. I decided to make a run for the front doors.

Tiles shattered at my feet. I stopped.

Enoch's tone was dead calm. "Get back here, girl, be-fore I show you what this gun does to flesh and blood."

Eyes lowered, I turned. The mosaic faces of the lion an the lamb had been destroyed—a cruel, irrelevant bit o irony.

Enoch steered me down the corridor on the ladies' side. tried to drag my heels, hoping Dr. Peabody would wake u and phone the police—assuming he was still alive. Bu Enoch was a strong man. The more I resisted, the harder h shoved.

We came to the basement door.

My heart, already hammering, increased its tempo "Don't make me go down there, Enoch…please." This tim my fear was no longer repressed. And this time the fear wa rational.

He jabbed the gun into my side. "Keep moving."

I took the first step, bracing myself for the saggin boards. But Travis had repaired the stairs. So much fo hoping that Enoch would fall through them.

Getting desperate, I tried a different tack. "Why don't w just forget this ever happened, Enoch? I'll give up the leas and m-move back to Minneapolis."

"Nice try. Might've worked too, if you'd kept on forget ting the way you have all these years. Lucky for me, you husband clued me in."

"What?" For a moment I forgot my impending mortal ity.

"It was Donald who let me know you're a sleepwalker.'

"Why?" The sting of Donald's betrayal on top of every thing was too much.

"He wanted me to talk you into goin' back home. Tha man's still got it real bad for you." At the foot of the stairs he shoved me. "Keep moving. We haven't got all night."

My mind struggled with the ramifications of Donald's bi mouth. He must have told Enoch how I'd injured my hands ow I never remembered anything the next day. What a onvenient loophole for a corrupt attorney.

"But you spoke to me the night you came in with the nife. I could've identified you."

"No, I spoke to Lizbet. When you sat up lookin' like a ombie, I knew you wouldn't recall a thing."

"That was a pretty big risk."

"A calculated one. Only thing I didn't anticipate was that tupid hypnotist." We came to the boiler room, and he ushed me. "Get in there."

Flashbacks appeared of my mother's body. I saw myself n the same spot. I stopped, incapable of entering the room.

A knee to my kidneys was enough to persuade me. I fell o the floor as Enoch slammed the door shut.

"Sweet dreams, Lizbet." I could hear his laughter from he other side.

I scrambled to the door, but there was no handle. Travis ad warned me never to let it shut. I was trapped just the vay I'd been at two years of age when I'd found my mother ead.

Hammering against the door, I pleaded with Enoch. "Please, let me out. It doesn't have to end this way!"

"Save your breath. There's not much air, and you're onna need it."

He was right. If I stayed calm, eventually Travis would ome home. Or Dr. Peabody would find me.

After a few minutes, my optimism vanished. I heard the ound of a body being dragged down the stairs—Dr. Peaody's, no doubt.

Then I saw the wisps of smoke curling beneath the door. My attorney had set the place on fire!

"Enoch!" I started pounding, knowing it was useless. He'd already left.

Backing away from the door, I assessed the odds of su
vival. The Silverbrooke was made of stone so it couldn't b
totally destroyed. But the basement was like a tinderbox, ful
of old crates and wood scraps. The doctor and I would b
dead from smoke inhalation long before the building suf
fered any real damage.

I crumpled to the floor, pleading to whatever highe
forces were listening. Within minutes I succumbed to th
swirling poisons.

I DON'T RECALL being rescued, but it must have been he
roic. Even now Travis is too modest to go into any detail. S
I'll just tell you what happened from the time I awoke in th
hospital.

An oxygen mask covered my face. I felt as though m
lungs were on fire. The first thing I saw after opening m
eyes was Travis, his anguished expression proving I was stil
alive.

He was holding my hand, stroking it gently. "Don't tr
to talk, Genny. You're gonna be all right."

Even if I'd wanted to, I couldn't have spoken. Yet Travi
must have read the question in my eyes.

"You weren't burned," he said. "You just suffered smok
inhalation. Dr. Peabody's going to be okay, too."

He went on to explain that Enoch and Lurlene Sarrazi
were long gone. No one knew where.

Travis hadn't stayed long at Calder's. They'd started ar
guing, and Travis had stormed off in a Texan fury. But h
admitted his lousy mood had more to do with Enoch tha
his relationship with Calder. Something had come to hin
while he was visiting his uncle, and he knew that I would b
in danger if I were left alone with Enoch.

As soon as he entered the bathhouse, Travis saw smok
coming from the basement. The main room in the cellar wa

already in flames, and he might not have reached us except for another kind twist of fate.

The thermal water had been hooked up that afternoon. The first thing Travis did from the stairwell was smash the pipes and flood the basement with spring water.

Some gut instinct must have told him we were down there. The water revived Dr. Peabody who managed to stagger outside on his own. Travis had found me unconscious in the boiler room and carried me outside.

It was probably just as well that Enoch had, by then, disappeared. Otherwise Travis might have been tempted to kill him with his bare hands.

"I never should have left you," he kept murmuring that day in the hospital.

I longed to reassure him that it wasn't his fault. I should have confided in Travis, despite Enoch's counsel. Travis had already had his suspicions. If he'd known what had transpired during my therapy, he might have pieced things together sooner.

But that was my mistake. I swore to myself in that hospital bed I would never keep secrets from Travis again.

"You know what finally hit me about Enoch?" he said.

I waited mutely for his answer.

"When you and I saw him the morning after Hepzibah was killed, one of the first things Enoch said was there were only thirty-five documented cases of homicide committed by sleepwalkers."

I knotted my brow. *So?*

"Why would a lawyer know a statistic like that off the top of his head?"

Silently I blessed Travis for being a mystery buff. He was right. It was a strange detail for someone to know. Especially since I hadn't yet told Enoch about my sleepwalking. Of course Donald had taken care of that, giving the lawyer an opportunity to research precedents and decide what to do.

The police arrived that afternoon to tell me, somewhat superfluously, that the murder charges had been dropped. Dr. Peabody had given a statement, and the fingerprint reports had come back.

My prints were on the knife—I'd touched the handle while I was in bed—but there were none in Hepzibah's house. If I'd killed her in a sleep state, I would have likely left fingerprints everywhere. I hadn't been wearing gloves to bed. For all his careful planning, Enoch had slipped on that one.

Travis was reluctant to leave me alone in the hospital, but the nurses insisted I needed my rest. There was a police guard outside my door. That was the only reason Travis acquiesced.

I slept fitfully until the next morning when I had my next visitor. Donald came in, wearing dark glasses and a somber expression.

The sight of him sickened me, but I was too weak to express my emotion. I had only enough strength to whisper. "Why are you wearing sunglasses?"

Slowly, he removed them. My revulsion faded. I didn't know whether to laugh or cry. Donald Ashford had the biggest shiner I'd ever seen.

"Who did that?" I croaked.

"Your cowboy."

Travis, the dear man. What were we going to do about his temper? I turned to Donald. "Why did you tell Enoch about my walking in my sleep?"

"I'm sorry, Geneva. I had no idea what he was up to. I only came down here to win you back."

"But you had no right..."

"Don't you think I've realized my mistake? Good Lord, I've been torturing myself ever since this happened."

I knew Donald was more than capable of self-torture. It was still small consolation.

"Is there anything I can do to make it up to you?" he said.

"Yes. Leave."

"But try to understand, Geneva. I still love—"

"Don't say that . . . please."

He lingered at the door for a few minutes. Tears were spilling down his cheeks. Fighting tears of my own, I turned my head away.

Later that day in the hospital, Travis came in with his Uncle Calder. Adversity had finally brought them together, but I didn't care what the reasons were. As long as the fences were mended.

Calder offered his deepest condolences. He admitted to having harbored an initial resentment that I had taken over the lease. But he knew nothing about the clandestine events of twenty-six years ago. He hadn't even been living in Hot Springs then. And I had no reason to doubt his word.

The good news was he'd gotten a call that morning from Lurlene Sarrazin. She and her husband were in the Caribbean. The night of the fire, a private jet had been waiting at the airport to take them away. Lurlene, who'd never questioned her husband all through their marriage, had thought it was some kind of romantic surprise.

But there was apparently no romance. Lurlene had phoned Calder in a state of panic. Enoch was drunk and abusive. She wanted to come home and didn't know how.

The police were duly informed of the Sarazzins' whereabouts. Lurlene was given safe escort home, and extradition proceedings were initiated against her husband.

NEARLY A YEAR and a half have passed since all of this began. Enoch was eventually brought home and convicted of murdering Hepzibah and Bill Swann. The prosecution prepared an impressive case against Enoch after establishing that Calder had left the golf course early the day Bill died, leaving him alone with Enoch. Enoch was also convicted on a number of other charges dealing with my abduction and is now serving concurrent life sentences.

Further investigation, based on Bill Swann's files, revealed the reasons behind my kidnapping. The people I had called Mother and Father had actually had a daughter named Geneva. She was born in Chicago and died of meningitis at eighteen months of age.

The Zloczewskis had been regular patrons of the Silverbrooke, so Festus must have seen Geneva as a baby or at least known about her death. My grieving mother—or stepmother, I still don't know what to call her—was struck by my resemblance to her late daughter. Given the paternal background Enoch revealed to me, that's not hard to understand.

She must have nagged her husband to adopt me. Knowing her as I did, I can appreciate why my father eventually gave in. And as he was my true father, love, however misguided, must have played some role in his decision.

The problem was that my real mother, Pearl, would never have agreed to give up her illegitimate child. I remember how much she loved me. I remember how happy I was when I was her daughter. The argument she had with Father was over money. She had refused to sell her daughter, even to the man who'd fathered her.

Festus and Enoch, lured by the prospect of financial gain, had arranged for me to take Geneva Zloczewski's place. I had nearly thwarted their plans by getting lost on Hot

Springs Mountain, but they had managed to work around that problem.

The Zloczewskis did not return to Chicago where their real daughter had been born and died. They had spirited me to Boston where no one would know that I was a substitute child.

I harbor no grudges against them. The Zloczewskis had loved me in their way and had provided a good home, no small feat considering the guilt they must have suffered.

I decided to keep the name Geneva, although now I'm known exclusively as Genny McCabe. Travis and I were married last summer. He and Calder have become partners on two other leases on Bathhouse Row. We run the Silverbrooke as a bathhouse, the second building as a bed and breakfast, and the third as a museum. Calder is still battling government officials to get permission to open his casino.

I no longer walk in my sleep. In fact, since I've been married, my sleeping habits have changed dramatically. Travis is a wonderful husband, and I love him dearly. But as he warned me months ago, he does snore.

Now I'm an insomniac.

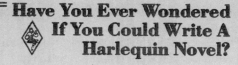

Have You Ever Wondered If You Could Write A Harlequin Novel?

Here's great news—Harlequin is offering a series of cassette tapes to help you do just that. Written by Harlequin editors, these tapes give practical advice on how to make your characters—and your story—come alive. There's a tape for each contemporary romance series Harlequin publishes.

Mail order only

All sales final

Wonderful, luxurious gifts can be yours with proofs-of-purchase from any specially marked "Indulge A Little" Harlequin or Silhouette book with the Offer Certificate properly completed, plus a check or money order (do not send cash) to cover postage and handling payable to Harlequin/Silhouette "Indulge A Little, Give A Lot" Offer. We will send you the specified gift.

Mail-in-Offer

OFFER CERTIFICATE

Item	A. Collector's Doll	B. Soaps in a Basket	C. Potpourri Sachet	D. Scented Hangers
# of Proofs-of -Purchase	18	12	6	4
Postage & Handling	$3.25	$2.75	$2.25	$2.00
Check One				

Name _____

Address _____ Apt # _____

City _____ State _____ Zip _____

ONE PROOF OF PURCHASE

To collect your free gift by mail you must include the necessary number of proofs-of-purchase plus postage and handling with offer certificate.

HI-2

Harlequin®/Silhouette®

Mail this certificate, designated number of proofs-of-purchase and check or money order for postage and handling to:

INDULGE A LITTLE
P.O. Box 9055
Buffalo, N.Y. 14269-9055